Lisa,
Thanks for your friendship and support.
Storm dogs always,
Larry Derbert

Requiem for a Vampire

Larry L. Deibert

Mundania Press

Requiem For A Vampire Copyright © 2007 by Larry L. Deibert

All rights reserved under the International and Pan-American Copyright Conventions. No part of this book may be reproduced or transmitted in any form or by any means, electronic or mechanical including photocopying, recording, or by any information storage and retrieval system, without permission in writing from the publisher.

The scanning, uploading and distribution of this book via the Internet or via any other means without the permission of the publisher is illegal, and punishable by law. Please purchase only authorized electronic editions, and do not participate in or encourage the electronic piracy of copyrighted materials. Your support of the author's rights is appreciated.

This is a work of fiction. Names, characters, places and incidents either are the product of the author's imagination or are used fictitiously, and any resemblance to any actual persons, living or dead, events, or locales is entirely coincidental.

A Mundania Press Production
Mundania Press LLC
6470A Glenway Avenue, #109
Cincinnati, Ohio 45211-5222

To order additional copies of this book, contact:
books@mundania.com
www.mundania.com

Cover Art © 2007 by SkyeWolf
SkyeWolf Images (http://www.skyewolfimages.com)
Book Design, Production, and Layout by Daniel J. Reitz, Sr.
Marketing and Promotion by Bob Sanders
Edited by Heather Bollinger

Trade Paperback ISBN: 978-1-59426-482-5
eBook ISBN: 978-1-59426-481-8

First Edition • August 2007

Production by Mundania Press LLC
Printed in the United States of America
10 9 8 7 6 5 4 3 2 1

Warning: The unauthorized reproduction or distribution of this copyrighted work is illegal. Criminal copyright infringement, including infringement without monetary gain, is investigated by the FBI and is punishable by up to 5 years in federal prison and a fine of $250,000.

Dedication

To my children Laura and Matthew, my wife Peggy,
and my mentor, Edgar award-winning author, Mark Graham.

A New Life

Her eyes fluttered open. How long had she been asleep? *Unconscious? Dead?* She felt dead, for although her senses seemed to be more finely tuned than ever before in her life, Lani could not feel her heart beating. She felt so cold, not only on the outside, but also throughout her inner being. Every nerve ending tingled with cold.

Looking down at herself, she noticed that she was naked. As her eyes made a sweep around the warehouse in the dim light, she was surprised that she could see everything so clearly. Lani saw Marcus's body lying a few feet to her right side, his head severed from his body, apparently by a large shard of glass from the broken window. The glass was deeply imbedded into the wooden floor just above his shoulders. She cried out in horror at the sight and screamed; her brain unable to assimilate what had occurred. Lani turned her head away from the sight, but after a few moments of sobbing, she regained her composure and, looking at him again, she noticed that his face appeared at peace, more serene than she had ever seen any living person. It had seemed that the weight of the world had been finally lifted from him.

When she saw her cloak, Lani wanted to pick it up, not only to cover her nudity, but to give her some warmth for the coldness she felt was becoming more acute with each passing minute: she reached out for it, but the forgotten shackles impeded her reach short of her goal. Her mind began to race; *how would she be able to leave this place being bound to the wall itself?* There was a gnawing in the pit of her stomach. She was hungry and did not know how much time had passed by since she had last eaten.

Suddenly, everything came back to her and she became agitated and frightened, gasping out loud. "Have I become like him? What was he anyway? Vampires simply did not exist; they were merely stories told by delusional people who enjoyed scaring the living Jesus out of those who would listen to them; still, I saw his fangs and felt them tear into my neck." Lani remembered feeling him drink her blood until she passed out. Was she dead, yet not? As she began to recall the events leading up to this moment, she thought that her parents would be worried sick.

They had allowed him to take her for a stroll after only meeting him that very evening. Marcus had hypnotic eyes and her folks enjoyed listening to him speak of Europe, from where he had recently arrived. He promised them that he would have Lani at their hotel door before the bell tolled nine. After they spoke together for a few moments, her parents acquiesced to his request, allowing her to walk with him for the better part of two hours without a chaperone. Lani was mesmerized by his charm and was more than willing to go with him.

She became rather frightened when he led her, arm in arm, to the warehouse district, eleven blocks from the hotel restaurant, but he assured her that his intentions were honorable. The night air was beginning to get quite chilly and she feared a storm was imminent. *That should be the least of my worries,* she thought.

"Lani, I want to show you the building I have purchased. I plan to turn it into a manufacturing facility of a type I had visited in Europe, but better, once all my assets arrive in America. I have great plans for a new business venture, never before seen in this country. Please allow me to show you my dream." *Your nightmare!*

When they stepped inside, she looked around the huge, empty building, wondering what his venture could possibly be. She looked into his face, seeing that it had perceptibly changed, hardened somewhat, and nervously asked, "What type of business do you want to open, Marcus?"

Hearing their footfalls as they strode over the wooden floor was disconcerting to her as he replied; "I have the plans in my office. Let's step inside and you can peruse what I intend to do in this building." She noticed his smile had a touch of wickedness in it and she felt a shiver run up and down her spine, yet she was eager to learn more about this strangely compelling man.

He unlocked the door and they stepped inside. A shaft of moonlight streamed down onto another empty floor. As her eyes adjusted to the light, she saw a few crates stacked in the corner, reaching like stairs up to the angled windows that were located near the ceiling. A dark cloth hung down from one side of the window frame. Looking around the room, hoping to find a desk or a table with plans lying on top of it, she saw there was none. On the floor against the far wall was a mattress, and what appeared to be chains hooked into the bare studs a foot or so above the floor. Lani was very confused, her eyes darting to the mattress, then to the window, and back again, when Marcus suddenly and roughly grabbed her, dragging her to the mattress. He threw her down, causing a huge cloud of dust to be released from the floorboards, and Lani began to cough spasmodically.

As she struggled to break free from his strong hands, she cried out, "What are you going to do to me?" *He's going to rape me!*

She became very frightened. As his eyes turned a bloody red and his features hardened, he opened his mouth, revealing two long, sharp canine like teeth. He fell upon her and she felt a sharp pain in her neck where his fangs cut through flesh and into her artery. Her hot blood spurted into his throat and she became sickened, hearing him swallow several times, as she weakened and lapsed into darkness.

When she awakened, he was standing over her, looking exactly as he did when she had first seen him, with the exception that his skin appeared sunburned, his paleness turned fire red. She tried to speak, but her throat was parched, making talking extremely difficult. He gave her a cup of water and Lani drank in small sips. Finally she asked, "What have you done to me and what are you?" Her eyes were wide with fright as she struggled to free her hands from their prison. She grunted, moaned, and kicked out at him, screaming her lungs out until she could scream no more.

When she composed herself, he began to speak. His deep, gruff voice was fraught with emotion as he answered, "Lani, you may not believe this, but I *am* a vampire, the last of my kind left in the world."

Her voice was filled with curious rage as she replied, "You are correct, sir! I do not believe you! Vampires are creatures that only exist in the minds of the insane and the foolish, yet I saw you grow fangs and I felt you drink my blood. I don't understand how this can be?" Remembering the sound her blood made as it rushed down his throat brought on yet another wave of hysteria, this one lasting even longer than the first, as Marcus just watched her let it all out.

He brought a stool over to where she was lying and sat down, wanting to tell her everything, yet not really knowing how. After a few moments, heavy raindrops pelting the roof replaced the silence. Suddenly agitated by the storm, Marcus stood up and began pacing; his hunger was growing and he wanted to kill her: he *needed* a mate. Once she was a vampire, many questions would not have to be asked, for she would instinctively know what she had to do to live, yet he felt he owed her some explanation about his existence.

Sitting back down on the stool, becoming sexually aroused at the sight of her exquisite beauty, he said, "I didn't believe in such creatures myself when I was attacked, killed, and passed through death into immortality." He looked at her through incredibly sad eyes and added, "Lani, I have been a vampire for nearly two thousand years!"

Lani couldn't speak, could barely think. This simply was not happening to her. Her head began to spin and she blacked out again, only to awaken a few minutes later to feel his sharp teeth in her neck as he sucked more blood from her. She tried to fight him off, but she was too weak and he was much too strong. She collapsed into unconsciousness once again.

When she awakened, Marcus was staring through the windows at the rain, which was slamming into the glass. She thought the sound of the heavy drops hitting the window was incredibly loud, afraid that the glass would break and they would become soaked. Lani realized that being soaking wet was the least of her problems at the moment, but it was something she hated nevertheless.

Marcus had felt her awaken and turned toward where she lay, concern etched in his face. A moment later, his expression changed to joy because she was so beautiful and he longed to have a mate again.

Continuing her struggle to free herself, her voice full of anguish, she asked, "Why are you doing this to me? What have my family or I ever done to you to make you do whatever it is you are doing?" Her eyes burned into his as she implored, "Please stop this insanity and take me home. My parents aren't rich but we could give you some money, if that is what you are after." Lani full well knew that he was not after money, but she hoped she could talk him out of the vile things he was doing to her.

He walked over to the mattress, sat back down on the stool and began to explain why it was so important that she was the one he had to be with, and make like himself.

"I lived near Rome, the son of a farmer, and I fell in love with a beautiful woman named Theda." His eyes reached deep into the past, and the pain in his stilled heart was etched upon his face, hardening him as he fought for control of his emotions. "In those days, Lani, it was very difficult for a person of my stature to pursue a woman of higher class, but I was fortunate that my father was well liked by many of Rome's elite and I was able to elevate myself considerably higher than my friends."

Marcus once again stood up and began to pace, occasionally looking up at the window, the rain striking it even harder now, forcing him to talk more loudly than just moments before. He turned toward her and said, "Theda and I became lovers and eventually we married, moving into a home on my father's land, enjoying each other's company and working hard to provide ourselves with some fineries, yet basically living from planting to harvest. We survived and we loved each other so much."

Lani interrupted, asking for more water, and as Marcus held the cup to her lips, allowing her to drink her fill, she saw him looking at her as though he was seeing her inner being. Though she knew she was in mortal danger, the feeling was strangely wonderful.

The ancient vampire tenderly wiped the few remaining drops of water from her lips with his fingers, a tear forming in the corner of his eye. *When had I last cried?* He continued with his story.

"About a year after we were married, Theda announced that she was pregnant. I was elated at the prospect of becoming a father, knowing that if

I had a son, the family name would continue. I took her hands and danced with her. I was going to be a father and my father would become a grandfather. There was so much joy in my heart that it nearly burst: the pride I felt was incomparable to anything I had ever experienced in my life."

He closed his eyes, and when he opened them, tears began to flow again as he continued.

"Because times were hard, I joined the Roman army to supplement the family income, while father, mother and Theda worked the fields and the vineyard. I was sent to Sicily to help quell a slave rebellion and the fighting was fierce.

"A few hours into the fourth day of battle, I was grievously wounded in the thigh by a spear. My blood spurted out in horrendous amounts, quickly weakening me. Night was falling and there was no way to get back to a rear area for treatment. I cut off a piece of my tunic with my knife, and wrapped the cloth tightly around my wound. The flow of blood decreased, but I passed out from the loss of so much of my life force. When I returned to consciousness, I felt someone sucking at my wound, drinking my blood. I began to fight him off and when he stopped drinking, he looked at me through red eyes. The man edged closer to my face and sank his incredibly long teeth, like the fangs of a wild animal, into my neck, drinking more of my blood. The pain was unbelievable and I passed out again. When I awakened, he was laying there, his head separated from his body. Apparently I had beheaded him before I passed out, although I don't remember that to this day." Marcus stopped telling his story, rose to his feet and began to pace again, truly agitated by the storm. He pressed his hands against his ears as though the noise was hurting him and he pounded his fists against his chest as though trying to harm himself, though she didn't know why.

A few minutes later, a more composed Marcus continued. "The sun was beginning to rise, and the heat was becoming unbearable. My skin began to smoke as though I was burning up. I saw a cave in the near distance and raced toward it, hoping that the shelter from the direct sunlight would help ease my pain. Each moment was agony as I ran toward the entrance, but once I crawled inside its mouth, and the cooler shade it provided, I felt much better, although I now felt hungrier than I had ever felt. Rummaging through my pack, I found some dried meat and bit into it ravenously. As I chewed, I became extremely nauseous, but I swallowed, immediately regurgitating the food. I could not understand why it would not stay down. I decided to try to see how serious my wounds were, wanting to treat them in some way. As I began to rip off the makeshift bandages, a small dog joined me in the cave. He appeared as though he was starved for both attention and food, but I was too concerned about myself to see to the animal."

Marcus stared deeply into Lani's eyes; his intense, dark eyes burning into her very soul and said, "My wounds were healed, as though I had never been speared. I felt my neck where the man had bit me and there was nothing there either. I was confused and quite frightened. What had happened to me? The dog, feeling that I was not a threat sided up to me and I could smell its blood, instantly knowing what I would have to do to live another day. As I felt fangs growing in my mouth, I grabbed the dog, bit into it and drank it dry, dropping the lifeless carcass to the ground after I finished. I now knew what I would have to do to live this new life. Less than ten minutes had passed, when I felt the dead animal stir. I looked toward it and saw the vile creature it had become. When the dog leaped at me, I lopped off it's head. Now, as an immortal, I knew not only how to dispose of my victims, but also how I could be destroyed." He sighed, and then added, "Lani, I have killed a human or an animal every day for nearly two thousand years.

Lani reeled in shock. She had always been a dog lover and to have this man, who professed himself to be a vampire, tell her he killed a dog in this manner, made her scream again, the reality now sinking in. She thrashed about in her chains. His story was unbelievable, yet she knew it was true. After her screaming finally subsided, she opened her eyes, once again seeing the monster he was. She defiantly spat in his face. With intense rage, he fell upon her saying, "My dear, except for the blonde hair, you are the reincarnation of Theda and you will be my eternal bride." Marcus's sharp teeth once again found her neck and he began to drink.

Recalling all that had happened repulsed her. *Am I now indeed a vampire, doomed to live life eternal, drinking the blood of humans and animals to keep me alive?* She prayed in earnest, as she had since she was old enough to know what prayer was and the importance it had in her daily life. As a minister's daughter, she had to be on her best behavior at all times, even though she wanted to be like the other children and have some fun. Lani felt that she was treated differently because of who her father was and it made growing up difficult at times, although she was probably more knowledgeable about the world than her friends. She laughed maniacally, and at great length, in the deserted building, knowing that no one would be able to hear her, nor rescue her from what she may have become, but how would she even be able to continue life, being chained to the wall. Perhaps she would die before she even had to do what Marcus did to live—a life of drinking blood, killing animals and people to survive, the only one of her kind in the world.

As her fury intensified, she cried out, "God, I am one of your children! Why have you forsaken me and allowed me to become like him?" She looked over at the beheaded body of Marcus and as her hate for her creator—*God?*

Marcus?—grew, she threw her arms forward. Enraged, she pulled the chains free from the wall. She was amazed at her newfound strength. Lani quickly scurried over to Marcus and, as a dog would lap water, began to lick the blood congealing around his body. A large splinter of glass from the broken window had severed his head from his body and the glass was still imbedded in the floor. She quickly pulled it out and tossed it aside; giving her the room she needed to bite into his neck to extract whatever blood she could drink. Instinctively she knew there would not be enough to sustain her for long, but the drink was enough to warm her and give her the strength to hunt for a victim. Lani went out into the storm, her chains dragging behind her, clattering on the cobblestones. The newly born vampire stopped, for fear she would be heard, and broke the manacles around her wrists. She could now quietly approach the vagrant she saw cowering in a doorway. As he gathered his well worn coat around his trembling body, searching for more warmth from the wet garment, she silently approached him, watching him shake from the unbearable cold he was enduring as best as he could.

Lani could smell him, not his body odor from being unwashed for so long, but the rich scent of warm blood coursing through him and she was delirious with it. Lani again felt her fangs growing; forcing her to open her mouth for fear that she would pierce her flesh with the sharp canine teeth. All of her senses were heightened at this point and as she saw him in his discomfort, trying to warm himself more, she could also hear his heart beating; the wonderful sound was drawing her closer to him. The scent of his blood became stronger, more alluring than it had been only moments before; saliva began to drip from her mouth, running down her chin, much like a rabid dog. As a newborn animal would, she knew what she had to do, although she was momentarily repulsed by what it would mean. Despite the fact that she had briefly fed from Marcus, the blood she had taken was nearly depleted. She needed to drain this man of his life in order to be fully reborn into this new life of vampirism and immortality. Lani finally came to the realization that she was no longer a child of God, but was a bride of Satan, her hunger for blood and killing replacing her thirst for knowledge of her Lord and Savior. Lani briefly looked upward, snarling and quietly laughing at some unknown, unseen entity before continuing her pursuit of her new life's treasure.

She came upon him, but before she was able to consummate this new beginning, he turned toward her and saw a face that nearly frightened him to death, almost denying her the reward she was seeking. Lani knew this could not happen. In less than a heartbeat she was upon him, pinning him to the door with her body, sinking her teeth into his jugular vein, almost gagging as pint after pint of hot blood ran down her throat, its heat rejuvenating her, strengthening her, healing her. It only took her a few moments to figure out how to keep sucking and swallowing, not allowing a single drop of the precious liquid to escape her. It was the most exciting, terrifying experience of her life *death* and as he fell to the ground, a leg beating the cobblestones several times before his eternal sleep. She smiled, loving *hating* what she had just done and with absolutely no regard for the dead, she threw him over her shoulder and carried him to the river, cutting his throat with a sharp piece of metal she had found by the riverside. Lani then weighted the body down with a few large rocks and tossed him into the water. She certainly would not want him to become a vampire, recalling what Marcus had said about cutting a victim's throat, denying the corpse eternal life.

After she tossed the vagrant's body into the river, watching him sink to the bottom, a shaft of moonlight had appeared, the rain having ended sometime during her rebirth. She stared at her reflection in the water. Her once beautiful blonde hair, now matted with mud, was hanging down around her face, her curls completely gone. A face that was once pure now cast a reddish hue from the blood circulating through her system, warming her to a temperature many degrees lower than humans, but warming her nonetheless. Her bright, blue eyes now seemed lifeless; they were simply objects through which she was able to see. Lani's lips were rich with the color of blood, and seemed larger then they had been when she was alive. They were turned downward and she wondered if she would ever be able to smile again. She closed her eyes, hoping it was just a dream, but when she opened them, she once again saw the despicable creature she had become, loathing herself, yet determined that she would live this new life to the fullest extent. *Why? I must kill to survive.* She once again looked toward heaven, receiving no sign that this cup would be lifted from her. God had forsaken her and she would never pray to Him again.

Lani went back to the warehouse and disposed of Marcus's body and head, now feeling a terrible sadness for her 'father', and she cried as she watched him sink beneath the surface of the water. Later, when she returned to the warehouse, she searched the place, trying to find out something more about him before she would move on and do what? She certainly could not go home and she really had no place to stay, not that the warehouse was bad, but she was accustomed to better lodging. She was certain that she would be able to find a rooming house in which to live, wondering what she would do to earn money for her keep.

In a large crate, she discovered Marcus's journals, written in several languages. A number of the journals were written in English, the cover of each one bearing a certain time period. Thumbing through the pages of one, she learned that he had lived in England for nearly one hundred years prior to coming to the United States. She also found several thousand English pounds, which she would be able to convert into dollars: money that would certainly sustain her for quite some time to come. She'd be able to afford quality rooming in a nice section of town.

As she waited for the sun to rise, Lani thought about her parents and what she would do after seeing them again. *Can I even see them again after what I have become?* It was a riddle more perplexing by the moment. If she told her father she was a vampire, what would he say to her: she was quite certain her mother would faint dead away, in total shock and disbelief, but what her father would do would be quite a different story, indeed. He would surely think her to be a demon, sent to him by the devil himself, and then she would have to kill him, for he would have her pursued to the ends of the earth, if necessary, to end her evil life. She became aware of a single beam of sunlight dancing upon the concrete floor, less than two feet from where she was sitting. Lani reached out to grab it, as she used to try many times in her childhood. When her hand broke through the beam of light, she pulled back because it hurt her, nearly burning her flesh. She had forgotten that part of Marcus's story for that brief moment, learning for herself the danger of direct sunlight.

Lani scanned the room, searching for a place the sunlight would not find, yet, with the exception of crawling inside a crate, there was nowhere to hide from her newest enemy. She remembered seeing the black cloth hanging by the window and with only moments to work, she raced up the makeshift crate ladder and pulled the cloth across the broken window, shutting out much of the light. A beam had passed over her arm with little discomfort; this new knowledge suggesting that any part of her body that was covered or shaded from direct sunlight would not be affected, but she needed time to prove her theory, choosing to wait until nearer to sunset to experiment again.

She walked about the room, stopping at the mattress, staring at the last place she was human, mentally reliving all that Marcus did to her and told her about his existence. The new immortal thought that now would be a good time to study his journals. She needed to piece together what he was all about, hoping the information would help with her survival. Lani gathered up the leather bound writings, sat down on the floor with her back to the wall and picked up the oldest journal, written completely in Latin. With her limited knowledge of that language she only hoped that she could understand enough of the words to muddle though. To her delight and amazement, she understood every word, a gift of the greatest magnitude.

The Journals of Marcellus Bratius

Shortly after my twenty-fourth birthday, I met Theda Urillus. She was sitting on a bench in the forum, idly playing with a little red cat. As she pulled a toy attached to a string, the cat would stare at it, as if anticipating its next move, then pounce on it and take the toy between its paws, batting it back and forth until she pulled the string again. Theda would laugh, throwing her head back, the deep blue of her eyes reaching upward to the light blue sky. Wisps of her black hair fell from the loose bun she had them put up into, and the breeze would catch the hairs and blow them about. A small hand would come up and gather them back together into the high pile of silken hair.

Theda was elegantly dressed; I thought perhaps she could be the daughter of a senator, merely out for a stroll with her pet. She was wearing a dress woven from the finest silk; its colors of red and gold gleaming in the sunlight. She was indeed the most beautiful woman I had ever seen.

I was carrying a basket of grapes to sell at the market, but I was so enjoying the incredible young woman playing with the cat that I put the basket on the stone walkway to relieve my shoulder of its burden. I had been carrying it for nearly three miles and I was growing fatigued. After setting the basket down, I took a long pull from the water bag I had hanging upon my shoulder, sating my thirst. As I wiped the sweat from my brow, I never took my eyes from her.

She noticed me looking in her direction and smiled. Her white teeth were dazzling and made my head swim. Her rich, full lips were the color of ripe apples and her cheeks were quite rosy.

As I continued my observation, and she kept looking at me, the red cat bounded from the bench and ran toward me, sniffing at my basket, rubbing itself against my ankles, purring. I picked the feline up by the scruff of the neck, causing the lady to flinch and furrow a brow, but I quickly let go of the fur and placed the cat in my hands, stroking it as I walked toward the bench.

"Good day, Miss, I believe this belongs to you," I said, handing her the cat.

"Thank you for bringing him back to me, kind sir, but I was displeased at the way you at first handled him. I would have preferred you would have scooped him up, rather then grabbing the scruff of his neck."

"I apologize profusely. You see, we have many cats around our farm and they like to be handled roughly. I merely did what I am used to doing, but I certainly would never try to anger a woman as lovely as you. Allow me to introduce myself. I am Marcellus Bratius, son of Arelius Bratius. I am in the city today to deliver my crop to market, hopefully for a good price."

She offered her hand to me for a kiss and introduced herself. "I am Theda Urillus, daughter of Senator Maximus Urillus. It was such a lovely day, I had to get out of the stuffy house to get some fresh air or I fear I would have perished in my musty quarters. I live not far from here if you would care to walk a lady to her door."

"It would be my pleasure and a bit of conversation with you would be a most wanted diversion from thinking about my burden."

"She frowned, albeit playfully, and replied, "Oh, so I am now a diversion from you burden, after you have been so gentlemanly. Perhaps I have misjudged you in this brief period of time."

I had noticed the twinkle in her eye and the corners of her frown trying to pull her lips upward into a smile and I said, "Good lady, a Bratius never would be so crass as to use the company of a beautiful woman as a diversion. It was merely a poor choice of words. What I had meant to say was that a walk with you would be a journey of the first rank."

Her house was only about a ten-minute walk from the forum and we continued to chatter like magpies.

When we arrived at her home, I saw it was quite large with many statues placed about the yard and a gazebo standing sentry by the pool; a fountain spurting water into the otherwise unmoving water. The ornate carvings on the doorway revealed the lineage of the family Urillus and their rise from working class to the elite of Rome. I was certain that I would marry her someday within the next year or so, and I began to plight my troth by asking her if I could see her on the morrow when I returned to the city once again.

She offered me her hand in response with a mere nod of her head, along with a smile, and I kissed the soft flesh laid out in front of me.

"Theda, I must leave now for the sun is beginning its descent and I must get to the market, then walk home before darkness falls. Until tomorrow, my dear, I bid you good day."

"Marcellus, when you arrive tomorrow, I will be waiting by the pool and there will be a goblet of wine and some bread inside the gazebo for you. You will be hungry upon your return, I am sure."

"Thank you, Theda. I look forward to lunch with you tomorrow, but now I must leave."

That night I did not sleep well, the face and voice of one of Rome's most attractive women stirring me awake many, many times over. Though I longed for daylight and looked forward to my trip to the city, I was also quite tired and needed rest that would not be coming all too soon. I got up and splashed water on my face, accepting the fact that sleep would not come and I should perhaps do something to keep my mind occupied until dawn. I checked the stock, cleaned a few stalls and sang to myself to pass the time, finally seeing the sun begin to rise, golden tendrils of light washing over the greens and browns of the surrounding landscape. God's earth would be nothing had he not given us sunlight to warm us and provide its energy to the very foods we live upon. I loved the sun, because the night offered little compared to the daytime.

Later that morning, after reaching the city and selling my goods, I raced to Theda's house, finding her sitting inside the gazebo, a jug of wine and a loaf of bread at her side. She smiled and waved when she saw me approach and I collapsed on the floor next to her, the scent of her perfume driving me mad with desire, yet I had to remain above reproach if we were to begin a courtship and then, hopefully marriage.

We courted for over a year, finally being given permission to marry, with my bride electing to live with me on my father's farm, displeasing her family somewhat, but they were understanding about our feelings.

Theda and I were married for about a year when one day, as I was toiling in the fields, she came out to me, carrying a water bag. It was extremely hot, hotter then it had been in some time. Rainfall was next to nothing, and crops were suffering. After I thanked her and took a long swallow of the tepid liquid, satiating my thirst, she excitedly uttered, "Marcellus, we are going to have a baby. I missed my time two months in a row and I am quite certain I am pregnant." I whooped and hollered, grabbed her and twirled her around, laughing like a madman.

"Marcellus," Theda happily screamed, "Put me down before I get dizzy." Her laughter filled me with joy.

I stopped twirling her and gently placed her back on the ground, tiny dust balls rising from the impact of her bare feet, and hugged her with all my might. "I'm going to be a father, Theda. If it is a boy, the family name will continue and my father will be so happy."

Seven months later our son, Darius, was born and he was as beautiful as his mother. I knew it would be difficult to properly raise him because hard times had fallen, so I decided to join the Roman army to supplement the family income while father, mother and Theda continued to work the farm.

The slave wars in Sicily were threatening to spread into Italy and I, along with many other soldiers, was sent out to quell the spreading rebellion.

Lani skimmed over the part about Marcus becoming a vampire, having already heard it but began reading after where he beheads the dog.

I knew that the blood from the dog would not be enough to sustain me, and the battlefield lay less than one hundred yards away. After sunset, I approached the carnage and litter of battle; I was overwhelmed by the scent of so much blood. Many of the wounded had not lost much of their life essence, but were unable to move due to exhaustion.

My best friend Julius heard me approach and in a hoarse, soft voice implored, "Help me! Have you any water for I am parched?"

When I kneeled beside him and told him who I was, he smiled weakly. I could see by the condition of his legs that he would never walk again and I felt it was my duty to end his life, a life that would be continued only by the scraps of food he would be able to beg, living an existence that he would never be able to accept. I placed the bag to his lips, allowing him to drink his fill. I kept looking at his neck, delirious with his scent. Before he knew what was happening, I began to drink, absorbing the life force of my friend, making him a part of me, forever.

His bloodless corpse was stone white, and after I had gently laid his head back on the ground, I took out my knife, and slit his throat, also slashing the wounds my teeth had made in his neck. I was learning so quickly.

A few nights later I returned home to see Theda and Darius one more time before moving on. She lay upon the bed sleeping, her chest rising and falling with each breath, her mouth slightly open. I wanted her more at that moment then ever before, yet knowing that it would not be possible, for she would never understand what I had become and I could not allow her to live a life like the one I was learning to live. I left her room without as much as a backward glance. After spending a few moments with Darius, I kissed my son then went to look in on my parents. My head slumped and my stilled heart was full of pain, I walked from my house to begin my long journey as one of the living dead.

After finishing that journal, Lani picked up the most recent leather bound volume and began to read about Marcus's trip from England.

I have just arrived in America. The crossing actually went better than I had expected. No one outwardly gave any thought to the missing passengers and I was never seen taking a human life, not that it would have mattered, but it made my journey all the more pleasant. The most revolting incident of the trip was having to suck the life from the fattest woman I have ever seen in two thousand years. Her taste lingers inside my veins, which is most disgusting. Hopefully, after running a few more humans thorough my bloodstream, it will go away. Just sitting here, thinking about her, chills my bones and leaves me feeling rather wretched.

Although my disgust lingers, I will share her story because I found it quite compelling. I recall standing on the deck of the Mary Montague, talking with the captain, and smoking a very fine cigar. After Captain Lambert left me alone with my thoughts, she strolled onto the deck.

She came out of the dark into the moonlit spot where I was standing. I was so appalled at her appearance, yet I couldn't help but stare at her. She was about five feet and three inches tall, and must have weighed nearly two hundred and fifty pounds. Wilhelmina Stanley strode up to me, her bulk moving in several directions at the same time. Her dress was the color of a ripe peach with a low cut neckline, revealing breasts the size of cantaloupes. Across her shoulders rested a red shawl, and a white bonnet covered her light brown hair. Her smile revealed yellowing teeth inside bright red lips located just above what appeared to be three chins. Her bright eyes danced when they saw me and with an arm and hand several times the girth of mine, she waved as she approached. I had wanted to put this woman out of her misery since the first day of the voyage, but she was too well known by many on board and would surely be missed. I had hoped that I would not be in close quarters with her until the final night, but my hunger was growing stronger, and I knew that she would be so easy to take. Some of the passengers had put up a struggle, but I doubted that she would.

When she was nearly upon me, I turned and bowed slightly, smiled and said, "Good evening, Miss Stanley, you are out of your cabin quite late tonight."

"Yes, I know", she said with an irritated voice, "I am quite famished, since I ate so little at dinner this evening. I think I may be coming down with something. My appetite isn't what it should be, but by morning I am ravenous again. Have you ever felt hungry at this time of night, Mr. Bronson?"

I had to suppress a smile, wondering if she had more blood inside her than the average person. I tried to stay away from obese people, as they sickened me when I bit into flabby body parts. The taste of human fat was revolting and it lingered long after consumption of a person's life force. I looked at her and replied, "Yes, my dear, as a matter of fact, I was thinking of retiring to my cabin for a bite. Would you care to join me?"

She seemed shocked that I would invite her in, cocking her head in incredulity at my proposal, but Willie, as her new friends called her, said, "I really could do with some food, and you are such a nice person, always the gentleman, unlike many men in London, who spurned me and called me horrible names. I don't know what will be said if anyone sees us going into your cabin together, but frankly, I don't care."

I believed that anyone seeing us together would think me a fool, or think her the luckiest woman alive, sharing time with a handsome man. I said, "Perhaps they will all be asleep and not even see us enter. We can have a few laughs and drink some wonderful wine. I have bread and cheese to nibble on. Does that tickle your fancy, Willie, if you don't mind me becoming too familiar?"

She giggled and offered me her hand for a proper escort to an improper rendezvous. *Deadly, Lani thought, running her tongue over her lips.*

Once inside, I took off her shawl and removed my jacket. She sat down on the edge of my bed, sinking a few inches into the mattress, and blew into her hands to warm herself.

I poured two glasses of wine, thinking that I may as well have a bit of sport with the fat cow before emptying her to her very soul, drinking in her warm blood and watching her die. I snickered to myself, thinking that her eyeballs would probably pop from her skull when she felt my fangs sink through her flesh and into her artery.

"Here you are, my dear, some wine to cut through the cold you must be feeling inside. You really were not properly dressed to be out on deck. You could have caught your death of cold had you been out there for any length of time."

I had been speaking to her as I handed her the wine and she noticed my foul breath, a curse vampires have to live with, and she probably never expected that from a man so elegant. She reeled back and covered her nose with her hand, a gesture I had witnessed so many times.

"I apologize, fair Willie. I fear I had eaten something yesterday that did not agree with me, and my odor is quite unpleasant."

She smiled, uncovering her nose and replied, "That is quite alright, Marcus. I also have bouts of mouth odor myself. I was not offended that you have unpleasant breath, but the fact that it is an odor I have never smelled before. It smelled quite like rotting meat, and I must admit it nearly made me nauseous. Please do not think me unkind for being so blunt."

I returned her smile and said, "I truly believe that you will never smell any scent like mine after tonight." Her glance was quizzical, but very short lived. We drank wine and she had some bread and cheese while we talked. Several glasses and more banal conversation ensued until an intoxicated Willie bared her soul to me.

"Marcus, I have only had one man in my life. I am thirty-three years old and I was married when I was nineteen. At that time, I was a stunning young woman, weighing less than half of what I do now. One night, after my husband of three years took me to a fashionable London eatery, and we were strolling home, talking of having a child soon, he was struck on the head from behind, falling to the ground. I didn't immediately know that the blow killed him, but it did." She began to sob and I offered her a handkerchief. After regaining her composure, she continued her tale.

"The assailant grabbed me and dragged me into an alley, disrobing me at knifepoint, then he raped me. After that humiliation, I hermited myself in my house, eating and eating as a replacement for the love I was missing. I knew that after being raped, my chances of finding another man to replace Bernard would be extremely slim and I ballooned up to my present weight. I am so embarrassed with myself, Marcus, but perhaps a man like you could help me regain control of my life, after we arrive in New York. Would you help me please?"

She was such a pathetic wretch, tears filling her eyes, as she held out her arms to me, wanting me to make her feel like a woman again. I tenderly kissed her hand, looked into those limpid pools and through my most vicious smile said, "Unfortunately, my dear, you will not arrive in New York!"

Her eyes grew wide with fright as she saw my teeth grow longer and sharper, my face hardening into what I had become so many centuries ago, and even in her horror, she was transfixed by my appearance. I laughed loudly as drool dripped onto her face and into her open mouth. Already in shock, her silent scream reaching no one's ears, I drove my fangs into her fatty neck, finding the artery. I held her down on the bed as she clawed at the sheets with her dirty, uncut nails, her legs kicking into thin air. I had to suck so hard to get her blood into me and her enlarged heart was pumping furiously. She looked up toward the ceiling of the cabin and muttered, "Lord, why have you set this monster upon me. You took my husband, and now you take me. I hate you." With that said, she died, filling my brains with all of her memories.

As Lani closed the journal, she felt empathy for Wilhelmina Brantley, but only for a moment, since her human emotions were withering away like tree leaves in Fall. She then picked up the leather bound volume that bore the date October 20, 1840. Marcus must have written this last night while I was sleeping, she thought.

October 20, 1840.
When I saw Lani in the restaurant earlier, I could not believe how closely she resembled Theda, with the exception of her blonde hair, of course. I was going to follow her and her parents, finding out where they lived, and then I would stalk her, drawing her to me through hypnotic suggestion and they make her as I am. We would feed throughout eternity together, happily taking the lives of humans all across this country, expanding our knowledge and I would be able to tell her all my adventures of two millenniums. Lani Jorgenson would be my bride.

As I listened in to their conversation at the dinner table, I learned that this was Lani's twenty-first birthday and her father and mother acceded to her wishes to come to New York to dine at a fancy restaurant and to see a show in a nice theater. I found out that they would only be in the city for one more day and I knew I would have to act quickly, or possibly lose her forever, and that could not happen.

When the waiter came to my table to take my order, I asked him to give Lani and her parents a bottle of wine with my compliments.

After he carried out his order, he came back to my table with instructions that I was to join the family at theirs. I walked over to the Jorgensons and introduced myself.

"Good evening. I am Marcus Bronson and I could not help but overhear you talking about the young lady's birthday. I am new in town and I thought it might be a way to make the acquaintance of someone who might be able to tell me a bit about this wonderful city."

Lying will certainly be a huge asset in this new life, Lani mused as she continued to read.

Reverend Jorgenson rose from his seat, the silver cross around his neck casting off the light it had captured, imperceptibly stinging my eyes, momentarily taking me back to the time when Christ was crucified. I shook the reverend's hand and recalled that day.

⁂

Jesus was nailed to the cross, his earthly life nearing an end. Through telepathy, I asked why God had done this to me, forcing me to live off the blood of his children, hiding as a hunted animal.

Christ looked down upon me and mentally replied, "My Father has not done this to you. It was the will of Satan that evil would walk the earth in the guise of man…" At this moment, he passed from life and I learned no more After hearing those words, I did believe that He was not responsible for my creation, that I was indeed a child of the devil, wanting to die for the sins I was committing every day, yet relishing eternal life, having been immortal for over one hundred and sixty years at the time of his crucifixion.

⁂

"…And this is my daughter, Lani, who, today indeed, is celebrating her twenty-first birthday."

I bowed and kissed her hand, just as I had done with her mother a moment before. Reverend Jorgenson continued, "Please sit with us, as we are also tourists in New York."

I feigned disappointment that they were not natives of this city, but I sat down and said, "Perhaps later I will find someone who can tell me how to get around town. I have just arrived from England and I am staying at the hotel across the street, however, I was hoping that you would be able to tell me where to go to get some US currency, since I am only in possession of pounds and schillings. I certainly hope this establishment will accept payment with foreign currency, or I may find myself in serious trouble with the proprietor." I smiled and noticed Lani totally captivated by my European charm.

"I wouldn't worry, Mr. Bronson. I am sure that many businesses in this city have handled more than American dollars over the years, but if there is a problem, I will trade our currency for yours and exchange it before we leave for home tomorrow".

"Where is home, Reverend?"

Lani answered, not wanting to be left out of the conversation, momentarily shocking her mother with her forwardness. "We live in Bangor, Maine, Mr. Bronson."

I smiled at her, wondering how she would taste when I bit into her, replying, "Miss Jorgenson, I am sorry, but I do not really know where Maine is in relation to New York. My knowledge of America is quite limited, I'm afraid."

She blushed at my smile, but recovered quickly, answering, "Maine is several hundred miles north of New York, it being the farthermost state on the east coast, bordering Canada, and it is well known as the best place to get lobster in the United States. Have you ever had lobster, Mr. Bronson?"

"No, I haven't, Miss Jorgenson, and please call me Marcus."

We conversed for over an hour, drinking two bottles of wine, after which I hypnotically suggested that her parents allow me to take Lani for a walk, telling them that I would return her to the hotel before nine o'clock, although I knew that they would never see their daughter again.

I brought Lani here and drank from her. We talked at length. I told her what I was and what she would become and why and then she fell asleep. Tomorrow she will become immortal and I shall have my bride.

Lani closed the journal, waiting nightfall, her hunger growing with each passing moment, the last vampire on the face of the earth!

DAVID

She hungered for him, more than she had ever hungered for anyone in her century and a quarter of vampire life. Lani Jorgenson had grown tired of animal blood and human blood in bags and bottles, stolen from local hospitals and blood banks. She needed to feel the carotid artery explode into her throat, releasing the essence of the warm life she was taking, as it coursed through her veins, radiating through her body, killing the coldness she felt immediately before consumption. After she had satisfied her needs, she would be filled with remorse, not wanting, but needing to do this, assuring her survival for one more day: One more life would be taken to give her the strength to carry on with her existence, her curse throughout eternity.

David Forrester lay next to the mysterious woman he had met three weeks ago. Although he knew very little about her, Lani had affected him as no other woman before. She would go out with him any time of day, but she preferred evening dates. He would pick her up at her apartment and they would go out dancing or to a movie, but she would never allow him to take her to dinner. "I only eat one time a day, and that is generally lunch," she would tell him repeatedly after he'd ask her to go with him to a restaurant. The one time she accepted, she ate nothing and only drank wine, while he pigged out on steak, potatoes and a salad, followed by cake and coffee. The lady had amazing willpower to sit there and watch him eat, he thought.

Lani saw David for the first time at an outdoor concert starring Bobby Vinton and Lesley Gore. The venue was being staged at the home of Phillip and Betty Grayson, owners of Grayson Talent Agency in San Diego, where Lani worked as a secretary. The Graysons were known throughout the business as people who took care of their employees, almost to the point of treating them as family.

He was standing beside the bar, drinking a glass of beer. His stunning good looks drew her toward him and as she approached she studied him at length. David had dirty blonde hair, wisps of it falling over his ears and forehead. He had just taken off his sunglasses, revealing his large, brown eyes. Dressed in white clam diggers, blue button down shirt, white sneakers and no socks, his golden tan revealed his love for the sun. She noticed him smile as he saw her approach and his white teeth were nearly perfect inside lips the color of brick. When he lifted his glass to his mouth, his biceps bulged under the sleeves of his shirt.

Lani finally arrived at the bar, stood beside him and said, "Can a lady get a drink here?"

He looked at her, lost in her beauty. Her skin tone was creamy white with a hint of an early tan, and her oval face was framed by shoulder length blonde hair. Her small, regal nose was set between two sad looking, blue eyes and her mouth, lips ablaze with blood red lipstick, was set in a bit of a pout, as she waited for him to answer her.

"Yes, ma'am, I can get you whatever you would like. And what would that be?"

"Red wine would be nice." She extended her right hand and said, "Lani Jorgenson. And you are?"

"David Forrester. Part time journalist and part time chauffeur. Whatever I can do to make a buck, I'm your man." He took Lani's hand, and was taken aback by how cool it felt to his touch.

She noticed his inquisitiveness and exclaimed, "Cold hands, warm heart!"

David smiled and, with a nod of his head, said, "I like that, Lani. I like that a lot."

In the early part of the twentieth century she had discovered a formula she could apply to her skin, allowing her to appear as though she spent time in the sunlight, although she could do nothing to keep her from being cold most of the time. There were many human qualities she had occasionally missed, but being a vampire gave her the ability to stay awake 24 hours a day, consuming millions of words through her voracious reading. She continued writing in her journal, a record of this life, which one day she would share with the world. Although she enjoyed this type of existence, she knew that someday she would grow tired of not being able to enjoy the pleasures that humans could enjoy; a simple meal, the aromas filling her brain's pleasure center; marriage and childbirth, sharing the joys and heartbreaks of life's pursuits.

As they stood there watching Lesley belt out one of her hit tunes, "Judy's Turn To Cry", David walked behind the bar and poured two inches of wine into a crystal goblet. He handed her the drink.

While the concert progressed, David would go behind the bar to serve drinks and tell jokes. When bartending slowed down again, as Bobby Vinton took the stage, David was able to spend some time with Lani, refreshing her drink, and they began to chat again.

"You said you were a part time journalist, David. Do you work for a local newspaper, or what?"

"Well, I submit stories from time to time to different newspapers, but most of my journalistic achievements were when I was in Vietnam for a year as a stringer with the Washington Post."

"You're from back east?"

"Yeah, I grew up in a little town in Pennsylvania. Macungie. I'm sure you never heard of it. You?"

She shook her head and replied, "Bangor, Maine, but I left there some time ago and haven't been back."

"Do you have family there, Lani?"

She shook her head and her sad eyes were downcast. "My parents died a long time ago and I've been on my own for a few years now."

He nodded and said, "Yeah, both mine are gone, too. That's why I decided I wanted a little adventure and went to Vietnam to find out what was going on there. In less than a few months, I knew we should have gotten out, but I think we'll be there for a long time to come."

"How about your chauffeuring duties? Celebs?"

"Some, but mostly businessmen. The Graysons set me up in business and I can do as much or as little as I want. They know I like to set my own hours and come and go pretty much as I please, and that suits me just fine."

"Do you work for the Graysons, Lani?"

She had been sipping her wine, nodded her head, then she answered, "Yeah. I've been with them for a few weeks doing secretarial work, but to be perfectly honest, I don't think I want to be a secretary for the rest of my life."

"Yeah, I know what you mean, but you have to admit, the bennies you get for working for them are pretty okay. It would cost a bundle to see Bobby and Lesley in concert somewhere, and here we get them for free, plus all this great food and drink. Have you tried the lobster salad yet? It is really good."

"No, I had a bite before I came over, just to avoid all the rich food that's being served. A girl has to watch her figure, you know."

He looked her up and down, and said, "I don't know if you have to watch your figure, but I sure like looking at it." He glanced at his watch and said, "I get off duty in about a half hour. Would you like to go for a drive later?"

"Sure, David, I'd love that."

※

Now, twenty-two days later, she lay there, sharing his warmth; cuddling and kissing like two normal people in love. David's desire was growing by the moment and he wanted her more than any woman he ever wanted before. Lani suddenly, expertly, mounted him and they made love with unbridled passion.

David enjoyed watching Lani as she worked him, her downward thrusts matching his upward ones, her long hair draped her face as he held her firm breasts in each hand, her nipples taut and hard, the old heart shaped necklace she always wore, swinging freely between her breasts. Occasionally he would lean her toward him and take one into his mouth, teasing her with licks and little nibbles of pleasure. They had taken it slowly at first, their foreplay lasting for nearly an hour. She would tease him with her hands and tongue, stroking and sucking him until he was nearly ready to burst, crying out with anticipation when she would stop and begin to kiss him, hard and long, her breath still unpleasant, but tolerable. Her underlying, unknown odor was masked by mouthwash, and she constantly chewed breath mints. Although he couldn't figure out the scent, he was intrigued by its muskiness.

When she mounted him again, he could feel her body grow colder, except for the place where they were joined, and his confusion grew. All the women he ever had were always warm during sex and yet Lani was the complete opposite. He was suddenly frightened, but so engulfed in his passion, fucking like it was the last time he would ever make love, that his fears receded.

As they climaxed together, she screamed, an animalistic cry emitted through human vocal chords, the sharp, wounded sound piercing his brain to his very soul. Lani collapsed on top of him, her head falling to the pillow above his left shoulder. Her nostrils flared as she smelled his hot blood flowing through the thin membrane of his artery, driving her near mad with desire, a burning hunger that needed to be satiated, freeing her from the emptiness within, the residue of yesterday's meal having been flushed away—a sea of red urine. Her need was so great that she nearly swooned when she drove her now un-recessed fangs through the unresisting skin of his neck, seeking out the blood tunnel through which his life force was speeding, his heart pumping faster as the neurons in his brain received the message—pain—and sent it back through his nerve endings.

Her teeth felt like white-hot needles as they broke through the artery, his pain center alerted to what was happening. David cried out and thrashed around, attempting to escape what he knew was impossible. Vampires simply did not exist. As she continued to feed, his head was spinning, coherent thought slipping away into blissful unconsciousness. His heart was straining, having to pump faster to get the now reduced blood supply to his brain, for once his brain shut down, nothing else would matter, for once the ability to reason and react is lost, all hope is gone.

Lani was regaining her body heat, as David's blood soon became hers, the taste of it exquisite as the fine wine she had sipped at her birthday party, one day before becoming a vampire. She wanted to suck every drop from him and then rip his heart from his chest to lick and chew as one would an after dinner mint, but her love for him would not allow his destruction. When he lapsed into dark oblivion, she stopped herself, allowing him to live. She felt his heart beating and knew he would survive, but she knew she could not stay in this city any longer.

David lay on the bed, his chest heaving as his heart continued to hammer inside, forcing the greatly diminished blood supply through arteries, veins and the larger capillaries, new cells being reproduced, albeit slowly, but being produced nonetheless.

Lani sat with him. She had already packed all her belongings into her brand new Ford Mustang. Before morning, she would leave and drive until she felt she was far enough away to not want to return to him. The past few weeks had been a living hell as she satisfied her lust with the blood of derelicts; homeless people no one cared about. She drained them, cut their jugulars, and then tossed their bodies into incinerators or weighed them down, sending them to the depths of the murky bay, hopefully to never be brought up to the surface again, although it wouldn't matter at all if any did rise, for they would just be dead bodies.

When David finally began to stir, Lani kissed him and said, "Sleep, my love. You have had a terrible nightmare and when you awaken, you will have forgotten me, and your strength will return. I do love you, as I have never loved another human before and someday we will be together again." She heard him sigh as her hypnotic suggestion calmed him and she detected a smile upon his lips.

Lani washed up, gathered her purse and walked out the door, never looking back.

He awakened less than thirty hours later, blinking his eyes several times to focus on the unfamiliar surroundings. As he pushed himself up from the pillow, his head exploded in pain caused by his unknown low blood pressure. David winced and clutched the sides of his skull; trying to ease the discomfort he was experiencing. After a few moments he began to feel better, although he was still weak. His neck felt stiff and sore and when he put his hand there to relieve some of the tension, he felt the wounds, not knowing what they were. David's mouth tasted like a combination of breath mints and, unbelievingly, blood. Perhaps he had bit his tongue sometime in the past few hours; he looked at his watch, noticing that the hands showed an earlier time then he had remembered.

David threw the sheet back; the need to piss becoming greater then any other feeling at the moment, and he saw he was naked. He was perplexed as he stepped to the floor, the soft shag carpeting comforting his feet as he slowly made his way to the bathroom, clutching onto the bed, a chair, and then the doorjamb for support until he stepped upon the cool tile of the bathroom floor. He grabbed the sink as a wave of nausea overcame him and he puked up great amounts of yellow-green bile from his empty stomach. After he finished, he turned on the water, cupping a hand under the flow and bringing it up to his lips, taking several swallows, his head still bent over the basin.

His desire to urinate was getting stronger, but he felt too weak to stand. Before sitting down, he noticed some bloodstains inside the bowl. The pattern appeared as though blood had been poured in there and splashed up the inside walls, the flush not quite getting it all. He made a mental note to check his urine after he finished to see if he had been bleeding, although he wouldn't have a clue as to why. He sat there with a thousand questions going thorough his mind and no answers forthcoming. After he urinated, he checked before flushing and saw that the blood wasn't from him and he was very confused.

The pain in his skull grew by leaps and bounds and he took three steps back to the sink, opening the medicine cabinet to hopefully find some aspirin, but the shelves were bare, and remarkably, extremely clean. There wasn't even a ring mark from a cup on the glass shelving, nor was there a spot of toothpaste. It was almost as though the cabinet had never been used at all. Save for the blood in the basin, he had noticed that everything in the bathroom gleamed and it smelled as if a pine cleaner had recently been used.

He closed the cabinet and stared at the face in the mirror. David was twenty-eight years old, but he noticed that seemingly overnight *or was it longer?* his face had seemed to age somewhat; looking a bit sallow in places His once smooth forehead now had lines etched into the skin below his dirty blonde bangs. David opened his eyes wide and saw red blood vessels had popped through the whites of his eyes, and his brown irises seemed a little dull. His large lips were the color of a sun bleached brick, nearly bloodless looking. Remembering the wounds he felt, he looked at his neck and saw what appeared to be two large pinpricks, yet the skin around them was not pushed in, but rather was pulled out, almost as if something had been sucking on his neck. It was quite a perplexing discovery, yet he was transfixed by what he was looking at. His analytical mind could only suggest that an animal, or possibly a bat had feasted upon his blood. *Here in the apartment? Outside?* He knew it wasn't a leech, because when he had been in Vietnam last year, several times he had gotten some attached to him while out on patrol with an American advisory team. Nothing was coming to him as he continued to stare at the wounds in the mirror.

After returning to the bedroom, he put his clothing on; his underwear had been neatly folded upon the seat of a chair while his slacks and shirt were draped over the back. When he bent over to put his shoes on, a wave of nausea hit him, but fortunately he only had dry heaves. David grew hungry as he looked around the strange apartment: not knowing where he was, whom he had been with, if anyone, or why he was even here.

The living room gave him no clue as to the identity of the owner. It was spotslessly kept, with bare walls, save for a still life painting of flowers in a vase. The light green shag carpeting had been recently vacuumed and the furniture was free of dust. He slowly walked into the kitchen, which, as the living room and the bath, was immaculate

Opening the refrigerator, he found nothing to eat, and the only thing inside was what appeared to be a half bottle of red wine. David opened it and was ready to take a drink when he smelled that it was not wine, but blood. He nearly dropped the bottle to the floor, his heart skipping a beat at this discovery. All of the cabinets were empty, as was the silverware drawer and there was not even as much as a box of crackers to be found.

He walked back into the living room and went to the door. He opened it and looked up and down the hall. Spotting a newspaper a few doors away, he walked down the hall and picked it up. Looking at the date, he was once again stunned—he had lost three weeks of his life to his recollection. He slumped against the wall, shaking like a leaf, totally dumbfounded at this discovery.

As he walked back to the apartment, he noticed the number 513 on the door, but that didn't mean anything to him except that he was on the fifth floor of a building somewhere in…? He walked back to where the paper lay on the floor and picked it up, taking it back to the apartment with him. He smiled, remembering his days as a paper boy—the carrier would get a miss for non-delivery on his bundle sheet the next morning.

David re-entered the apartment and strolled back to the bedroom once again. He opened the closet doors to find no clothing hanging. All the drawers were empty and it just appeared as though no one had lived here at all. *Is this my place? Do I have amnesia and rented an apartment without remembering? Why was there a bottle of blood in the fridge? What bit me?* So many questions and no answers. He sat down on the edge of the bed, trying to put this all together, but nothing made any sense at all.

He felt so tired and decided to lie down again, just for a minute, but when his head hit the pillow, he was instantly asleep.

❧

When he awakened, he felt much better, but the questions he went to sleep with would not go away and he was truly baffled. He did some mental testing on himself, trying to find out how much he remembered about himself, yet concerned that there could be holes in his memory. What happened to him that he could not remember the last twenty-two days of his life? Did he do a short version of the Rip Van Winkle? Suddenly, without any warning, a vision, lasting no longer than a fraction of a second crossed behind his eyes—a woman with blonde hair and a killer smile, but that was all he got out of what he had seen in his mind's eye. No name, no recollection of where she lived, or even who she was. Perhaps it was someone from his past whom he had forgotten for a long time. He fell back to sleep again.

David awakened, feeling more refreshed, yet still not knowing where he was or, once again, how long he had slept this time. He sat up, a bit too abruptly, and his still low blood pressure sent signals to his brain to move slowly, which he did as he stood up and walked into the bathroom to urinate again, this time able to stand without feeling too dizzy. There was still a slight red stain in the toilet bowl and he just shook his head, resigned to the fact that he had no idea what that meant. After he finished, he stared at himself in the mirror; his stubble was beginning to grow into a light beard. This told him that he had been in this room for perhaps two or three days without shaving. Where he had been before that, he had no clue. His stomach rumbled and he decided he had to go get something to eat, for he was hungrier then he had ever been, even though he had gone without food or water for two days on one occasion in Vietnam, when with a three man team, they wound up inside a Viet Cong camp, having to lie still until the enemy soldiers departed.

David left the apartment building and walked a few blocks until he came upon a restaurant. He went inside and when he smelled the odors of various foods cooking, his hunger immediately became more pronounced: he was ravenous. After seating himself, a waitress came to the booth to take his order.

She wrinkled her nose a bit as she stood by him and David finally realized that he had not washed in at least several days. His body odor was offensive, even to his own senses now that he was aware of it.

"I'm sorry, Miss. I was working pretty hard and I guess I should have showered before coming to eat, but I am so hungry I just couldn't wait."

She smiled and said, "Not to worry, mister, you smell a lot better then some of my regular customers do. What can I get for you?"

He looked up into her eyes and for a moment, another face was transposed over hers. It was only a brief instance, but it triggered his memory. The waitress looked quite a bit like Lesley Gore, which led him to remember the blonde woman he met at the Grayson's party, although he could not remember her name. *Was she the mysterious resident of the room he had just been in?* Perhaps more would come back to him after he got some food inside him.

"Sir?"

David shook himself from his trance like state and replied; "Two cheeseburgers, fries and a cup of coffee should do it for me, for now." He handed her the menu and after she brought his coffee, he added two spoons of sugar and a little cream, sipping it, so as not to aggravate his empty stomach.

After he had eaten, he reached into his wallet for some money and saw his driver's license. He now knew who he was and where he lived, and more memories were beginning to rebuild in his brain. Perhaps he could find a photo of the mysterious woman, or something that would give him a lead as to what had happened to the missing time in his life, still horrified at the fact that his memory had so many holes in it.

His apartment was on the other side of town, so he figured that he must have driven over here. As he walked the street, he noticed his car parked along the curb, a citation stuck between his windshield wiper and the windshield. He looked it over and saw it was for illegal parking, so he tucked it in his shirt pocket, planning to go to the police department to pay it and to tell his story, once he figured out what his story was. David unlocked the door to his '63 Chevy Corvette and sat behind the wheel. He glanced over to the passenger seat and once again was treated to a fraction of a second vision of the blonde woman. Before driving away, he checked out the back seat and the floor on the passenger side to see if there were any clues to the woman's identity, but, as always, his car was immaculate.

David arrived at his apartment building and when he walked inside, he checked his mailbox. There were a few advertisements, an insurance bill and a business card from the Grayson Agency. Written on the back were the words, David—Where the hell are you? You blew a driving job and Phil is pissed off. Call him ASAP.

He walked up to the third floor and saw three newspapers in front of his door, so he now knew that he was at that other apartment for two full days, and probably three nights. *With the blonde woman?* Scooping them up and unlocking the door, he went inside, heading to the fridge to hopefully find a cold beer, which, fortunately he did. He popped the top and drained it in a few swallows, tossed the empty into the trashcan and helped himself to another. When he strode into the living room to sit down and think, a pain shot through his skull and he fell into the chair, breathing in short gasps, his eyes closed tightly to ease the throbbing. After a few moments, the feeling passed and he felt a little better, but the beer had already run through him and he needed to use the bathroom.

David urinated and then washed his hands. He checked the medicine cabinet to see if he had any aspirin to relieve his headache, and when he opened it, he nearly retched after seeing the bottle of mouthwash that was inside. It was hers! She had spent time in his apartment, so he now knew that she was more than a one-night stand. As his memory was once again jogged, he raced into his bedroom and pulled open the nightstand drawer so quickly, it fell to the floor. The contents spilled onto the carpeting and he smiled when he saw his journal, knowing that the answers to a great many questions would be just inside the cover. He picked it up and began flipping through the pages until he came to a page on which was scrawled a few sentences, including the name Lani Jorgenson. When David saw her name, a flood of memories was released from the darkness into the light. He read, no consumed, each word on each page, his picture of Lani becoming more complete with each entry. When he finished, he cried out in exquisite joy of his discovery, and then he cried out in extreme agony.

The flashback only lasted for a few moments, but in that brief period of time, David remembered everything about the beautiful, blonde woman he had been seeing for over three weeks. He pictured her sharing his laughter and his pain when he talked of good things and bad things, yet she had shared so little with him about herself; her mystique had always been one of the main reasons he wanted to keep seeing her. She only allowed him to take her out to dinner one time: she drinking wine, while he ate ravenously. One time he had seen her watch him from the corner of his eye and she appeared to be upset with the fact that he was enjoying his food so much, almost as though it was a form of torment to her. When confronted about her refusal to eat something, she had always come back with, "I've eaten earlier, and I only eat once a day," or, "I'm really not hungry, David, but you can have whatever you want."

He stood up and went to the refrigerator for another beer and when he opened it, he remembered finding the bottle of blood in her fridge. David threw up in the sink and after a coughing jag; he slammed the refrigerator door shut and went back to the bedroom to lie down on the same bed that he had shared with Lani. Even though it was unbelievable, and he knew that no one would believe his story, he now knew that Lani Jorgenson was a vampire and he vowed that he would destroy her before he was laid to rest.

Central Park

Even after all these years, Central Park remained one of her most favorite places to visit. Granted, she had never gone overseas to experience many of the wonders of Europe, but she truly enjoyed these 843 acres in the middle of Manhattan. It was always one of the easiest places to find victims, alone and ill prepared to be killed by a vampire, and she had killed many while roaming the topography that was created by nearly 20,000 workers. She had read somewhere that over three million cubic yards of earth were moved and some 270, 000 trees and shrubs had been planted to create the park

Lani strolled through the Columbus Circle gate and started her walk north, observing families gazing at the myriad of vegetation nestled in the middle of a sea of skyscrapers. Walking the streets of New York on a July day was sometimes brutal for humanity. The heat from the sun reflected off concrete and steel, baking passersby. Exhaust fumes from the thousands of vehicles speeding by on a daily basis was quite nauseating as well. A walk through Central Park helped eliminate these discomforts. Even though it was still hot, the thermometer had reached 88 degrees, the breeze flowing through the shade trees helped to lessen the effects of the New York climate.

As she walked, she began to recall the time prior to the park's construction, remembering that she was extremely annoyed when she found out about the plans, since thousands of New York residents were uprooted to create the park. How she had enjoyed roaming through the streets at night, preying upon the unsuspecting poor, people who would never be missed, for they were the scum of the earth. When she was in a really destructive mood, Lani would annihilate entire families, dumping their bloodless corpses into the swamps for the vermin which inhabited those areas, allowing them to feast as well as she had. As the memories came flooding back to her, she smiled wickedly, causing a passerby to stare at her as though she had lost her mind, thinking her to be one of the retards, *mentally challenged*, who were brought here to be looked upon in disdain. As the black man continued to stare at her, Lani gave him the finger and allowed him to see a little bit of her teeth, scaring the absolute shit out of him as he boogied on down the road. She felt him turn his head to check out her backside and she simply raised her right hand and threw him the finger without even looking at him, laughing heartily. She continued her stroll, once again reliving that one particular day in 1859.

※

She remembered that on the day the park opened, sometime in the winter, thousands of New Yorkers skated on the lakes constructed on the site of former swamps. If any of the bodies she dumped there were ever found, she never heard about it, and she wondered if anyone ever checked out the tiny punctures in necks, wrists or inner thighs of Irish pig farmers or German gardeners, whose bloated corpses, *what was left of them anyway,* may have risen to the surface. Back in those days, disappearances were the rule, not the exception, although many people kept disappearing in today's world, some of their own volition. She clearly remembered the gentleman who came to her rescue after she had fallen on the ice, being laughed at by a few children who had skated circles around her. Lani had tried many things in the last nineteen plus years of her new life, but skating was not one of her fortes, even though she had tried it many times as a child. The man skated over to her to offer assistance to a damsel in distress, but when he saw her splayed out, her skirt thrown upward, revealing her bloomers, he had to chuckle, first causing Lani to be angry and then to smile and laugh along with him.

He grabbed her arm and as she braced herself with the other, he pulled her to her feet, nearly toppling him over as she fell into his chest. He wrapped his arms about her to prevent her from falling over again. His scent was delicious and Lani knew she had found her victim for the night.

"Pardon me, sir, but I am a novice at skating and I fear I attempted to go beyond my limitations." He was a quite good-looking man, she thought. He appeared to be in his late twenties or early thirties, tall, about six feet even, handsomely chiseled face with large brown eyes, black hair and handlebar moustache. His lips were full and his nose was a bit large, but it fit his features fine. With the exception of a missing tooth, an incisor, his smile was charming. His dark eyes sparkled when he looked into hers, although she could see a bit of sadness in them.

"That is quite alright, Miss?"

"Lani Jorgenson." She smiled at him, looking radiant and capturing his full attention.

"Miss Jorgenson, I have been observing you for some time, and I could see that your skating skills were less than average. I must admit I was hoping that somehow I would be able to rescue you, perhaps even to get the chance to talk to you extensively."

"Sir, you are being a bit presumptuous, perhaps. How do you know that my husband will not appear very soon and bash you for being so forward with a total stranger?"

"Edward Cummings is my name, and now we are not total strangers since we know each others name. Personally, I don't believe there is a Mr. Jorgenson, for if there were, he most certainly would not allow the most beautiful woman I have ever seen out on the ice alone to fend for herself, now would he?"

"Mr. Cummings, you certainly do study those you wish to get close to. You are correct, though, there is no Mr. Jorgenson, but there are times that a lady must see what the man is going to do after hearing about a husband, in order to find out what kind of person she is going to be dealing with. I hope I am making myself clear, for sometimes my words do not come out correctly."

"Yes, Lani, if I may be so bold?" She nodded her approval of the use of her first name. "I perfectly understood what you said, and I agree that a lady cannot be too careful who she speaks to in this day and age. There are many scoundrels lurking about who would take advantage of a young woman alone among so many strangers, but let me assure you, I am not one of them."

"Edward, if I may, you certainly don't appear to be a scoundrel, and I do believe I could enjoy skating with you, if you would be so kind as to help me along."

Sometimes Lani really liked to string humans along before their destruction, especially a man like Edward who was so obviously attempting to get her into his bed, and if she felt like playing with him for a while, he just might succeed. Although she did not consider herself promiscuous, she did enjoy sex from time to time, plus it gave her a release from the fire that constantly burned from within her soul. *Do I still have one, I wonder?*

Edward held onto her lightly, yet firmly, guiding her around the ice, making gentle turns until she began to develop a rhythm between her feet and the surface of the lake, until she felt that there was no exertion involved. Lani almost felt human for a few minutes, something she had not felt for a long time now. As she skated, she paid more attention to the people on the lake, hearing bits and pieces of conversations of love, friendship and turmoil, one couple arguing like mad about the state of their finances. Yet most of the humans were having so much fun cutting figure eights into the ice and laughing at themselves when they would make mistakes and fall down. She pictured herself skating with her friends Elise Roberts and Laura Deibert when they were young teenagers, as the boys would taunt them and show off their own skills. How they would laugh. A tear came to Lani's eye as she thought about the first time she met them.

Elise was a gangly, green-eyed teenager, having turned thirteen just about a month before. She was very tall for her age; especially back in those days, Lani mused, having reached a height of five feet nine inches at that tender age. Over the next few years Lani and Laura would be amazed at the amount of food she could eat and still stay skinny as a sapling. Elise told her new friends that she was "all arms and legs, and I don't know what to do with them," and the three of them would laugh. She originally hailed from a small town in Florida and was not happy when her parents decided to move to Maine, for Elise loved the sunshine and would always have a beautiful tan, nearly year round. But her father's business was failing and he had an opportunity to move to Bangor and become a partner with his Uncle Marvin at his granite quarry. Though Elise was upset, she quickly found out that she liked winter and learned how to skate almost immediately. It became her passion and almost her downfall.

Laura had lived in a sleepy little town in Pennsylvania, but after the death of her father, her mother fell in love with a traveling salesman, who was based in Bangor and after courting for about a year, on and off, they married and headed up to Maine, arriving a few months before Elise. Laura was also tall for her age, a twelve-year old standing five feet eight inches, with dark brown hair, and the neatest dimples when she smiled, which she did frequently. Her brown eyes danced with delight as she animatedly discussed her goals and dreams. She wanted to become a teacher and impart all the knowledge she would acquire to her students, helping them to grow into fine young citizens of this country, but on that fateful day, her dreams were nearly shattered.

Just outside of town was a rather large pond that saw quite a bit of use. In the summer, many children could be found swimming in the tepid water, while in winter, the frozen surface was perfect for those who wished to ice skate. Elise and Laura were in the same class in school and almost immediately became friends. Lani was a home school student, and only saw the other kids in the late afternoon and on weekends, but on this particular day, the three of them met at the pond to skate.

When Lani approached Elise and Laura, she heard them laughing loudly and smiled, hoping to have found two new friends. She walked over to the pair, who were looking her over and when she got within a few feet, she said, "Hello, my name is Lani Jorgenson. Who are you?" She held out her hand in greeting and Elise shook it first, replying, "Hi, I'm Elise Roberts.

Laura next shook hands with her and offered, "I'm Laura Deibert."

The three girls talked at length about their families and friends and school but Elise was anxious to get onto the ice, probably to show off her skills, so the three girls put on their skates and went out on the ice. Elise did indeed show off her skills, and her two friends enjoyed watching, applauding her when she did intricate turns and spins.

Dauntlessly, Laura showed the girls that she too could skate very well and Lani and Elise applauded her efforts as well.

Unfortunately, Lani was not as adept at skating. She could do okay in a straight line or large circles, but to do something fancy would just cause her to fall down, but she was very strong mentally and physically and never got hurt

A few days during the past week had been relatively warm for late November and today was no exception. The sun shone through the bare branches of the giant trees lining the pond, and the light danced upon the different shades of ice. As the sun made its way higher in the sky on this Saturday morning, some of the ice was beginning to melt and small cracks were appearing on the surface. The three girls were oblivious to this fact and kept skating toward one of those places, getting precariously close several times, not hearing the ice breaking the closer they got to that area.

Laura and Elise found two round poles that may have been left there by some of the boys who had used them to play with the hickory nuts that were strewn about. A boy would pick up one of the green nuts, throw it in the air with one hand, while holding the stick with the other and try to swat it as far as he could when it fell back down. The sticks were a few feet long and the girls began to twirl them in their hands as they skated toward the thin ice again. They had played this game before, but never on the ice. They were standing on top of one of the cracks, while Lani was practicing making a figure eight and Laura yelled to her. "Hey, Lani, watch this."

Lani stopped and edged closer to the two friends and watched, as Elise and Laura would twirl the sticks with one hand, throw them into the air and catch them. Sometimes one would drop her stick, retrieve it and try again. One time they both threw the sticks high into the air and they came down a few feet further onto the thin ice, which was cracking more, yet only Lani heard it.

She yelled, "Look out!" Her two new friends laughed at one another, skating toward the sticks. The weight of both of them in the same place was too much for the ice and it broke, sending them into the freezing water of the pond below, disappearing briefly before rising to the surface.

Laura screamed, "I can't swim," and grabbed hold of Elise's dress, desperately trying to stay afloat. As Elise reached out to get a handhold on the ice, the weight of Laura along with their soaked clothes pulled both of them under, but Laura would not let go. She was frightened that she would drown. Underwater, Elise struggled to pull Laura's hands from her dress, but to no avail. Both of them were starting to gasp for air when Lani plunged into the frigid water. She grabbed Laura's arms and managed to get her to the surface and pushed her onto thicker ice where she was able to catch her breath. Elise had become disoriented by her lack of air and was no longer in the small pool created by the broken ice, but had drifted a few feet away and was searching for the hole in the ice to get out.

With Elise's air nearly depleted, Lani saw her and grabbed her around her waist leading Elise to the hole. Lani gave a hard kick with her legs and brought both of them to the surface where Elise gasped for the air rushing into her lungs at last.

After pulling Elise onto the ice, Lani pulled herself up. When the three girls were safe, Lani got them moving, so as not to catch pneumonia. They walked to her house, which was the closet of the three.

Lani's mother saw them coming up the path, wet and cold, and made them all come inside and take off their clothes. Mrs. Jorgenson had each girl wrap themselves in blankets and sit by the fireplace until they warmed up. She also fed them soup and hot tea until their clothing dried out and Elise and Laura were able to go home.

Elise and Laura thanked her for saving their lives, and as Lani's thoughts came back to the present, she wondered where they were now. The last thing she knew was that Laura did become a teacher somewhere in Pennsylvania, and Elise married a young man named David and moved back to Florida. She closed her eyes wishing she could see her friends one more time.

༄༅

After wiping her tears away, still seeing the faces of her friends, Lani turned toward Edward and said, "Let me go, now. I think I can do this on my own. You have been a wonderful teacher, but now you must let your little bird fly alone."

He nodded his approval and let go of her arm, watching her gracefully glide across the ice, making nice tight turns to avoid hitting any of the other skaters. After her second turn around the lake, he applauded her newfound expertise and she skated over to him, delighted with her accomplishments.

"Lani, I am truly amazed with how quickly you learned to skate like that. Are you sure you never skated before?"

"Edward, I have not skated since I was a teenager, and that was so long ago."

"I hardly believe you are much older than twenty or twenty-one now, so how could that have been so long ago."

She flashed a grin, knowing she had almost been caught with her words, finally saying, "Yes, you are right, Edward. I am twenty one, but my teenage years seemed like they happened over twenty years ago."

"Would you like to talk about it, unless, perhaps those years were not the best of your life and you'd prefer not to talk about them? We could go for a sandwich, if you would like that, Lani." He had pulled a pocket watch from his vest and in the fading light saw that it was almost three PM, but the cloudy sky made it appear to be much later.

"I'm not really hungry, Edward, but I would certainly like a glass of wine, or possibly a brandy, if that would be alright with you? You, of course, may eat something if you wish."

He took her arm in his and said, "Wonderful! I know this great little café a few blocks from here. We could warm up some and perhaps you'd allow me to take you to the theater this evening. I know there is a wonderful minstrel show playing at the Fifth Avenue Theater."

She nodded her approval and they strolled to the café. The street was nearly deserted, those still out there scurrying home for dinner and possibly a lot of good conversation later. Walking was treacherous as there were many icy patches on the cobblestone pavements and on the streets, but they got to the café without falling. Lani drank a brandy and watched Edward annihilate a roast beef sandwich along with two pints of ale. He was becoming a bit tipsy, which might inhibit his sexual performance, but his thinned blood would flow so much more quickly. Lani almost hated the fact that she was going to kill him, because he was actually quite fun to be with, but she knew she could not get close to anyone, or it could ultimately lead to her destruction.

Afterward, with darkness approaching, they walked back to Central Park where they strolled the paths, both of them enchanted by the accomplishments of those who created it. She wondered how it would look with all the trees and flowers in full bloom, suddenly realizing that she would walk these paths for who knew how long. Marcus lived for nearly two thousand years, an amount of time she could not yet comprehend, yet when she looked into a mirror, she saw that in nearly twenty years she had not aged one millisecond. *How many centuries will I walk the earth? What will humankind accomplish in that time?* She had read all of Marcus's journals and had been truly amazed with his descriptions of how technology evolved since the beginning of the first millennium.

Her arm was hooked in Edward's, but she could not put her head as close to him as she would have liked to because of her rather large sun hat. Until she knew that she could spend a certain amount of time outside in the daylight, her awareness of being in the direct sunshine without some form of protection, like sunhats and long sleeves, could prove to be disastrous, causing her bodily harm. That first day, when she discovered what direct sunlight could do to her, immediately opened her eyes to the dangers she would have to deal with as an immortal, though she kept looking for an answer to her problem. Lani looked toward him and said, "Edward, I really don't think I could enjoy the theater tonight after spending so much time on the ice. I fear I have grown a bit tired, but if I am not sounding too unladylike, I would enjoy having you come up to my flat for a cup of tea or coffee and then we could go for a stroll later."

Edward was momentarily taken aback for he had never had a woman ask him up to her room for refreshments. *Sex?* He replied, "That would be marvelous and I will assure you that I will be a gentleman at all times."

Lani gave him a deliciously wicked smile and said, "I certainly hope so, Edward. I truly do."

Was that a double-entendre? He wasn't quite sure of her meaning, but he hoped that she was perhaps a tad promiscuous.

Her apartment was above a pawnshop on Harper Street, and by the time they arrived, Edward had seemed to sober up some, probably in anticipation of a sexual interlude with the incredible looking woman on his arm. After she unlocked the door, they walked up the filthy, narrow stairs, single file. Lani bared her teeth at a rat that was eating a few crumbs of bread it had found lying about. The loathsome creature squealed after seeing Lani in full vampire mode and scurried into a small hole in the wall. Edward, two steps behind her, never saw her do this, although he heard the rat squeal. It seemed as if the rat was not squealing in anger at being interrupted, he thought, but in fear of them for some reason. He had never heard a rat sound frightened before, but the sound it made had Edward shivering some, wondering why it would be frightened of two people.

When they entered her small, sparsely furnished apartment, she turned on the gas light beside the door and hung her cloak and hat upon a hook in the closet next to the door. Lani took Edward's coat and his bowler hat and hung them up as well.

"Edward, please take a seat while I freshen up a bit and then we will drink some wine and talk of pleasant things."

"That would be wonderful, Lani. There is nothing I would enjoy more than some stimulating conversation with you. *At least until I can get your clothing off and fuck you with reckless abandon.*

As Edward relaxed on the divan, gazing around at mainly bare walls, Lani strode into her bedroom and took off all her clothing, wrapping herself in a robe, before walking back out to the kitchen for a bottle of wine and two glasses. When she brought them back into the sitting room, Edward smiled at her garment, now realizing that there would be sex in his immediate future.

For about a half hour they sat talking about their childhoods and what they were doing now. Of course, Lani had to make up quite a few lies to keep the conversation going, wanting to know who Edward was before adding him to her growing list of deceased lovers. He was the bookkeeper at Moore Brothers, a small manufacturing business, specializing in hinges of all types and sizes. "Having been there for eight years now, I think someday soon I will be asked to step up to sales. My knowledge of the products is limitless and I have been known to be able to encourage buyers to choose our line when filling in for one of the company's representatives."

The conversation drew quiet for a few moments and Lani said to Edward, "Would you like to kiss me, now?"

Edward nearly blushed at her forwardness, but he was dying to taste her lips, breasts and that hot, wet place. He sided closer to her and took her in his arms, slightly repulsed at her less than sweet breath, but he was so aroused that it did not matter one bit. As he kissed her, she pressed her breasts into his chest and reached between his legs, squeezing his manhood, which was already hard. Lani smiled and gently pushed him away, opening her robe to reveal her naked body to his roaming eyes. Edward nodded his approval and his lips danced over her nipples as he slipped two of his fingers inside her. She moaned in response, taking his head and pushing it downward, having him taste her salty wetness.

She climaxed and Edward stood up and removed his clothing, revealing a rather nice body. Lani laid back on the divan as Edward got on top of her, moving slowly at first and then faster, his urgency becoming primary over her needs, now. After he exploded, he fell on top of her, exhausted and elated, Lani bared her fangs and went for his throat, his blood rushing into her mouth as he thrashed about, screaming for her to stop. "What are you doing to me, Lani?" She stopped and withdrew her fangs, pressing her hand to the wounds, so as not to get blood on her furniture and allowed him to see what she had become.

His eyes bulged with incomprehension as his mind reeled, seeing her teeth, red with his blood, her eyes the same color, and her breath now reeked of death, his, he was sure. "This cannot be! Vampires do not exist!"

"I'm sorry my darling, but I do indeed exist and just to let you know before you become part of me, you were a marvelous fuck." Lani buried her fangs back into his neck and drained him.

Afterward, she gathered his clothing and took him down to the basement, throwing his bloodless corpse into the small, overworked furnace, adding more coal to quicken his disappearance. She went back to her apartment, satisfied in two ways, opened her journal and began to write about her latest victim.

֍

Lani shook off that memory as she continued on her journey through the park. The flowers were in full bloom and she always loved the smell of fresh flowers. Hundreds of conversations were in progress. The couple walking a few steps in front of her had just come out from a restaurant where he had proposed to her. They were in animated discussion over wedding plans. She could hear the strains of so many different types of music being played on walkmans, both cassette and CD. Black people would be primarily listening to rap and soul, while Caucasians enjoyed a variety of country, alternative and oldies. Lani always enjoyed music because it represented such diversity among the people, yet most of it went back to the roots she had remembered, the congregation of her father's church singing hymns with such feeling and she felt a twinge of humanity, wanting to be able to live like a normal person, yet knowing that could never happen. She was over one hundred and seventy five years old and she could never go back.

She remembered how her love of music forced her to come to the vigil across from the Dakota on that December night over fifteen years ago, the day after John Lennon was murdered. She very much enjoyed The Beatles because they were the best band at the time of her relationship with David, the man she loved more than any other man on earth, although, thankfully, she had not run across him in nearly ten years.

Lani strolled up the small hill and stood by the spot marked with a simple memorial to John Lennon; the place that would soon be named Strawberry Fields after one of his best-known works, a song she listened to often, enjoying the lyrics, wondering how they came to him. She remembered the young man she had taken that night; he was so sad and alone, telling her he had to come to the vigil because without Lennon, his life would become meaningless and he wished he could die and be with the man he loved so much.

"Yes, I know what you mean, Richard," she said, after brief introductions were made. "John was like the best writer ever, you know! His music will live forever, but there will never be any new stuff and that bums me out big time."

"Lani, you understand how I feel about the man's music, but there was more. When I listened to his songs on my cassette player, I would actually get an erection. I think I was in love with him, which is really weird because I don't think I'm gay. I'm twenty seven years old and I have been in a number of relationships with women, unfortunately not for any length of time, but I never even considered having sex with a man."

She could smell that he had been smoking pot and was probably becoming delusive about Lennon, but that didn't matter; she was hungry and needed to eat soon.

"Are you here with anyone, Richard?"

"No, I came up by myself, all the way from Aberdeen, Maryland!"

"Does anyone know you came up here?"

"There is no one, Lani. My parents are both dead and I live in an apartment by myself. Most of my friends don't even really hang out with me anymore because I like to smoke shit and they don't, so I kinda stay to myself most of the time."

"Bummer, man. Wanna go for a walk in the park with me?"

He looked around at the crowd, knowing there was safety in numbers, and he was afraid to go deep into Central Park because of the muggers. "I don't know, Lani, lots of bad shit happens in this park at night, I heard."

"Yeah, shit happens, alright, but I know the safe places to go. I've been walking these paths most of my life and, trust me, it's okay. I have some coke and we can do a line if that interests you"

Cool, that's something I always wanted to try, but you don't find a hell of a lot of snorters in Aberfuckingdeen, Maryland." He laughed loudly, causing a few heads to turn their way, but only briefly.

"Okay, dude, let's boogie out of here and you'll feel something you'll never experience in your life again, and you can bet the house on that, brother."

They walked through the park until they came to the lake, which was totally deserted at this time of night. She said, "Are you ready for a truly one of a kind experience, Richard?"

He had smoked a joint on the way to the lake, offering her some, which she accepted, even though she rarely used any kind of drugs, not knowing if they would have any lasting effect on her existence. "Lani, I am ready, girl."

Even before he had completely finished that sentence, she was on him, knocking him onto the grass, and finishing him off before surprise completely registered on his face. After she licked her lips, she said, "Say hello to John for me, Richard." Lani slashed his throat with the razor knife she always carried and dumped him into the lake. He would be found, but it would look like another Central Park mugging and murder to the NYPD.

※

The sudden backfiring of an old car brought Lani back to the present. She sat down on a park bench and spent some time watching some children at play while a group was setting up at the band shell. Apparently there was going to be a concert, and depending on how good they were, she thought she'd give a listen. It felt so good being able to enjoy the bright sun with no fear of bodily harm, her immunity was completely built up, as she knew it would, and Lani was looking forward to a long life of both day and night hunting. With air travel as speedy as it was now, she planned to visit every continent on earth, beginning in the very near future. Her only concern was David, because she knew he would never end his pursuit; she felt like that guy on the TV show back in the sixties who was convicted of killing his wife and the damn police lieutenant wouldn't let him have any peace, always hounding and hunting him. She really wished she could make love with

David one more time, but she knew that could never happen, because he was just getting too damn old to fuck, but seemingly not too old to chase after her. Hopefully he'd die before he got another chance, the last one being too close for comfort, but she vowed she wouldn't kill him unless it was absolutely the only way out for her.

As humans kept walking by her bench, totally unaware of what she was, Lani studied them, hoping she might find someone with whom she could spend the day and part of the night. Her sexual appetite had grown to the point where she could hardly get enough of it, but selecting partners just on appearance was difficult at best. Looking at some of the women walking by elicited smiles from them but it had been a long time since she had a lengthy relationship with a woman.

The band had begun to play country music and the lead female singer looked remarkably like Reba McIntyre, and she really sounded good, as well. Lani listened to a few numbers as she continued to scope out the human traffic in front of the bench, her hunger growing at a rapid pace. One man continued to stare at her from just inside her periphery and although he was cute, she could see a wedding band on his hand. He was probably in the city alone, hoping to get lucky with some young chick and then go home to a wife who was probably just into straight sex, or none at all. She considered taking him for a ride, but decided against it when she saw the woman approaching her.

She was about five feet six inches, flaming red hair falling over her shoulders, creamy skin, green eyes and small, pouting lips. Her eyes seemed to be searching for something until they rested upon Lani's gaze. The vampire began to laugh heartily as the woman got closer and she stopped in front of the bench and said, "What the hell are you laughing about, bitch? Do I look fucking funny to you, or what?" Her Brooklyn accent seemed not to fit her appearance, almost like the time at a convenience store in Lancaster, Pennsylvania, when a gorgeous young woman waited on her. The woman could have won any beauty contest, but when she began speaking in a Pennsylvania Dutch accent, Lani almost lost her cool; it sounded so funny.

Lani stopped chuckling and replied, "I'm sorry, Miss. I wasn't laughing at you, I was laughing at the printing on your body suit." The woman was wearing a black spandex body suit, which was molded to her incredibly athletic body. Over her breasts were the words VAMPIRES SUCK! "That is so absurd it is extremely funny, I think."

"Why's that, honey? You a vampire or something?" The woman had her hands on her hips in a defiant posture, eyes glaring at this stranger whom she felt was insulting her, anyway, even if she was just laughing at her outfit.

Lani's eyes grew wide, finally realizing that the woman had to be kidding. How could she know? "Yes, as a matter of fact, I am a vampire," Lani replied, softly. Would you like to become one?"

The woman sat down beside her and said, "Sure, it probably beats being a hooker. I guess. Plus I get to live forever and never grow old, right?"

Lani simply nodded and asked, "Do you do women, Miss?"

"Meyers, Nicki Meyers. Yes, if the price is right."

"And what might that be, Nicki?"

"Two hundred an hour, or you can have me all night for five big ones." Suddenly she realized that she could be making a deal with a detective, and asked, "Are you a cop?"

Lani studied her, shook her head, and said, "Do you have a pimp you have to report to?"

"No, I work alone, always have. I split from home about five years ago and I've been doing okay on my own, but I'm only going to hook for a couple more years, then I'm going to retire on my investments."

"If you are free now, we could go to your place and I'll turn you into a vampire before the night's over."

Nicki looked at her and said, "Yeah, right! I was only pulling your leg. We both know vampires don't exist, but I am ready for some action. It's been a while since I was with a woman, but you are really good looking and I'm already getting turned on. Maybe we better get going before I jump you here and now." She placed her hand on top of Lani's and was confused feeling how cold she was on such a hot day. Lani merely smiled and shrugged her shoulders, adding to Nicki's confusion even more.

The two women hailed a cab and took the short ride to Nicki's apartment. When they entered, Lani was really impressed with the elegance she was witnessing. Nicki had purchased some fine antiques and the paintings gracing her walls had probably set her back a bundle. "You certainly have great taste, Nicki. Many of these paintings are extremely valuable and are definitely good investments."

"Lani, you seem to know pretty much about this stuff for a chick of what, about twenty two or so?"

"I only look young. You should know that vampires never age. I am almost a hundred and eighty years old!"

"Yeah! Well you hold your age well!" They both shared a laugh, but not about the same thing, Lani thought. This girl was going to be so easy. She hoped the sex would be as much fun as the teasing she was doing to her.

"Lani, would you like something to drink, or are you ready to get down to business?"

"I'd like a glass of wine, if you have some, preferably red."

After walking into the kitchen, Nicki stuck her head back inside the doorway, looking at Lani, saying, "I guess vampires only like red wine, but unfortunately I only have white."

Lani smiled and replied, "White will be fine, Nicki."

While Nicki was busy in the kitchen Lani strolled to the window and looked down on the people scurrying to and fro, cell phones popping out of suit coats and briefcases, doing business on the run, never slowing down. A young boy of perhaps twelve or thirteen had just expertly picked the pocket of an unsuspecting middle-aged man wearing a thousand dollar suit. The young thief happened to look up where Lani stood, but when she smiled at him, he doffed his baseball cap and ambled away with absolutely no fear of getting caught.

Nicki brought the wine to the window and as she handed Lani her glass, she said, "Hell of a city out there, isn't it? Everyone seems to be so caught up in their own little worlds they don't know when to stop and take a breather. Shit, most of them will be in the ground before they see fifty. Too much fuckin' stress going on today; everybody trying to get rich quick, the way it seems."

"What about you, Nicki? You're trying to get rich quick in your profession, before your looks are gone, aren't you?"

Nicki looked at Lani for a few moments, and replied, "Yeah, like I told you in the park, I don't want to hook forever; just long enough to get me set for life, so I can kick back and take it easy."

"Don't you want to do anything to occupy all the time you will have on your hands? Sometimes having a lot of time is a real pain in the ass. You always have to find things to fill it with, although not having to work is a blessing, I guess."

"You sound like you live the good life. You rich or something?"

"Like I told you, I've been around for a long time and I've amassed a fortune along the way, sucking the blood from many rich guys and a few rich gals, taking stuff from them that I could convert to cash easily."

"No shit? Well, if I want to become immortal, we better get it on so you can drink from me and give me eternal life."

They went into the bedroom and after stripping, Nicki began to fondle Lani's breasts, saying, "Hey, man! You are really cold, not just your hands, but also your whole body. You're pretty pale looking, too. Do you feel okay or are you getting sick?"

When Nicki looked into Lani's reddening eyes, seeing her teeth grow longer and longer, her face hardening, she screamed, then laughingly said, "Lani, you weren't shitting me! You are a vampire! Awesome!"

"Nicki, I am so sorry I have to do this, but you should know that vampires are only in it for the blood. You're history!"

Lani bit into her, not seeing Nicki smile, actually believing that she was going to become immortal, until her last conscious moment; she then knew she was dead.

The vampire knew that there would be questions about this death, so she dressed her and sat her in a chair, placing a lit cigarette in her hand, after taking a few drags. She knocked some red ash from the butt onto Nicki's body suit and waited until the material began to flame. Before long, her body was engulfed in fire and after the overstuffed chair began to burn, Lani quietly and quickly left the building. She crossed the street and watched as Nicki's whole apartment became engulfed in a hot blaze. Lani was now able to walk away, satisfied that the death would be ruled accidental. It was however a shame to burn all those fine paintings.

Jordan / Brad

She loved to walk along the shore at dawn, the sand pushing between her toes, cascading over the tops of her feet and falling back down creating mounds beside the indentation of her soles. The tiny grains, as they made their journey, caressed and stimulated skin and nerve endings, causing her feet to tingle with every step. Looking out over the ocean, she could see the tops of low hanging clouds turning red from the rays of the now rising sun, entrails of light spreading across the waves, touching her blonde, nearly white, hair, briefly turning it the color of peach. The sound of the waves lapping at the shore, as the water raced to and fro, helped to cleanse her mind of her relationship with Marty Walsh, her husband of seven years, terminated only last week.

Jordan Walsh, a recent transplant to the Grand Strand of South Carolina had spent the first thirty-four years of her life as a resident of Macon, Georgia, first with her ultra strict parents, Peter and Martha Strange, and then with Marty, since their wedding in 1992. Her divorce had now enabled her to resume painting and writing short stories, two passions she acquired during childhood. She had given them up to help her former husband grow his business, a clearinghouse for old toys and comics, recently becoming an Internet company.

The Stranges were actually sorry to see Jordan divorce Marty since they were positive that he would become wealthier then their wildest dreams and would be able to give her everything they couldn't. Both of them were occasionally distraught with the fact that they kept Jordan close to the vest and wouldn't allow her to explore the world on her own, but that was because Martha had been sexually molested, though not raped, as a teenager, and Peter did not want anything like that to happen to his only child. He had never told his daughter what had happened to her mother and Martha kept it locked deep in the recesses of her mind.

After Jordan married Marty, Martha became more withdrawn except on those rare occasions that her daughter and son-in-law would visit them, making her dull eyes sparkle again. She missed having Jordan around. Her daughter would make her laugh with some of her short stories and Martha also loved to watch her paint, the brush inside her nimble fingers flying over the canvas, vibrant colors covering the white surface in a flash. By the time she married Marty, she had painted thirty-one canvasses, mostly landscapes and rustic looking homes that had sprung forth from her vivid imagination.

As she continued to stroll along the same path she had been taking for the past month, Jordan once again saw the pale young woman looking down at her from the flagstone patio of a quite large beach house. She had seen the woman several times since having started her pre dawn walks and had noticed that the woman always appeared sad, her eyes seemingly searching for something too far away to see. Jordan would usually smile and wave, only receiving an elongated nod of the head in return, a smile never forming on the young woman's face. She was however, intrigued by the woman's demeanor and posture and desperately wanted to paint her, having now completed four portraits of friends, and one of herself. She decided that today would be the day to approach the woman with her request.

After the woman on the beach waved at Lani, she did an unusual thing by turning and walking toward the house. Lani felt a stirring inside that had not surfaced in over seventy years. With the exception of a rare one-nighter, that was the only time she had taken a female lover, tiring of her in less than a month, but the approaching woman re-ignited those feelings once again. She truly hoped the woman was a lesbian, or she would have to kill her before having any fun with the tall, gorgeous blonde who was now ringing Lani's doorbell.

The vampire casually walked back through the patio door, into the living room and down the six steps to the foyer. She hungered for blood *or was it sex* even though she had eaten less than twelve hours ago.

As she watched the young woman walk toward her door, Lani thought about her most recent victim. He was a golfer, perhaps playing a few holes after work. She saw he had hit a shot into the woods bordering her property, while she was out for a stroll in search of something or someone to drain. Only six pints remained in her refrigerator and she longed for fresh blood, plus the thrill of the kill. The thefts of blood in nearby hospitals were beginning to put the police on edge, and she could not afford to get caught posing as a hospital employee when she went in to steal a meal in a bag.

The man was searching for his ball when Lani approached. He looked up and smiled at the beautiful, young woman dressed in a powder blue jogging suit and red sneakers, her hair tied back in a ponytail, her bright blue eyes stabbing knife-like into his.

"Hi, there. Lose this?" She was holding his number 4 Titelist, its once pristine white cover marred by a few ugly brown scratches from the tree it had hit, falling at its base. Lani stood a few feet away, watching the handsome man stick the head of his club deep into the lush, green fairway, after seeing his ball head toward the trees After he walked into the woods, she tossed it to him and he caught it in his left hand. His right hand held a three iron to ward of snakes. The woods of South Carolina were ripe with them.

"Thanks, Miss. I guess I need some more work on my game to keep the damn ball in the fairway. You play?" He began twirling his club like a majorette would her baton.

"No, I've never taken up the sport, although I do like to play mini golf sometimes. Four hours of sweating has never appealed to me." His scent was beginning to drive her wild. "Have you been playing long?"

He began to bounce the ball up and down on the face of his club, hoping to impress the woman. Who knows, he thought, maybe he'd get laid tonight. She wasn't wearing a wedding band. "I've been addicted to this game since I was a teenager. My father took me out with him one time and I was hooked after making a par on the third hole I ever played. Do you live around here or are you merely looking for stray golfers?" He smiled and chuckled, hoping to have her realize that he was teasing her and not being an asshole.

She returned his smile, saying, "I've always had a fondness for stray golfers, but yes, I do live around here." She pointed toward her house, although only a portion of it could be seen through the dense foliage. "My name is Lani Jorgenson," she said, extending her hand toward him as she closed the distance between them until they were only one pace apart.

He stepped toward her, clasping her hand, gently but firmly, asserting his masculinity, she thought. If only he knew she could crush it with a mere squeeze. He replied, "Brad Carson." Her hand was cool to his touch, even though the temperature hovered near seventy degrees.

She noticed his concern about her less than normal body temperature and joked about it saying, "You know what they say; cold hands, warm heart." She remembered saying that to David all those years ago. As soon as she said that, his gaze dropped down to her breasts, voluptuous, even in a jogging suit.

As he held her hand, he could feel Lani warming with his touch, almost as though she was drawing his body heat away from him. It felt discomforting, but not at all unpleasant. Just staring into her eyes seemed to make him feel that she wanted to be near to him.

The warmth from Brad's hand stirred her hunger so much for his essence that she wanted to take him right here, right now, but she couldn't: someone might see her feeding and that would neither be very good for Lani, nor for the person who happened upon her drawing the life from her victim. It would certainly mean one more dead person on her list of almost fifty five thousand victims in the past one hundred and fifty nine years.

She came out of her semi-trance and asked, "Brad, would you like to come up to my house for a drink? I can drive you back to the clubhouse later;

unless, of course finishing your round would be more important to you?"

Brad smiled, definitely sure that he would be banging Lani in short order, and he wanted to do that very badly. Living alone and working sixty-five hours a week didn't open many avenues for sexual interludes, and he had not been with a woman in nearly a month. "Lani, I'd love to come up for a drink. Will you be able to put my clubs in your car or would you like me to walk back to my car and drive it back to your house? We could have dinner, if you'd like? After all, a girl must eat, right?"

"Brad, I can honestly tell you that I am truly starved, and a bite would really settle my stomach. I get butterflies whenever I meet a nice guy like you. Tell you what, let's stroll on up to the house and you can throw your clubs in my garage and pick them up tomorrow when we get your car. We'll have a drink, freshen up a bit and I'll fix you a steak. How's that sound to you?"

He answered her with a smile and a nod, too blown away to speak. *She is already inviting me to spend the night. I am going to get lucky with this beautiful woman!* Taking her hand in his and pulling his golf cart, they walked through the woods to the house.

They had barely taken two steps into the foyer when Lani kicked the door shut and passionately kissed him. Brad was surprised and taken aback by her forwardness, even though he wanted to get her into bed as soon as possible, but he responded. When she opened her mouth to slip him tongue, he noticed her awful breath, but his manhood was beginning to rise and he didn't care. She rubbed it through his slacks and he began to gasp in pleasure and readiness but he said through his panting, "Lani, we have to stop for a moment. I haven't had a woman in a month and I'm afraid I'll climax before I'm inside you."

She pulled her hand away, smiled and replied, "Okay, Brad. I understand how that could happen. Want to take a cold shower with me so we can calm ourselves down, It's been a while for me, too, and I'd like to make it last. I really liked you from the moment I met you, Brad."

Taking his hand in hers, she led him down to the basement to an oversized shower stall. They undressed, both eyeing each other up, their separate hungers growing at a feverish pace. Once inside the shower with the door closed, Brad not noticing that she had locked it, they began to kiss, and Lani actually felt like having sex with him before his demise. At least he would go out happy and leave a good-looking, bloodless corpse, she thought, bemused at the fact.

Although she was disappointed that his cock was one of the smallest she had ever seen, especially for a man his size, she had learned many tricks over the years to please herself and make him feel like a Clydesdale, even if it would only be for less than an hour at best. Lani hated long relationships, but she truly loved David; perhaps that is why she let David live when she could have killed him so easily. Love was an emotion that was seldom in her vocabulary or her life.

She turned on the water as they kissed. Brad squeezed her breasts, a little too hard she thought, but what the hell, it was the last time he would ever tweak a tit so she let him do his thing. Brad stopped kissing her on the lips and began to kiss her neck, keeping one hand on her left breast while the other one moved downward to that moist place he longed to be inside. As he rubbed her clitoris with his finger and continued to play with Lani's nipple, she moaned loudly, making Brad feel like he was pleasing her more than she had ever been pleased in her life. He would never know that he was one of thousands before him.

Brad continued on his downward journey, stopping briefly to suck her tits and bite her nipples. When he did this, Lani bared her fangs, although he did not see, and she cried out in pleasure, pushing his head down further until he was licking her where his finger had just been. After she exploded, he stood up and entered her, stabilizing her against the wall, holding her butt as he thrusted. She wrapped her long legs around him, jockeying herself into a better position, and making him feel quite Herculean as he continued to pump, spewing into her after only a dozen or so thrusts. Brad felt better than he had in months and when his heart settled down to less then a hundred beats a minute, he guessed, he raised his face to her, desperately wanting to kiss her again and again and his eyes, large with fear, saw what she had become. Fortunately he didn't have to see her that way for long because she grabbed his hair and pulled his head to the side, biting him with a ferocity even she had not experienced in a long, long time.

As she drank, Brad began to lose his grip on her and she slipped down his body. She stopped sucking momentarily to wrap her legs around him tighter, as blood began to spurt from the two punctures in his neck. He tried to get a hand up to the wounds to stop the flow, but she held his arms and went back to her feeding. She felt his heart stop pumping, but she continued to eat, wanting to get as much out of him as she could. As he died, Brad's corpse collapsed on the shower room floor. His head made a horrible noise when it cracked open. Brain fluid seeped out and was washed down the drain. She then proceeded to slit his throat, even though she gave a moment's thought of allowing him to become a vampire. She ached for eternal companionship, and she really did like him

After making sure all the blood was washed away, Lani turned off the water and left the shower to towel off and get dressed. She picked up Brad's lifeless body, looking at his open mouth in what must have been a silent scream, and she threw him into the backseat of her car. She drove to a pier, weighted him down with several large rocks she had found, and tossed him into the ocean for the fish to feast upon. She drove to the club and put his clubs in his car. She drove his car several miles away. The vampire then hailed a cab for a ride back to her house. After paying the cabbie, she walked back to the club and returned home in her car.

❧☙

A knock on the door brought Lani back to the present and when she opened it, she said, "Yes, may I help you?"

"Good morning, Miss. My name is Jordan Walsh and I would like to ask something of you. Every day now I've seen you standing on your deck as I walked by and I'd like to paint your portrait, if I am not being too forward. You have a remarkable looking face, but your sad eyes are what have really captured my attention. They seem to bear the burden of generations, yet they sparkle so." She had extended her hand outward, waiting for the woman to accept it, yet she didn't until Jordan finished speaking.

While greeting her guest, the vampire replied, "I'm Lani Jorgenson and I'm flattered that you would want to paint me, a total stranger. Have you painted many portraits?" Lani ushered her inside, walking to the kitchen with Jordan trailing her. "Would you like some coffee, Jordan? Do you mind if I call you by your first name?"

"I would absolutely love some coffee, Lani, and I'm glad we can be on a first name basis, even though we've just met."

While Lani made a pot of coffee, licking her lips at the thought of drawing out Jordan's life force, she said, "I would very much like to hear about your painting abilities to see if I would want you to paint me. I had a portrait done once before and I wasn't truly satisfied with the work of the artist. Before I acquiesce, I would like to see some samples of your work and of course we would have to come up with a fair price for your work."

Lani turned toward her guest, who was looking around the kitchen, her mind somewhere else.

"A penny for your thoughts."

She looked up at her hostess, smiled and said, "I'm sorry, I was just remembering what it was like to have coffee in a similar kitchen with my husband."

The vampire was ready to dismiss any thoughts of taking this woman, but instead replied, "Have you been married long?"

Jordan's eyes turned downward, staring at her empty ring finger, and when she looked back at Lani, stated flatly, "Marty and I have been recently divorced." The vampire smiled again as she asked, "Any kids?"

"Thank God, no. Marty was so caught up with his business that there was hardly ever time for sex, let alone having children. I guess at 34, I'm running out of time to have any, especially since there is no man in my life now, nor in the immediate future. How about you?"

"No, there's no Mr. Jorgenson, nor is there a man in my life right now, either. There were a few times when it got close, but the guy usually disappeared, never to be seen again." *Thousands of men!*

"I hear that from so many women. Guys just don't seem to want to get caught up in a lasting relationship and they wind up splitting, usually after getting what they wanted out of the time together with the woman."

Lani brought two steaming cups of coffee to the breakfast bar, hopped up on a stool and said, "I guess I was lucky in one respect. I always got everything I needed from my brief relationships, leaving my partners drained at the end."

Jordan raised her cup in a salute saying, "You are lucky, then."

They drank coffee in silence for several minutes, both of them thinking about the other, although not in quite the same way. Lani broke the silence by asking, "Could I see samples of your work? If I like what I see, we could set up a schedule, if you wouldn't mind painting me here. I love this place and try to be here as much as time allows."

Jordan finished her coffee and said, "That would be great. Would you like to come to my place or should I bring some canvasses over her for you to look at? I only live down the beach a way, perhaps less than a mile. We could walk to my house together, or I could call a cab, if you think it too far to walk."

"I'd love to walk there with you. It will give us some time to talk. If you're free for the next hour or so, we could go now."

Jordan smiled and replied, "That would be great, since I have nothing going until this afternoon."

"Okay. Let me grab a jacket and we'll take a walk."

Twenty five minutes later, Lani was standing in Jordan's studio, gazing at all of her works, noting the fine attention to detail and use of rich colors." This stuff is very good. Have you sold many pieces? I see three or four that I would like to buy and hang in my house."

"I'm flattered, and no, I haven't sold many paintings yet. I guess I haven't pursued customers like other artists have, since I'm pretty much okay money wise. Even though Marty and I divorced, he insisted that I should have a percentage of the business we built together, which was a substantial amount. My financial advisor said that I should never have to get a conventional job, if I lived within reason, and didn't make extravagant purchases. That arrangement suited me fine, since it allows me all the time I need to paint and write."

"You're a writer, as well?"

"Yes, I have written a number of short stories and I have had a few published. Someday I want to write a book on painting, and then perhaps sit down and pen the great American novel, perhaps a historical look at a family through several generations."

"That sounds fascinating, being able to research the past, tracing a family genealogy to its roots and watching it branch out, connecting with the trees of other families." Lani smiled to herself. Her eyes danced as she remembered her own past, even though she never really gave much thought to finding out about her ancestors. She felt that that part of her life was not worth knowing about, but she now considered doing some research of her own.

"Do you know anything about your family tree, Lani?"

"No, I never really got into it, but you are stirring some embers deep in my soul and building a fire for knowledge of my family's roots. My stepfather *Is that what Marcus was, since he was responsible for my rebirth* was originally from Europe and I was told once that his roots went back to nearly one hundred and fifty years before the birth of Jesus."

Jordan was truly amazed by this fact and said, "Could I do research on your family, Lani? It sounds absolutely fascinating, and would probably make a great book."

Realizing that she had taken the conversation to a depth from with there would be no return, Lani answered, "Jordan, I think that would be a wonderful idea, for later on, but right now I am truly excited about you painting me and the two of us beginning a long lasting relationship."

Jordan, feeling stirrings she had not felt since her one brush with lesbianism back in high school, wondered if it was time again to try to love another woman. She certainly did not have much luck with men, not even really caring much about the lack of sex with Marty, but she was so much older than Lani and didn't know how her new friend would react to one of her advances. She'd have to play it slow, until she knew that this would work, for Lani was certainly a beautiful woman, but would she be interested in a gay relationship?"

Lani picked out the paintings she wanted and she and Jordan loaded them into the back of Jordan's 1991 Ford station wagon, They hopped in the car for the short ride back to Lani's house, although by road, it was nearly twice as far as it was walking along the beach. Both women were quiet during the trip, but Lani was becoming very nervous. As much as she wanted Jordan's blood, since her scent was becoming unbearably wonderful in the closed quarters of the car, she also wanted her sexually, and not just for one night, and Lani was unprepared for the type of feeling she was now having. As a vampire, blood and destruction were her pleasures, but the human part of her wanted that comfort and closeness that would be found in a relationship with Jordan. She'd have to bide her time and not kill Jordan until she was sure that she had had enough of her.

They arrived at Lani's house and took the paintings into the living room, placing them by the walls where Jordan thought they would look best. Lani laughed when Jordan picked up a canvas and placed it against the wall upside down, while Lani had her eyes closed, wanting to see how the painting would look against the wall. The two women were hysterical over what amounted to nothing, yet you would have thought that it was the funniest thing a person could witness. Jordan was beginning to get peculiar feelings about Lani and she didn't know what would become of them.

"Okay, Jordan, I'll close my eyes again while you put the painting against the wall again, but this time, turn it around." When Lani opened her eyes and looked at the painting, a seascape at sunset, she really liked how it looked against the pale blue wall. "Yes, that is perfect there. It is such a wonderful painting, Jordan. I love it, as I love all the work you have done. I think it is time to talk business, now. I would really enjoy you painting me."

As they drank coffee and talked about art, Jordan listened intently to Lani's description of a painting she really loved, done by an obscure artist in the late 19th century. It was almost as though she had witnessed the painter at work, when she spoke of the way he mixed his colors to get that perfect shade. Jordan knew that the painter had disappeared shortly after finishing the work Lani was talking about. Rumor had it that the painter, Arthur Gilmore, had run away with a young blonde woman he had been seen with for several weeks before his disappearance. Jordan recalled reading an article about Gilmore somewhere and she was pretty sure that the reporter had alluded to a sketch of the woman, and had written that foul play could have been involved since Gilmore was reputedly worth several million dollars, most of it in art and gold, assets that could become liquid very quickly. Jordan made a mental note to try to remember in what publication she had read this story. A story like that would make a wonderfully, exciting novel.

"...Jordan? Are you still with me? You look as though you are a million miles away."

"I'm sorry, Lani. Something came to mind that I need to research. If you don't mind, I'm going to get going now but I'll be back tomorrow, at, say ten thirty, and we can begin your portrait."

"That would be great. I am really anxious to see how you capture me on canvas, and I must say that your price was more than fair." Lani escorted Jordan to the door and they waved to each other just before Jordan hopped inside her car. Lani closed the door and leaned back against it, closing her eyes and allowing her fangs to grow; she bit her own wrist just to taste Brad's blood, hunger overtaking her body and soul. She ran into the kitchen, threw open the door and ripped open a bag of type O blood, holding it high above her upturned face, allowing the thick red essence to flow into her mouth like syrup, her joy of finally having a drink etched on her face like a child opening a present at Christmas.

Jordan leaped from her car and raced up the steps and into her house. She reached down and scooped up a handful of mail, taking a moment to see what had arrived. When she walked into her office, she had already looked at a large card announcing a three-day sale, fifty to seventy percent off; Victoria's Secret had sent her another catalog. Jordan placed on her desk a letter from Marty, a statement from MasterCard, and People magazine. She discarded the VS catalog and the three day sale card into the trash can wondering how many trees were cut down to make all this paper, advertisements that most people didn't want anyway and more of a burden on the mailman's back. Her letter carrier, Ralph, always complained about the amount of mail he had to carry each day, yet he always said, "Job security, Jordan. That's what all this junk mail is and I always tell my customers to keep it coming, for once it stops, many of us will be thrown out of work.'" Jordan would answer, "Hey, Ralph! I ordered more catalogs to help you keep your job," laughing as he threw her the finger, knowing he could because he knew her pretty well.

She sat on her leather chair and began going through her file cabinet, which was in total disarray, needing purging and alphabetizing of everything she had thrown in there. After searching for about fifteen minutes, she found the article and after rereading it, dialed the phone number listed at the end of the column. After five rings someone lifted the phone from its cradle and answered, "Hello, Jake Kelly here."

"Mr. Kelly, my name is Jordan Walsh and I was talking to someone today who spoke about a painting done by Arthur Gilmore. I had remembered reading your article about his disappearance and you made mention of a sketch of the woman involved."

"Yes, there is a sketch of her in my files somewhere, but I don't know what good it would do you since that was nearly one hundred years ago and the woman is long dead."

"Did anyone ever come up with a name?"

"Not off the top of my head, Mrs. Walsh, but if you really want to know, I can try to find out for you. My schedule isn't very pressing at the moment." Jake Kelly was sitting at his desk, an open bottle of Jim Beam bourbon in his left hand and a glass with three fingers of the dark liquid in his right. The phone was turned on in speaker mode. Mr. Kelly spent more time pouring booze than he spent banging the keypad lately. At sixty three he was just about ready to pack it in, but he wanted to finish out the year first, then he and his wife would take off for Florida to a nice retirement community where he would begin to flesh out his third novel, still hoping to sell the first two. "Do you have a fax number where I can send the picture and any more information I can find." As Jordan told him, Jake Kelly wrote it down, after throwing down the drink and setting the empty tumbler on his desk pad. "Okay, Mrs. Walsh, as soon as I find everything, I'll get it out to you, ASAP.

"Thank you, Mr. Kelly. I appreciate it and look forward to your fax." She hung up the phone wondering what the hell she was trying to discover about a one hundred year old disappearance, even if it would make a good novel, true or untrue. After a moment of thought, she stood up and began to pack up her travel kit with everything she'd need to begin Lani's portrait.

⁂

Several days had passed and the portrait of Lani was coming along really well. Each day they had a three hour sitting and Jordan would allow Lani to see the progress she was making, with Lani making suggestions to enhance her image.

After the fourth session, when Lani came around to check the daily progress, she got closer to Jordan than ever before, brushing cheeks, a rush of something coursing through her body, Jordan's scent becoming stronger. When Lani pointed out a spot in the background she felt could use more color, Jordan turned her head and looked deep into Lani's eyes. Their faces moved toward each other and they kissed, hard and passionately. Jordan abruptly stood up, maintaining her lip lock with Lani, ignoring her unpleasant breath, something she had been aware of since their first meeting, and put her arms around the younger woman, her sexual arousal nearing a peak. After a long kiss, Lani breathlessly said, "Let's go to my bedroom, Jordan." She took her guest by the hand and they calmly walked upstairs and fell onto the bed, tearing at each other's clothes, licking and sucking one another until they both exploded in waves of pleasure. Lani had to turn away because she did not want Jordan to see her exposed fangs, which appeared during every lovemaking session, whether with men or women.

Jordan stroked the vampire's hair with one hand and rubbed her naked back with the other, saying, "What's wrong, Lani? That was fantastic, I thought. I hope I pleased you."

Lani had settled back into a more human mode, turned toward her newfound lover and replied, "Nothing is wrong, Jordan and yes that was amazing." She tickled Jordan and whispered, "Wanna do that again?"

Jordan smiled and tweaked Lani's nipples, nodding her head, unable to speak as a catch came into her throat. Her friend had now become her lover and things might get a bit sticky from here on in. She thought about how she had not received anything from Kelly so she called back earlier that day, getting his answering machine, hoping he would fax her today. Surprisingly, as she was thinking about this, her fax machine was beginning to spew out several eight and a half by eleven pieces of paper, one showing the sketch of the woman involved with Arthur Gilmore.

After several more rounds on the mattress and a sexual escapade in the shower, while they were toweling each other off, Jordan said, "Lani, I hate to leave, but I have some work I must do at home, but I could come back later and stay the night if you would like me to."

Lani turned toward her lover, exposing her incredible, albeit white body to Jordan. She drank the vision in as one would a fine wine, slowly, a smile crossing her lips. Lani said, "Jordan, I believe I am in love with you, but I am not ready to commit to overnight relationships at this time. Perhaps in a few days I will change my mind, but right now let's leave it to our session time and a few hours afterward." Lani took Jordan's face in her cold hands and kissed her full on the lips again and again as Jordan rubbed her lover's breasts. They broke free and after dressing, Jordan drove home feeling better then she had ever felt, even with Marty. Perhaps she truly was a lesbian. She went upstairs to bed without checking her fax machine.

Jordan / Lani / David

After Jordan left the house, Lani went out hunting. She needed blood and the few bags she had wouldn't do it. The vampire needed to feel the explosion of blood after biting through flesh, deep into an artery. She longed to hear the heart of her victim straining to pump the ever decreasing supply the human body needed coursing to all of its parts, keeping them working properly with the oxygen it supplied. She raced down the beach to watch Jordan undress and hop into bed, and she could see her rubbing her clitoris with her finger. Lani wanted to go up there and turn her into a vampire, to have someone to go throughout eternity with, but she could not do it. Did she love this woman as much as she loved David, still, even though he was very old now, and still hunting her? Lani knew that David was in Myrtle Beach because she had not only felt him, but last week she saw him. Somehow he was able to track her movements pretty closely, and it was becoming quite disturbing.

Her keen hearing picked up the sound of sneakers pounding the sand: a lone runner perhaps? She looked in the direction of the sound until she saw the man jogging down the beach, alone. He appeared not to have a care in the world, not knowing that his life was just about to end.

Lani bared her fangs, saliva dripping down her chin: she was so hungry and raced toward the man, pouncing upon him and in one swift movement bit through his neck, but he turned away at the same moment, his blood spurting into the air, splashing onto the sand creating little black spots as it soaked into individual grains. As he prepared to scream, Lani put her hand over his mouth and said, "Shush, my friend, we don't want to disturb the good people who may be sleeping." As she spoke, blood spewed onto his face, mixing with his tears, his eyes growing larger with fright as he finally realized what was happening to him.

She smiled sweetly for a moment and then bit him again, viciously and ravenously, drawing the blood from him at an alarming rate. He knew he was dying and would not be able to stop this woman, yet he continued to fight until he breathed his last. Lani fell upon him, feeling his erection and smelling how he shit himself as his sphincter muscle relaxed after he died.

Lani abhorred the scent of excrement, but it was quite common among her victims and she dealt with it.

After licking the remaining blood from her lips and the wound around his neck, she walked into the ocean, dragging his body, forcing water into his lungs so he would drown. Lani had cut his throat with a sharp shell she found on the beach, forgetting to bring her straight razor. She knew that there were small sharks in the vicinity and she hoped they would move toward the body quickly and feed upon it. If and when he was found, his body would have been gnawed on by the ocean predators, leaving no evidence of a vampire. There were more people beginning to believe that such creatures really existed, but she didn't want to give them information to feed upon. Sometimes she wondered if she may not have done a proper job of slitting a victim's throat and that perhaps she was not the only vampire left, but she was absolutely certain that she would feel it there were any more of her kind in existence. It was even quite possible that one or more could have survived during Marcus's reign. She shook the thought from her mind.

Lani paced: she wanted to be with Jordan, perhaps almost as much as she had wanted to be with David all those years ago. He was still constantly on her mind, even after their last meeting, which nearly led to her demise.

The year was 1986 and she had not seen David in over twenty years, but she felt his presence, and wanted badly to see him. He would be almost fifty years old by now, but she figured that he would still be a handsome man, and she fantasized often about having sex with him one more time before his death, preferably by her. *Will I be able to kill him?* She thought she never could because her love for him was so strong. It took her many years before she finally understood that David was so much like her father, the only other man she had ever loved; in fact, it was at her father's grave where she felt him. Her mind went racing into the past.

Lani had gone back to Bangor only one time since that fateful day in 1840. It was ten years later and she longed to see her mom and dad once more, hoping to hold them both in her arms and beg for their forgiveness.

When she walked into the home in which she had spent the first twenty years of her life, she cried out in pain, wanting more than ever to have the curse lifted from her and become human again. She had missed this part of her life more than she could have ever dreamed possible. Both of her parents were gone for the day, as she knew they would be, but she needed to see her house again.

Her mother had kept her bedroom just as she had left it before setting out on their trip to New York. Lani sat on her bed, feeling its softness and warmth and she decided to lie down upon it, momentarily savoring her past.

She had so many memories of her mother telling her stories and her father reading to her from the bible, teaching her God's ways: ways she could never live under again, though she longed that she could. She sat back up and opened her nightstand to find all of her pretty things inside a velvet-lined box. Opening it, she discovered the ring Calvin Brennan had bought for her, professing his love on her eighteenth birthday, shortly before a runaway horse and buggy killed him. She slipped it on her finger and decided that she would take it with her, as she would the necklace she had found, a gift from her father.

Lani was lost in her thoughts and never heard them come into the room.

"My God, you have returned our daughter to us, Lord!" Her father exclaimed his joy at seeing his Lani, believing for years that she had indeed been killed by the stranger with whom they let her walk. He raced over and hugged her, feeling how cold she was.

Her mother had clutched her hand in her own and said, "Child, you are so cold. Are you ill?"

"Mother, father!" The joy in her dead heart was something she would treasure for as long as she lived. "Please sit down, for what I am about to tell you, you will not believe, but every word is true."

For nearly an hour, Lani spoke of her new life and what had transpired in all these years. "If you wish to kill me now, father, you may. For, if I leave this house, I will continue with what I need to do to stay alive. Please release me from my eternal damnation, father!"

Lani's father was mesmerized. His daughter was a vampire. Impossible! Creatures like that simply did not exist, but if they did, wasn't it his responsibility to remove the blight from the earth, saving all of humanity. He looked deep into her eyes and said, "I cannot kill my own flesh and blood, Lani. I am sorry." He placed the necklace around her and kissed it, blessing the inanimate object that would bind them till eternity.

She hugged them both, for the last time, and walked out of their lives forever, wanting to have died, yet happy to be alive. She never saw her mother faint, or her father pray to the Lord to not take his daughter, no matter what she had become.

Over the years she had found out that her mother never recovered from seeing her again, and she died the following year, but today, May 17, 1986 was the one hundredth anniversary of her father's passing and she wanted to come to his grave. The day was as gray as the feelings she possessed at this moment.

※※

As she knelt down to place some flowers by his headstone, she felt a hand upon her shoulder. "Hello, David," she said without even looking at him.

After she stood up and faced him, his features devoid of any emotion whatsoever, he acknowledged her with only a simple nod of his head.

She studied him. His face had taken on a few wrinkles, and his beard was beginning to show some gray. David's hair was shorter, but it only carried a few gray highlights. He had put on a few pounds, but she knew that middle age would do that to a man. When she closed in to kiss him on the cheek, he pushed her away.

"Don't ever touch me again, you vile creature," he uttered with a contempt born of over twenty years of rage for this woman he once had loved.

Lani smiled defiantly, looking around at the number of people in the cemetery and said, "I don't think you would do anything stupid to defile this place of rest, especially with all of these onlookers, now would you, my love?"

He swiveled his head and looked at the number of people, many whose eyes were trained upon him at this very moment. "No, I would not do anything here, Lani, but when we leave the grounds, I will do everything in my power to destroy you. You are a blight upon humanity and I have not been able to live a proper life in all these years, hoping to one day meet you again and end your existence." His words were accompanied by drops of spittle, which wound up upon her face, pissing her off to the point where he saw a little of her fangs, something he hoped he would never see again, ever.

"Now how about giving me a kiss and we'll talk about old times." She bumped up against him, smiled and said, "Is that a sword under your jacket, or are you happy to see me, David." She grasped the blade through his long coat, rubbing up and down over the length of the weapon. Lani stood up on her toes and licked his ear, saying, "That's a mighty long sword you have there for me. How about the other sword, David? Does that still get long and hard for your women? She squeezed his manhood playfully, yet it was enough to stir him. "Yes, I see it still does get long and hard for me."

He pushed both of her hands away as she laughed heartily. "You'd love to take my head right about now, wouldn't you?"

"Lani, nothing in the world would give me more satisfaction than seeing you die."

"You know, all I'd have to do is scream and say, 'he has a weapon and he's going to kill me', and what do you think would happen then, my friend?"

"I guess you have me over the barrel for now, but I swear I will kill you someday, Lani. You can't keep living forever, destroying human life."

"David, most of the people I feed on are a detriment to society as it is, and I am doing everyone a favor, but you humans don't understand that, do you?"

"How can you expect me to understand that you kill in order to live?

Killing derelicts is still killing, Lani, no matter how you look at it. Obviously I will never understand."

Lani looked deeply into his eyes and said, "I could make you like I am and we could feed together and live throughout eternity. Remember how good the sex was between us, David, and you are still young enough to please me."

David was horrified, not ever considering what she had just said as a possibility. "How many more of your kind are there, Lani?"

"I won't lie to you, David. I am the only vampire left in the world, but I love you and I want you to be with me." She once again tried to get close to him and was pushed away, which angered her even more: her teeth flashed and her eyes reddened. Her voice grew hard with contempt and she said, "Perhaps I should kill you now, slash your throat and feed you to the fishes, Forrester."

"Perhaps you should, Lani, and end my lifelong torment. Here, I'll make it easy for you." He bent toward her, exposing his neck, and she was so close to taking him, even with all the people watching them, though they had no idea of what was going on, but instead, she merely walked away from him, worrying the beads upon the necklace she always wore, her symbol of another life.

As she thought about her father, she felt the swish of the blade that had missed her by less than an inch. She spun around and knocked it from David's grasp, threw him to the ground and fell on top of him. They were behind some shrubbery where people could not see them and she bared her fangs, her face not more than a foot from his and said, "Do you really want to die this way, David? I will drink from you and then slash your throat and feed you to the fishes!" Her breath was more horrid than he had remembered and although he did not want to live like this, his desire to destroy her was so strong that he pleaded for his life, hoping to have one more opportunity to hunt her down again and finally remove the world of the last vampire, a world that didn't even know she existed.

"Please don't kill me, Lani! I beg of whatever humanity might be left inside you." He struggled with her, closing his eyes, afraid that she would never consent to his request, but her grip on him abated and when he opened his eyes, he once again saw the soft features of her face, her eyes always sad looking. Her long blonde hair tickled his face and for a moment he was in love with her again.

She got off of him and said, "David, I will let you go because you know I still love you, but you must stop hunting me or I will have to kill you."

Lani walked away, leaving David on the ground, gasping for air, his heart hammering inside his chest, realizing how close he had come to the end of his life.

※

As the thoughts of David waned, she once again looked up at Jordan's bedroom window, deciding that now was not the time to go in there, but she had definitely made up her mind. Jordan Walsh would soon walk the earth as her companion throughout eternity.

※

David paced in his room, several miles down the beach. He knew that Lani was somewhere in Myrtle Beach, but he didn't know where. The article had said that a golfer had been missing, but it never said what course he had been playing, and with the Grand Strand having nearly one hundred courses, he would have a difficult time finding out where the man had played that day, unless he went down the list alphabetically and called each one to try to get the information he needed to continue his quest. The police department would not tell him anything since he was not a relative of the missing man, Brad Carson. He knew that Lani had probably been walking in the woods bordering the golf course, and had attacked him, but that still didn't give him a clue. In the morning he would begin calling all the courses to see if Brad Carson had played there recently, making up a story about finding his custom made pitching wedge and wanting to get it back to him. David finished his drink and went to bed, sleeping fitfully as images of Lani danced through his mind: Lani, the lover, and Lani the vampire, both images causing him to toss and turn until he finally stopped dreaming in the middle of the night.

※

Jordan had awakened at about three o'clock in the morning with a dry throat and a still wet bed. She crawled out from under the covers and pulled the sheet from the mattress, replacing it with a dry, fresh one she had stored in her closet. After finishing that task, she decided that sleep would not be forthcoming for a while, so she slipped into her robe, opened the sliding glass door and stepped out onto the deck for some fresh air. Looking toward the water, she noticed a spot of sand that appeared to have been disturbed by some kind of activity. She smiled, figuring it had been two zealous lovers, eager to get it on, not being able to wait until they got home. Jordan remembered having heard a scream shortly after going to bed, but she was too busy working herself to wonder what the man was screaming about, until she saw the sand. He had probably climaxed and screamed his passion, passion that she was feeling for Lani. In the morning she would go to her house and profess her love to her beautiful, blonde friend.

A stiff breeze came up and suddenly Jordan was freezing. She went back inside and closed the door, rubbing the chill from her arms, and then she lay back down upon the bed and grabbed the remote control from her nightstand. She began clicking through the channels; finally stopping when she saw a movie was on. The images fluttered in front of her eyes, which kept opening and closing as she fought the need for sleep. It was a musical, made sometime back in the late thirties or early forties, she thought, but there was something nagging at her brain as she tried to go to sleep, the image of a woman in the background as the dancers strutted their stuff on the stage inside the nightclub.

    Suddenly Jordan sat straight up, her eyes not believing what she was seeing. She hopped out of bed and raced to the TV, quickly sliding a tape into the VCR and pressing record/play, hoping that the camera would pan the audience again. When it did, Jordan nearly screamed at the top of her lungs. There, sitting at a table by herself was Lani Jorgenson, or a woman with an amazing likeness of her, nearly sixty years in the past. Jordan continued to watch and tape the movie, seeing the actress, or extra, three more times, the last time near the end of the film, hearing her speak for the very first time. It was only a sentence, but it was Lani's voice she was hearing.

    Jordan stood up and paced inside her room, wondering if she was seeing a woman who had to be about eighty years old, with the face and body of a twenty year old, but that couldn't be possible, could it?

    She went into the bathroom, peed, and after washing her hands, splashed water onto her face, trying to get rid of the tiredness she felt, for she could not go back to sleep, but she didn't know what to do. All of a sudden, she remembered the fax machine and she purposefully strode into her office, turned on a light and walked to her desk. She immediately saw that several faxes had come in during the day, the top one being the sketch of the blonde woman, matching Lani right down to the necklace she wore. Jordan gasped, knowing that she was falling in love with a woman of not only unknown age, but also what else? The only creatures that could live over a hundred years and still look youthful were myths, legends-vampires. Could Lani Jorgenson be a vampire? Jordan needed to find out more about her, so she sat down and turned on her computer, trying to find out if a woman named Lani Jorgenson lived in any other time period, even though entertaining that idea was totally absurd.

    An hour into her search, she came upon a website listing obscure disappearances from the nineteenth century. She entered Lani's name and was rewarded *horrified* by what she read. A woman matching Lani's age and description had disappeared in 1840, on her twenty-first birthday. Jordan printed the page and sat there for a long time rereading the news item and staring at the sketch of Lani.

    She called Marty and told him what she had found out and that she was really disturbed.

"Honey, it's probably all coincidence. Vampires simply do not exist, and you know that." Marty stifled a yawn from being awakened from a deep sleep.

"Marty, I understand we are dealing with something that is only put forth on film or in novels, but the similarities are remarkable, especially the necklace. Lani told me that the necklace was a gift from her father and that it was very old and had been in the family for over one hundred and fifty years. How could that be a coincidence?"

On the other end of the line, Marty Walsh was pondering what Jordan was telling him, wondering if she was going mad. Getting involved with a woman was one thing, but being deluded into the possibility that her girlfriend was a vampire, and nearly two hundred years old to boot, was not realistically plausible to his orderly mind. "What are you going to do about it, Jordan?"

"I honestly don't know, Marty. I guess I have to do some more research. Oh, I was also watching a movie tonight, but I don't know its title, but I know you and I had watched it a few times when we were together. You may even have it in your video library." She went on to describe the film, hoping that Marty would remember the title, for the TV guide didn't even list it.

"Sounds like "A Night On The Town", which was made in Forty One, I think. Why, what does that mean to you?"

"Coincidentally, the woman I am seeing, or her double was in the film and even had a speaking part near the end of the movie. Marty, it was Lani's voice. Plus, she was wearing the necklace."

"Okay, Jordan. I have to go out of town on business today, but I promise I will come over tonight and then you can introduce me to Lani and let me see the sketch and I'll watch what you taped. Maybe there is some kind of explanation. The actress could be Lani's grandmother, perhaps, which would account for the similarities in looks and speech patterns."

Jordan thought for a moment and then replied, "Marty, you are probably right. Come to my place tomorrow night about eight, and I will make sure Lani is here. I'll just sit on this stuff until you see it and then we'll go from there."

"Fine, Jordan. I'll see you tomorrow night, then. Bye."

He hung up without letting her say goodbye, so she shouted, "Asshole!" into the dead phone and slammed it back onto its cradle.

She was preparing to spend a long time at the keyboard, both researching and writing, but first she needed a drink, badly. Jordan stood up and stretched. She yawned and then turned around, staring into the face of Lani Jorgenson.

Jordan was floored and as she backpedaled away from her friend, she stumbled over her chair and fell to the floor.

"My, we have been busy, haven't we? To what do I attribute all this effort?" She waved her hand across the sketch, the article and the doodling Jordan had been doing while on the phone with Marty.

She grabbed Jordan around the neck, lifting her and raising her two feet above the floor, with Jordan trying to break her stranglehold, as her eyes were beginning to bulge and her air was completely cut off. Lani put her back down and said, "Answer me, bitch. Exactly what the fuck have you been looking for?"

Jordan coughed a few times, and then she swallowed the bile that had been rising in her throat. "Lani, how did you get in here?"

"Hey babe, when you've lived as long as I have, you can do almost anything. Locked doors have been child's play since about eighteen fifty five, if I remember correctly." Lani smiled, baring her fangs to Jordan for the first time. "Didn't you know that vampires were super strong and extremely smart?" I must admit, it took me until about an hour ago to figure out that you might be on to me after I talked about the Gilmore painting, but it finally sank in and I figured I had better get over here before you came up with more answers, but after seeing what you have on your desk, I guess I was a bit late."

Jordan asked, "May I sit down, or must I stand in the presence of a person so senior to me?"

"That's a good one, Jordan. I'll have to use that sometime, oh, but I can't, for no one is older than I, except for the two creators, three if you count Marcus, who was my creator. The other two, of course, being God and Satan." She hopped up onto the desktop and sat with her legs crossed, looking down at the woman she had been in love with, but no longer. "Let's go for a walk on the beach and I'll tell you my story."

Jordan knew that the statement was not a request, but a command, and if she had any hope of staying alive longer, she had to obey. They both walked from the house and strolled the beach. Lani told Jordan how she was transformed into a vampire and what her life had been like for past one hundred and fifty nine years. "I look pretty good for almost one eighty, don't I, Jordan?"

"Yes, Lani, you look very good." What else could she say? All the while that Lani was talking, Jordan was trying to figure out a means of escape, to live, but there seemed to be no way.

Lani stopped walking and said, "Unfortunately, lover, this is where it must all end, and although I very much want to drain your blood from your body, I will give you the option of death by bloodletting or death by drowning. It's your choice, but you know you must die."

"You let David live, why not me?"

"Because I love David more than anything, except living forever, but he has been a real thorn in my side, and two thorns I don't need. So, what's your choice?"

Jordan had been kneeling, running her hand through the sand. She looked up at Lani and said, "Neither, bitch!" She threw a handful of sand into Lani's eyes and open mouth, causing her to gag and scratch at her eyes.

While Lani was trying to clear her eyes and retching sand and old blood on to the beach, Jordan took off, running as fast as she could, her heart pumping, lungs straining for every molecule of oxygen she could take in, yet knowing it would only be a short stay of execution, for she could already hear Lani screaming her name, her voice becoming louder each second.

Lani was upon her in less than a minute, slamming her body into Jordan and knocking the wind from her. Jordan fell to the soft sand with a dull thud and turned over on to her back, seeing Lani, in full bloom as a vampire, staring down at her, shaking her head and laughing maniacally. "Jordan, I gave you a choice, but now we have to do this my way. Goodbye my love." She fell onto Jordan, sank her teeth into her neck and began to drink, slowly, savoring each swallow, as Jordan slipped mercifully into unconsciousness.

After Lani drank her fill, she slit Jordan's throat and dragged her into the water, drowning her and adding one more life to her growing list.

She went back to Jordan's place and removed all the offending evidence, taking it back to her house, where she burned it all. It was time to move on.

The Road North

The Plantation

After killing Jordan, she knew she would have to leave the area, and so Lani Jorgenson packed her belongings and threw them into the rear of her 1998 Ford Windstar, hopped in, and found her way to I-95. It was going to be a long drive, perhaps 10 hours or more, depending upon traffic and she knew she wanted to make one stop on the way.

It had been over one hundred and forty years since she last visited the plantation, enjoying the essence of so many young, strong blacks, reducing the slave population to half its normal strength, their disappearances puzzling the overseers and the master of the house a great deal. They had always had slaves run away, but they were eventually caught, returned and punished for their crime of desertion. The James river held many of her secrets from that time and occasionally she wondered if any of the bodies had floated back up to the surface, their once ebony skin the color of burned charcoal after all that blood was sucked from the very fiber of their bodies. Lani had to smile, recalling one particular slave who attempted to fight her off and nearly succeeded in killing her, an adversary she had never anticipated seeing in her immortal life.

The plantation, a tobacco farm of nearly two thousand acres was situated a few miles southeast of Williamsburg, and although Lani had forgotten its name, she recognized the house immediately after finding it. She had stopped at numerous gas stations on the way, searching for its exact location and finally, at a 7-11, the store clerk was able to give her the proper directions. He was young, probably not over 18, but she knew that he would not live to see his next birthday, for after a visit to the farm, she would come back here and take him, making it look like a robbery/murder. She felt that the store was set in such a manner that no one would see her do the deed and leave, once the lights were out.

Lani thanked him for his assistance and then drove the three miles to the plantation, parking her minivan on the shoulder of the road; a few hundred feet from the lane threading its way to the house. The trees guarding the entrance were majestic now, and she remembered when Burton Hennings had them planted, mere saplings at the time. Because of their enormous growth, she was only able to get a glimpse of the roofline of the main house, which appeared to be structurally the same after all these years.

She walked toward the house on the paved lane, recalling how, when it was still dirt, the wagons leaving the property, full with freshly harvested tobacco, would get hung up in the ruts after a particularly heavy rain and the blacks would curse and sweat as they utilized the combined strength of a dozen men to break the wheels free of the muck, enabling the driver to once again proceed to his destination. As she would watch the slaves work, sweat glistening upon their bare chests, she could hear their hearts pumping at a furious rate through their exertion. Lani could almost smell the blood circulating through arteries and veins, supplying oxygen to overworked muscles, which sometimes demanded more than could be given, the man's labor more than his body could tolerate, and she would then know who would be her next victim—the weakest of the lot, this particular time being Heywood. As she stood there, she recalled her days at the plantation.

The sun was vicious as the enclosed carriage made its way up the wide, dirt lane, lined with saplings, to where the magnificent house stood. Even from this distance, Lani could see how huge it was and she was quite impressed. Burton had described the house to her many times but to actually see it nearly took her breath away.

Four marble columns rose from the porch to the overhanging roof. As her gaze traveled upward she could see there were at least four rooms above stairs, facing the front of the house. Each window had a window box beneath the green shutters beside the glass panes. Each box, also the color of fresh tree leaves, was brilliant with flowers of many colors. A chimney rose from each end of the mansion, signifying two fireplaces for added warmth in winter. The clapboards must have been recently painted because their whiteness shone in the sunlight, and the house appeared brand new. Lani wondered if Burton had it painted for her arrival. She sat back and looked out from both sides of the carriage watching numerous darkies tending to the crops, mainly tobacco; however, Burton had a quite large vegetable garden that needed constant care. He always wanted to present fresh produce to his guests at dinners and parties. Burton told her many stories about the plantation after their lovemaking sessions, which lasted surprising long, considering his age. He was forty-six years old, but he was a wonderful physical specimen and sex with him was quite good she thought. True, he couldn't keep up with her growing sexual appetite, one of the benefits *curses* of immortality, but then again, no one could.

As she daydreamed, a tiny ray of light passed through the open windows of the carriage, drawing a diagonal beam in front of Lani's face. When she tried to grab it, she felt pain, but no burning. Her immunity was building, and she was sure that it wouldn't be too many more years before she would be free of the sun curse, although it would be longer than she thought it would be.

The carriage made its way up the steep hill and she could hear the labored breathing of the horse; its massive legs struggling to make headway up the steep slope. The driver kept cracking his whip along the flanks of the noble steed, causing the horse to whinny each time it was struck. Lani could see the fear in the horse's eyes whenever it turned its head outward. The horse was beginning to get too old for this kind of work and Lani was getting angry with the driver as he kept brutalizing the animal.

She briefly bared her fangs, wanting to take and destroy the driver now, to sate both her anger and her hunger. It had been some time since she killed the bible thumper on the train from New York to Richmond. She could still see him in her mind's eye and she reminisced about that particular kill to take her mind off of her hunger and anger.

***

He boarded the train alone and sat directly across from her on the long journey. Lani immediately disliked him and she didn't care whether he was married or not, he would not live another day. She smiled at him after a quick scrutiny. The man stood about five feet eight inches tall and weighed close to two hundred and fifty pounds, she guessed. His round face was topped by unkempt black hair, little wisps of gray forming at the temples. He wore it long and it nearly blended in with the blackness of his frockcoat As he stared at her through dark, brown eyes beneath bushy eyebrows, a smile crossed his thick lips and his wide, flat nose dripped snot into the man's full moustache. Though his beard was long, it was neatly trimmed.

They made small talk during the ride, Lani finding out that he had been recently divorced from his wife of seventeen years, she not having been in love with him for the past few. He left her with the responsibility of taking care of their three children, all girls. When Lani asked what had led to the divorce, the man, Evan McCabe stated, "Regrettably I was a heavy drinker and a gambler until I found the Lord, and perhaps after that I was very difficult with my wife and children, and over time they turned away from me. My ex-wife is a wonderful woman and I hope she finds a man she can be happy with for the rest of her life.

McCabe turned his face to the window and watched the scenery fly by until darkness covered everything. Lani waited until she was sure that everyone was asleep before quietly and quickly extinguishing his life. She lifted his beard and slit his throat, gently placing him in a sitting position, where he would appear to be asleep. The porter would find him long after the rest of the passengers had departed and it would appear to be a murder but the police would be confused about the absence of blood.

⚜

Lani came back to the present when the horse stumbled in a wagon rut, causing the driver to spew obscenities at it. She stuck her head out from the window to see the horse limping, knowing it would now have to be destroyed, for a horse with a broken leg would be worthless. She knew she would not be able to take the driver now because he would be busy destroying the horse and would have some of the field hands help him get rid of the carcass. Hell, they'd probably get to eat it if the driver wouldn't ask for too much money for the corpse. She would have to eat later, after everyone was in bed.

The horse lumbered the rest of the way to the front of the mansion and two blacks, dressed in fine clothing, came to the carriage. One opened the door for Lani, while the other placed a wooden box on the ground for her to step on, easing her exit.

When Lani stepped from the carriage and began to walk to the front door, the slaves followed with her luggage. Burton was waiting inside the massive oak door, a smile of joy crossing his face as he saw the new mistress of the house. Obviously they would have to stay in separate rooms until a marriage was arranged, but both knew that each other's door would be open twenty four hours a day.

"Lani, it is so wonderful to see you again, my dear. It has been much too long since we last met." He took her proffered hand and kissed it lightly, bowing at the waist as she curtsied for him. "You also look quite well, Burton. I trust you feel as well as you look?"

"Yes, I do. Thank you, but I think it is time for you to come in and freshen up. The trip must have been quite grueling for you."

"I must say, the train ride was quite long and dirty as I am still brushing coal dust from my garments, but it certainly was a speedy trip. I heard someone say that the train traveled at nearly forty miles per hour, however with frequent stops for water, the time was much longer than what the speed would suggest."

She looked around at the window boxes and smelled the flowers. "What wonderful fragrance, Burton? You have selected flowers that not are only beautiful to look at but they also have a wonderful scent. I also detect apple pies baking in an oven, and jasmine in the beds around the house. This is truly a magnificent place, Burton and I know it will be my home for many years to come," she lied with a straight face, knowing she would only be here for a few months at the most.

They went inside and Burton took her on a tour of the house. She marveled at the antique furniture, and the paintings that graced every wall of the house. On top of the fireplace mantel in the great room were porcelain figurines that the Hennings' had collected over the years. An ornate chandelier hung from the middle of the ceiling and was only a few feet over their heads.

Her bedroom was located in the middle front of the house and she opened the balcony doors and stepped outside to view the acreage spread before her. Thousands of acres of tobacco as far as the eye could see. The James River was the western border of the property and she hoped to dump many a body into it after feeding. *Yes, this place will suit me well,* she thought.

❧❦

A few weeks later, the vampire stood under a parasol, keeping her from the direct rays of the burning sun, watching a slave and taunting him, saying, "Heywood, a young, strong nigger like yourself should be able to hold your own with these other niggers who are much older than you, yet you grow weak from the strain. If Master Burton would see you not being able to carry your weight, he would whip you for sure."

Heywood stared back at her, knowing that she could just as well have him whipped, she being the Massa's woman since the death of his wife last year from the pox. Yet, she thoroughly enjoyed teasing those who were not performing as hard as the white folks thought they should. One thing Heywood noticed over the past few weeks was that whomever Lani taunted was found missing within a few days after her teasing, and this bothered him some, since he was now the one she was toying with. He would have to be careful around this woman.

The black man smiled at her and said, "Yes, Miss Lani, I am a powerfully weak nigger, for sure, but I done cut 'most fifty sticks of tobacco already today and hefting this wagon be taking all my strength away, but I be okay in a minute and we get this load rolling out of here."

Lani did not smile back at the slave, but she replied, "Heywood, if you put all your heart and soul into getting that wheel out of the mud, I will not tell Mr. Hennings that you are the weakest of the men around you."

Heywood knew that wasn't true, but what could he say except, "I'se thanking you, Miss Lani for letting me have another chance and I promises I won't let you down. You just watch ole Heywood put his back to this wagon wheel.

True to his word, the slave spit into his hands, rubbed them together, then gripped the bottom of the wagon, just to the front of the embedded wheel, and with a mighty heave, lifted the heavy wheel free from the brown goop that was holding it into the deep rut. She smiled and clapped her hands together, yelling out, "I knew that with a little motivation I could get you to work to your full potential, Heywood." Her mood abruptly changed and she curtly said, "Now, you get your black ass back to the fields and get that tobacco ready for the next wagon, you hear?"

"Yes'm," was all that Heywood could offer in return. His back was hurting so badly, probably having pulled a few muscles in order to avoid a whipping. His back was still raw from the ten lashes he was given last week for not informing on George, who Lani knew stole a pie from the window of the house, but did not tell the cook, enjoying the pain and suffering the slaves had to go through during the questioning. She couldn't figure out why these people would not tell on one another to save their own hides, but she really didn't care. As long as she could be amused, she was quite content to stay here until it became too risky of her true intentions being found out. She had been able to hide her existence all these years, so far, and she had no intention of getting caught now.

After dark, when most of the slaves were soundly asleep, groans of pain, and deep coughs were audible even at a distance of twenty yards from the shacks, Lani silently worked her way to the hovel that Heywood shared with fifteen other people. When she stepped through the open doorway, the stench of body sweat from sixteen people assailed her nostrils, and would have made a human gag, but Lani's acute nasal senses dismissed all odors except for the scent of blood. The fragrance of the essence of that many people in such a confined area nearly overwhelmed her with the lust to take them all. It would be easy and swift, but she knew she could not do it, wanting to stay on here for a little longer before moving north again.

She found Heywood easily enough, he being the largest of the supine bodies she gazed upon. Lani tapped him on the shoulder, seeing his eyes open even in the darkness, and she quietly shushed him before he uttered a sound, motioning him to follow her out into the courtyard.

After he followed her up the path toward the main house, wondering what he was getting himself into, yet not being able to resist her hypnotic eyes after he awakened, she turned into the woods and headed toward the river.

"Wha'fo you bringing me to da river, Miss Lani? Are you going to punish me for what I done today?"

"No, Heywood, I am not going to punish you, I am going to make you happy. I want to have sex with you. I always thought you were quite handsome for a darky and I am in need of a man. Since there are no young white men around, I have chosen you to satisfy my need."

"I don' unnerstand, Miss Lani. You is the lady of the house and the

Massa should be having you in his bed chamber?"

"Yes, Heywood, you are absolutely right, but Burton is over twice my age, and a young woman needs someone her age to keep a session in bed going for awhile." She squeezed his manhood, which was growing larger and harder with each squeeze of her hand. He was still single, not involved with any of the female slaves at this time, and she continued, saying, "If you don't freely have sex with me, I will be forced to tell the Massa that you attempted to rape me, and you know what that will mean." She drew her finger across her neck in a gesture of a beheading.

"Miss Lani, this not be right, dat I knows, but likes you say, if I doesn't do this, you could have me killed. You can even have me killed after I do this, but I guess I would die a little happier, knowing that I was able to have you one time. I admits, I has been taking looks at you every time you be in the fields, wondering what a white woman would be like, and now I guess I 'bout to find out."

Lani moved toward him and kissed him, his thick lips nearly engulfing her from the base of her nose to the bottom of her chin, and she was becoming delirious with his scent, wanting to kill him now, but also wanting to have him inside her, thrusting his huge cock in and out, quelling the fire in her loins, one of the human characteristics she retained and needed to fulfill from time to time. His large hands covered her breasts and he squeezed them as long as he could.

She pulled him down on top of her, and after a short time, they were both naked. He inserted his blood engorged penis inside her, thrusting as hard as he could, wanting to hurt her, yet enjoying his passion, slowing down to make it last as Lani scratched his back with her long nails, drawing blood and putting her fingers to her lips, licking the redness from her white fingers, whiter than Heywood could remember her being.

As he looked at her face, her moans of pleasure forcing her to keep her eyes closed, he saw something that frightened him. Her teeth were becoming like those of an animal and he finally noticed the horrible smell coming from her mouth. It smelled like death and he was confused about what was happening here. With each thrust she seemed to pull him deeper inside and when her eyes would open, they appeared red, as though they were bleeding.

Growing up in Africa, he had heard stories of vampires and although he dismissed them as legends and myth, he now believed that this woman could actually be one. Frantically he searched for a weapon as he continued to have sex with her. She seemed not to notice what he was looking for, enjoying herself too much. Through terrified eyes, Heywood noticed a piece of glass not more than a foot away from her head, lying at the base of a tree. He began to thrust harder, pushing her toward the tree and himself closer to the glass when she seemed to sense that something had changed his rhythm and had moved her body a significant distance across the soft grass they were lying upon. She opened her eyes to see him searching for something above her head and felt him reaching upward.

With the strength of ten men, Lani suddenly threw him off of her, and his surprise was noted through the whites of his eyes, and a silent scream. He landed just beside the broken windowpane. As she leaped upon him, her fangs bared and her eyes of fire staring at his neck, he grasped the glass and slashed at her, opening a three-inch long wound in her neck. She fell off of him to the side, holding the wound, which Heywood noticed, was not bleeding, as he attempted to get up and run from her, wondering if he would be able to make it back to the safety of his shack, or should he go to the house and tell Master Hennings what had just happened.

He had not taken more than four or five steps when she pounced upon his back, grabbed his forehead and pulled it toward the right, exposing the place on his neck, sinking her fangs deep through the skin. A sickly crunching noise could have been heard, had anyone been nearby: she began to drink, stopping while he was still alive, allowing his limp body to fall to the ground.

She wiped blood from her lips as it dribbled down her face, droplets racing to the inert form lying beneath her feet. Lani pulled Heywood to his feet and slapped him away from unconsciousness. When he opened his eyes and saw her, she was no longer a beautiful woman, but a vampire, an immortal unable to die, of that he was sure, after surviving his attack. He even noticed that the wound had closed and there was not even a scar where the glass cut through flesh and sinew. Heywood was breathing hard from a loss of blood and his mind was trying to accept the fact that the legends were true and as he opened his mouth, her hand flew over his lips, stifling his scream of pure terror.

Lani waited until he calmed down and then withdrew her hand, saying, "Heywood, how did you know I was a vampire?" She shook him as more words flowed from her mouth along with the smell of death. "Tell me how you knew and I may allow you to live!"

Heywood explained what he had seen while they were having sex and he also told her about the legends his father and grandfather had related to him back in Africa.

"Have you ever shared any of these stories with the other blacks on the plantation?"

"No, Miss Lani. I neber beliebed dem nohow! Please don't kill me and make me like you are!"

She grabbed his head again, exposing the other side of his neck and said, "I'm sorry, Heywood, but I don't believe you!" She sank her teeth into him and drank him dry. Sated, she sat there a moment, looking at his lifeless body, more upset that she was denied a sexual climax then his destruction.

After slashing his throat, Lani filled his pants and shirt with rocks and swam out about one hundred yards, allowing the body to sink to the bottom of the river where it would hopefully stay forever. She took the precaution of also slicing through her fang marks, making it look like just another nigger murder. She returned to the house, discarded her blood stained clothes and went back to Burton's bed, unsatisfied, but filled with warmth again.

In the present again, she walked up toward the house, noticing that it had been kept in marvelous repair and she had the desire to walk through the rooms to try to recapture that part of her life's memories.

As she thought about her last few days on the plantation, having a sexual experience with five more of the youngest blacks there, she was startled by a voice not ten feet from where she stood. In the past few years she had been taken by surprise on several occasions and she was wondering if she was losing her hearing, yet she could not go to a doctor to get checked out, unless she would kill everyone there, since they would find out she was not human.
"Hello, there, Miss. May I help you?"

She turned and looked into the dark eyes of Harrison Edmonds, owner of the farm. She smiled and said, "Yes, you may, sir. My name is Allison Vickery and I am a photojournalist doing research on old plantations of southern Virginia. I found this place on a website and since I was in the area I decided I'd pop over and take a look, if you don't mind." She decided to use a pseudonym since she was visiting a place where she had once lived.

"I don't mind, Miss Vickery, but I wish you would have called first and I could have set aside some time for us to talk. Is that your Windstar down the road, by the way?"

"Yes, it is, and please call me Ali. Unfortunately I had a breakdown," she lied, "and I've called AAA to come out to get me restarted, but I was told that it would be at least an hour, so I decided to at least look at the house, otherwise I would have called first. Are you leaving soon to go somewhere?"

"'Fraid so. I'm to give a lecture in Williamsburg tonight at the College of William and Mary."

"Are you a professor?"

He laughed and replied, "Guilty as charged. I teach a course titled 'Myths, Witches and Vampires of the South.'"

Lani's eyebrows rose slightly at the mention of vampires, but he seemed not to notice, since his focus had traveled down to her breasts before re-establishing eye contact.

"I was just about to ask you a stupid question, and so I will withdraw it before I insert my foot into my large mouth."

"Ali, I always tell my students that the only stupid questions are the ones not asked, so fire away."

She looked up toward the house and then back toward Harrison and said, "I was merely going to ask if you lived here, but for what other reason would you have asked me what I was doing here. Pretty dumb, huh?" Lani flashed him that radiant smile of hers once again, captivating him. She was really studying this man now. He was about six feet three inches, perhaps two twenty, solid throughout his body, revealed by the way his clothes molded to him. He looked like he was poured into his jeans and his t-shirt revealed a rather thick chest and large muscular arms. His light brown hair rested on the top of his ears, his left lobe sporting a diamond stud. His bangs swept to the right over a high forehead. Brown, nearly black eyes sparkled from beneath thick brows. He wore a neatly trimmed beard and a well-waxed handlebar moustache.

"Unfortunately, I must answer yes to that question."

"Unfortunately?"

He nodded his head and continued to look at the macadam beneath their feet. Looking back up he said, "It's a long story. If you don't mind coming up to the house now, I'll buy you a cup of coffee and tell you the whole sordid affair while I prepare for my lecture."

As soon as Lani stepped between the columns, and up on the porch, feeling the familiar wood beneath her feet, memories began to unfold as if she were watching a movie. She could see Burton standing at the top of the stairs, smiling at her whenever she would walk into the foyer. In just this brief re-introduction to the place, she could see that Harrison, or someone preceding him, must have completely restored this part of the house since everything looked magnificent, even down to the furniture of the past, possibly reproductions, or perhaps even the original pieces.

He had begun to tell her of the amount of money he needed to earn on the lecture circuit just to keep the taxman from taking the property and he also piqued her interest when he continued as he made coffee.

"I have always had a fascination for archeology and while researching this place after I bought it twenty years ago, I found a number of old post holes where the slave quarters were and I am trying to get some money together to rebuild them. Have you ever visited Carter's Grove near here?"

As Lani accepted the coffee, no cream or sugar, she shook her head in response, hiding her lie, a catch in her throat not allowing her to speak after he mentioned the slave quarters.

"Well, the Williamsburg foundation discovered the original foundations of two of the slave houses, shacks actually, and they built what they feel are exact replicas of the quarters, although we will never know for sure since none of us were alive back then. Anyway, that's what is keeping me in the poorhouse, but I really want to complete this plantation and open it up to the public. I have found some interesting information over the years and that's partially why I lecture about those three subjects. In fact, if you'd like to hear some stories about this property you could join me tonight."

"What will I do about my car? Triple A is probably on the way and I must find a place to stay tonight."

"Must you be anywhere tomorrow and any specific time?"

"Not really, since I was hoping to come here anyway and research my story and shoot some photos. What do you have in mind, Harrison?" She took another sip of her coffee, feeling its warmth course through her cooling body. She would need to feed before the night was through, and she certainly would not make Harrison a victim."

"Give them a call and cancel your service request and you can stay in one of the bedrooms here tonight. In the morning you can give them a call again and when it's running, you can nosy around the property and ask all the questions you want."

"Works for me, Harrison. May I use your phone, please?"

He took the phone from the cradle hanging on the wall and handed it too her. She proceeded to fake a call to AAA.

Later, at the college, Lani took a seat while Harrison lectured the class. He was articulate and amusing, enlightening and entertaining, capturing the rapt attention of everyone in the room, including herself. In her lifetime, she had met many intelligent men, but none as influential as this man. She was entertaining the possibility of staying here for a few weeks, perhaps even guiding him to the very places he was seeking, making it look like a coincidence, of course. She was so involved in her thoughts that she didn't snap out of her trancelike condition until she heard him say, "…the vampire or vampires killed a number of slaves in this area in the mid eighteen hundreds. Although it cannot be proven, since vampires are the result of active imaginations and legends handed down from generation to generation, there were certain facts that cannot be disputed. One slave in particular, named Heywood," Lani perked up at the mention of this name, "was found in the James River, weighted down by rocks. His neck was sliced on both sides, but there was evidence that he could have been in a fight, or, since the scratches he wore on his back were much like that from a woman, he could have been having sex. I prefer the latter, knowing that the woman of the house, one Lani Jorgenson, was known to have visited the slave shacks on a semi regular basis, and after every visit, a slave disappeared. I expect that she was observed and a journal kept of her movements, but she abruptly disappeared herself, and we will never know what happened to her. So, did or indeed, do, vampires exist? Thank you. Are there any questions?" Nearly every hand shot up in the air and Lani walked outside to get some fresh air and weigh her options, never seeing the older gentleman at the other side of the room perk up at the mention of her name.

※

David was in disbelief. He came to Williamsburg to listen to Professor Edmonds' lecture. While he was here, he thought he'd take a short vacation and visit Colonial Williamsburg, a place he had always wanted to visit but never had the time until recently. Fortunately, David had invested well over the years, plus he had won an incredible amount of money when one of his friends urged him to play a lottery. After taxes, the total came to over 5 million dollars, more than enough to allow him to continue with his pursuit of Lani, and now he just found out some new information.

※

Lani stood outside the college, looking up at the stars and smoking a very infrequent cigarette. She needed to think and smoking helped her thought processes. A horrible thought crossed her mind; she remembered that Burton had her portrait painted and it had hung in the great room at least until after she departed. And now, nearly a century and a half later she regretted not destroying it. Would Harrison see the resemblance and question her, if the painting still existed? She recalled watching a daytime soap opera back in the late sixties called Dark Shadows, laughing at the way the vampire was portrayed by the actor, and really being amused that nobody could figure out that he was indeed the person in the portrait hanging in the foyer of the house. The premise was so ridiculous, and now she was facing the same type of situation. She would definitely have to spend time with Harrison, and the kid at 7-11 just had his life saved. Lani could not kill anyone in this area, without rumors running rampant. Fortunately she had seen some cattle in a field nearby the plantation and she could take a little from each one to sustain her until she left this part of the South.

※

As Harrison was wrapping up his question and answer period, David waited for an opportunity to speak to him about Lani. He hoped the man truly believed what he lectured about because this could be the break that David was looking for. He had lost track of Lani when she went south years ago, and she was hiding her bloodlust very well, for the only news item that caught his attention was a story about a missing golfer near Myrtle Beach, but there was no information about a woman being involved. David saw the professor preparing to leave and strode up to speak with him.

"Excuse me, Professor. I just wanted to tell you that your lecture was fascinating. We have a common interest, Sir." He extended his hand in greeting and Professor Edmonds shook it vigorously.

"And what may that be, Mr.?"

"Forrester, but please call me David. Unfortunately, my laptop is back at the hotel, but I have documentation supporting your theory about vampires, including a picture of Lani Jorgenson that was taken when she and I were lovers in 1965. I believe it is the same woman who lived at your plantation over one hundred and fifty years ago."

Harrison looked at David, his brow furrowed and his mind searched for something to tell this man that although he lectured about vampires, he was not totally convinced that one had ever existed, but David seemed so honest that he wanted to hear his story in detail. "David, I really must run, but could you stop by my farm in the next day or two so we can talk?"

"Absolutely. I think you will definitely relate to the material I am going to show you."

"Wonderful! I have an engagement in the morning. Could you come over at about two o'clock?

David agreed upon the time and Harrison wrote the directions down on the back of his business card. They shook hands and Harrison walked out, wondering where Ali went. He had seen her leave the building after he began to tell the story about Heywood and Lani, and now with what David told him, plus knowing how much she resembled the portrait of Lani, hanging in the master bedroom, his curiosity was piqued. He would have to go slow with her, for if she was truly Lani, his life was in great jeopardy.

She stood by the car, smoking another cigarette, when her acute hearing picked up footfalls coming toward her. She looked toward the source of the sound and saw Harrison walking slowly, talking on his cell phone. As she strained her listening capabilities to the limit, she realized he was in an animated conversation with an unknown male, and she gathered that the conversation had something to do with a restoration project, presumably at the plantation, but Harrison muttered a terse "Goodbye," and snapped the phone closed placing it back in his briefcase.

When he saw her standing there, he waved and said, "What happened to you in there? I was in the middle of a story and I saw you stand up and leave. I hope I wasn't too boring?" He smiled at her.

She smiled back and replied, "No, you weren't boring. I just felt closed in and I needed some air. I came back in and stood just outside the door while you were taking questions, but I decided not to sit back down again." The lies were flowing like a river tonight.

On the way back to the plantation there was little chatter, both of them deep in thought about the subject of vampires, yet neither one wanting to raise a question to the other.

He stopped the car next to Lani's and she got out, walked to the back of the van and opened it. After grabbing a suitcase, she climbed back into Harrison's 1996 Rodeo and they drove up to the house, Lani's eyes darting everywhere in the dark, her mind's eye seeing the faces of the slaves she killed. Her anxiety was growing for she had never experienced flashbacks of that nature, ever. *What is happening here? So many questions and no one to ask them of?*

Upon entering the house Harrison said, "If you want to put your things away, you can use the bedroom up the stairs to the right, and the bathroom is one door down from your room. I'm going to throw on a pair of sweats and then I'll make us some more coffee. Are you hungry?"

"No, not really." She was famished but where could she find a victim at this time of night. Deciding she would wait until he was asleep to go out in search of blood, she put her hunger to the back burner of her mind for now.

Lani changed into sweats herself, after utilizing the bathroom, making sure she left no stains in the bowl for Harrison to wander about. She always carried a commercial toilet bowl cleaner in her travel case, applying the foam to the porcelain and scrubbing with a small brush until all the blood was washed away. The sweat suit felt good because without fresh blood, she was cold.

She bounded down the stairs and into the kitchen just as Harrison was pouring two cups of steaming coffee. He placed the carafe back on the tray, along with the cups and took them to the living room, placing the tray on the coffee table. They sank into the comfort of a soft, plush, blue velvet sofa and sipped their drinks. Lani's host had added a dash of brandy to the brew and it tasted wonderfully delicious, and as she drank, warmth returned to her. There were so many times she wished she could eat food, but solids made her nauseous and she couldn't keep them down, but coffee, especially laced with brandy was something she could drink gallons of when being denied of blood.

They both finished two cups of the wonderful black liquid over some small talk when Harrison suddenly said, "Ali, there is something I have to show you. Do you remember in my lecture when I talked about Lani Jorgenson, the woman who lived here before and could have been a vampire?"

She nodded her head and answered, "Do you really think vampires exist, or do you merely lecture about them to see what kind of response you will get from the students?"

As they walked up the stairs, he said, "I wasn't sure whether I believed in them or not, until tonight. I spoke with a man who definitely believes that Lani was a vampire, and I'm going to meet with him tomorrow, here at the plantation."

Harrison opened the door to the master bedroom and they walked in. There above the fireplace was the portrait of Lani and she stared at it, mesmerized, remembering every detail about the painter, hungering for him at each sitting, yet not able to consume him. She looked at the painting for a long time and finally said, "I bear a striking resemblance to that woman, don't I, Harrison?"

"Yes, you do, Ali. As soon as I saw you in the lane, I knew you were the woman in the portrait."

"That's preposterous! Lani Jorgenson lived one hundred and fifty years ago. How could I be the same woman?" She stared at him, waiting for him to continue.

"The man I spoke to this evening claims that he has evidence that Lani Jorgenson is alive and that he is searching for her." Lani didn't blink an eye with that statement but when he said, "The man's name is David Forrester," she uttered a small gasp and her eyes flew back to the portrait. *He must have been at the lecture, and I didn't even feel him!*

Suddenly she flashed her brilliant smile at him and in a calm voice said, "Harrison, even though you lecture about these strange things, you cannot possibly believe that man, Forrester. I believe you said that vampires simply do not exist! Let's just go back downstairs and have our coffee and talk of more pleasant things."

"Of course, Ali. You are probably right. Perhaps Forrester is deranged and merely attended my lecture to feed his delusions. He's probably coming here tomorrow to sell me something." They had begun to walk back down the steps when Harrison said that, and Ali stiffened briefly, but noticeably. Harrison wondered if he should have just kept his mouth shut, but the cat was out of the bag, now.

After they seated themselves in the living room again, Lani asked, "When is he coming here to talk to you?"

"I told him that I had an appointment in the morning so we decided on two o'clock."

"You have an appointment?"

"Actually, I lied to him. I thought we could go into Williamsburg for a few hours and I could show you around the historic area."

She brightened up, all talk of vampires momentarily dismissed, saying, "That would be wonderful, Harrison. My time is limited, but when you are talking to Mr. Forrester, I can take all the photos I'll need for my story, and I can interview you on the way to Williamsburg. It sounds like fun."

"Great, Ali. The visitor center opens at eight thirty and we can spend a few hours in town, grab some lunch and get back here before the salesman comes knocking at my door?" They both laughed and it was then that he noticed a peculiar, offensive odor coming from her mouth.

Ali finished her coffee and said, "Harrison, if you don't mind, I'm going to go to bed. I'm rather tired now. I guess if we are going out in the morning, I'll have to phone Triple A when we get back. Hopefully they'll get me up and running so I can get back on the road by tomorrow evening. Goodnight." She trudged up the stairs to her room as Harrison tried to figure out what he was going to do. He hoped by changing the scope of the conversation, she would become more relaxed, but he wasn't quite sure if it worked. One thing he found out was that if she was a vampire, garlic did not affect her, since he had added some to the coffee and brandy. "God, Harrison, you are really getting flaky. Vampires do not exist!" He muttered out loud as he turned off the lights and walked upstairs to his room.

Two hours later, Lani crept down the hall to Harrison's room. The door was slightly ajar and she could hear him softly snoring, deep in sleep. She didn't need the benefit of artificial light to find her way downstairs, quickly and quietly leaving the house by the rear door, nearly running toward where she had seen the cattle. She was starved and chilled: only blood would warm her now and she needed it badly.

As she made her way to the field, Harrison stepped to his window just in time to see his dog, a friendly Beagle, side up to Ali. She looked down at him and suddenly picked him up, her fangs sinking into his neck, draining him in seconds. Harrison was horrified. Ali was indeed Lani Jorgenson. Vampires did exist. He nearly dropped to his knees, his breath coming in quick gasps. What could he do? If she discovered that he had seen her, she would kill him for sure, or worse, turn him into a vampire, too! He contemplated calling the police, but that could mean more deaths. How do you kill a vampire? If garlic didn't work, would a stake through the heart? Would a cross protect him?

Minutes later, he saw her return to the house and he hurried back to bed, pretending once again to be asleep when she opened the door and saw him lying there. She knew he saw her because she saw him at the window. He had to die and this place had to be burned to the ground, all evidence of Lani gone forever.

Lani walked to the bed, blood still dripping from her lips and chin after taking the dog and small amounts from three of the cows in the field. As she approached, Harrison's breathing quickened. "Open your eyes, Harrison. I know you saw me and you now know that I am Lani Jorgenson."

He opened his eyes to see the maniacal look in her eyes and the blood on her face. "What are you going to do to me?" He stuttered; fear etched in every syllable.

"It was quite unfortunate that David was at your lecture tonight, for now I have to kill you and that is really sad because I had hoped that you and

I would have become lovers for a few weeks before I drained you. Also, never put garlic in a vampire's drink because it doesn't have any effect at all." She sat down on the edge of the bed and opened her mouth, the smell of fresh blood nearly nauseating him, her fangs were stained from her previous feeding and her beautiful face was replaced by a horrible caricature of herself, eyes red and bulging nearly out of their sockets, her skin the color of a mild sunburn.

He tried a new tactic, smiling he said, "You know I won't tell anyone about you if you let me live."

She laughed sardonically, adding, "Yeah, right, Harrison. And I still believe in the Easter Bunny. I am so sorry." She was on him so fast; he never even had time to cry out before feeling the two sharp punctures in his carotid artery. He could feel her suck the life out of him and his only regret as he slipped into darkness was that he would never finish restoring the farm.

After destroying Harrison, slitting his throat for insurance, she went back outside and brought the dog in, placing him on the bed beside his master. Fortunately, during their earlier conversation, Harrison told Lani that he could not build a fire because the chimney was coated with creosote and it could cause a fire. She blocked it a little more with some rags to make sure that the fire would indeed start and burn the place to the ground. If arson were suspected, the authorities would rule it out, given the nature of the blocked chimney. The fire would be considered an accident since no evidence of foul play would be found.

Lani unlocked her van and drove away as the sky turned red and the sound of sirens could be heard in the distance.

THE ROAD NORTH

COLONIAL WILLIAMSBURG

Lani decided that she would indeed visit the historic area before getting back on the road. After setting the fire and driving away, she pulled off the road about a half-mile away and raced through the woods to watch it burn. Firemen were on the scene already, but their valiant attempts to save the old structure proved futile. She had done her work well, and there would be absolutely no way to save the structure, and most importantly, the bodies inside would be burned to ashes, removing all evidence of vampirism. Momentarily Lani was saddened, because she really liked Harrison and hated killing him without having any fun. When she was absolutely sure that nothing could be saved, she got back in her car and drove into Williamsburg, stopping at a restaurant, prior to going to the visitor center. The immortal had an hour or so to kill, and she needed some coffee to help keep her warm again.

❦

After taking a shower, David felt more refreshed. He didn't sleep much, thoughts of Lani looming just behind his closed eyes, fueling the growing pain inside his skull. He awakened several times, trudging off to the bathroom to urinate or to take a couple of Tylenols. Harrison Edmonds actually lived where Lani was once the mistress of the house. David hoped that his talk with Mr. Edmonds would bear fruit, and perhaps give him some kind of lead to her whereabouts.

Since he had until the afternoon, he decided he would visit the historic area for a few hours. David hurriedly dressed and left the comfort of the room at the Williamsburg Inn, a place in which he could afford to stay since his recent good fortune. He had considered ordering room service for breakfast, but decided to drive to a Cracker Barrel instead: he stopped in the lobby to pick up a newspaper. The clerk saw him and said, "Good morning, Mr.

Forrester. I trust you slept well?"

Lying through his teeth, he replied, "Yes, indeed I did, Carlton." He read the young man's nametag, Carlton Binswanger. He appeared to be in his mid-twenties and was probably working at a dead end job, David thought, remembering that when he was only a few years older then the clerk, Lani had dramatically changed his life. God, he had been hunting her for almost thirty-five years. He finally decided that if he could not get any hard information from Harrison, it would be time to end the quest and enjoy his wealth instead of spending untold hours at the computer, searching newspapers online for clues to Lani's whereabouts.

He remembered when he first recalled every detail of that night in '65. Under hypnosis, he told the expert the entire story, even down to having a sketch made of her while he was under, but one night, after watching a horribly made vampire movie, he dreamt of her and felt her fangs drive into his neck, mentally hearing a sickening, crunching sound as they broke through skin, seeking his artery, rich with blood. David relived the entire episode, sweating profusely and being drained of all his energy. His memories were now intact.

David finally realized that the clerk was taking to him when he heard the words, "…the old plantation a few miles from here."

"Carlton, I apologize. I seemed to have been lost in thought and I didn't really hear what you were talking to me about, except something about an old plantation?"

The young man appeared somewhat annoyed at the fact that he had been talking for twenty or thirty seconds and Mr. Forrester didn't hear a word he said, but he smiled, nonetheless, and repeated what he had just said.

"I was saying that it was a shame about the fire at the old Hennings plantation. Apparently last night, the place burned to the ground. Preliminary reports suggest that it was a blocked flue in the fireplace. Mr. Edmonds must not have had it cleaned and it…"

"Excuse me, Carlton. I didn't mean to interrupt, but did you say, Mr. Edmonds. Could that have been Professor Harrison Edmonds?"

He nodded and replied, "Yes, it was, Mr. Forrester. Did you know him?"

"Agitated, he said, "No, not really. I only met him last night at a lecture. Do you have any more details? I certainly hope he was able to escape."

"I'm sorry, sir, but the professor and his dog were burned beyond recognition."

David merely stood there, pondering the situation and finally asked, "Was anyone with him when the fire occurred. Surely someone had to report it to the fire department?"

"The only thing I heard is that one of the firemen on the scene recalled seeing a Ford Windstar parked on the side of the road a few hundred feet from the entrance to the property earlier in the day. He also remembered that the vehicle was bearing a South Carolina plate."

A scornful smile crossed David's lips, remembering the article about the missing golfer. Suddenly the incident had Lani written all over it. *Could she have set the fire? Possibly, which meant she could still be in Williamsburg. How long would it take to find a Windstar with a South Carolina plate?*

"Mr. Forrester, are you okay? You look like you are a million miles away again."

"I'm sorry, Carlton, but I do have a lot on my mind; however, it is now time to go out into the world and explore history. I'll see you later."

David pressed the button on his key ring, allowing him access to his rented 1999 Toyota Camry. It was only a short drive to the restaurant, except he had taken business route 60 instead of the bypass and it took him a while longer to get there. Had he not made that mistake, he probably would have seen the blonde woman driving the minivan toward Colonial Williamsburg.

~~~

Lani pulled into the visitor center parking lot, noting that it was beginning to fill up very quickly and she was having second thoughts about getting this close to a great many humans. The scent of all that blood might drive her insane and not allow her to enjoy herself, for she really was looking forward to her brief visit. She knew that she would only stay a few hours at most and then get back on the road north.

When she walked into the visitor center, the even closer proximity to humankind and its marvelous scent assailed her nostrils, much like opening the cork in a bottle of fine wine, and she nearly became delirious, inadvertently clutching onto the gentleman to her immediate front, nearly pulling him down with her incredible strength.

He turned, prepared to offer the offender a piece of his mind, when he saw how ill the beautiful young woman appeared. She was white as a sheet and a foul odor was emanating from her open mouth, nearly causing him to gag, but he bravely put aside his revulsion, stating, "Are you ill, Miss?"

She smiled and said, "I guess I just had a bit of vertigo. I suffer from it on occasion when I am in close quarters. Once I purchase my pass and get outside, I'm sure I'll be okay. Thank you for your concern and I'm sorry I nearly pulled you down."

"My name is Lawrence Brobst and I am a doctor. If you think you need immediate attention I can give you a check up in my van."

"That's okay, Doctor Brobst. I'll be fine, really. I just need some fresh air, but I don't want to relinquish my spot in line, what with all the people who came in behind me. You see; I only have a few hours to enjoy Colonial

Williamsburg before I must get back on the road. If I still feel badly after we get back outside, perhaps a checkup would be in order. It has been some time since my last one."

As the line moved forward, more quickly now it seemed, or was it because her attention was drawn away from her incessant hunger by the conversation, she studied him. He was perhaps in his late fifties, no wedding ring, looked in pretty good shape and he was a wonderful conversationalist, yet all she could really think of was how he would taste if she decided to eat him. Time would tell.

They finally got their passes and stepped outside into the cool November air and she feigned continued vertigo, finally saying, "Dr. Brobst, I'd like to take you up on your offer.

He offered her his arm and they strolled together to his van, which was actually a mobile medical office. They stepped inside and she sat down on the proffered stool, while he took a stethoscope from one of the mounted cabinets. He was ready to place it against her heart when she said, "Doctor, is that really necessary. I would prefer if you placed your ear right against my chest?"

Taken aback, he muttered, "I beg your pardon, Lani, but I am truly a physician and in order to prescribe the correct meds for your condition, I have to check your heart, blood pressure and temperature, before delving further into your problem."

"Very well, then, do what you must."

He placed the stethoscope to her chest and after moving it around to several different places; he scratched his head and took her hand in his checking for a pulse, which he couldn't find either.

She noted his concern, a wicked smile crossing her face, and said, "What's the matter, Dr. Brobst. You seem quite perplexed!"

He shook his head slightly and looked into her eyes, which had seemed to acquire a massive amount of redness, and answered. "I'm afraid I am having a problem with my equipment because I cannot detect neither a heartbeat nor a pulse. If I didn't know better, I'd say you were no longer among the living."

"I'm sorry, doc, but I'm afraid I brought you out here under false pretenses, especially after finding out that you are a widower and have come here alone for a few days. You see, I am a vampire and unfortunately for you, Doctor, the life you have enjoyed all these years is just about to end.

Doctor Brobst watched her fangs grow and her face change into something more evil than he had ever seen in his life and still, he was so mesmerized, he was unable to speak or even move before she was on him, drawing his life into her body, the rich scent of his own blood wafting throughout the enclosed van. He died more quickly than she anticipated, possibly from a heart attack, since his heart was no longer pumping, making her job a little more difficult as she drank every drop. He tasted wonderful.

Using a scalpel, she cut his throat and then sliced through the wounds she had inflicted, eliminating all evidence of vampirism. She perceived no one nearby and stepped from the van, locking it behind her. Instead of taking the bus, she strolled down the path into the heart of the historic district.

Less than five minutes after Lani fed, David pulled into the parking lot. He exited his vehicle and strolled into the visitor center, spending twenty minutes in line before being waited on by a female cashier, whose happy face was contagious, causing David to smile in spite of himself. He was so wrapped up in the news of the fire that he forgot he was here to have a good time. Although Lani would always be on his mind, he knew that his search would end here, not wanting to pursue her any longer. He knew that he could not have prevented all the deaths she created, but perhaps he could have saved some lives along the way. After thirty-five years of hunting, only seeing her twice, he finally realized that he would never find her unless she made a really horrible mistake.

Lani was enjoying her stroll through the woods: she was sated and warm, feeling strong and truly marveling at what death had offered her that life never could have given her. She figured she would have been dead for over one hundred years, missing out on so much human technology, seeing wonders that her parents and friends could not have even imagined back in the horse and buggy days. Even the people who had lived here would be in awe of all the visitors tramping over earth they worked so hard to preserve after gaining freedom from England.

Arriving at the capitol, a beautiful building that had been completely restored on the original foundation, she looked up into a sky that was bluer than she had ever seen. A few wisps of clouds added a gorgeous detail to the sky, and the air smelled clean and fresh. The two trees framing the entrance to the building were rapidly losing their leaves and soon winter would bear down upon Virginia, causing more people to stay indoors, yet she was moving north to even more cold where she could take homeless people more quickly and less noticeably than in summer. She entered through the opening in the low brick wall that surrounded the Capitol and walked through the gate to a center courtyard where she sat among the other visitors waiting to enter and hear about the importance of this place. Although she was around many people again, the scent of blood was easier to overlook than inside a crowded place, its odor being dispersed to a much larger area.

Lani thoroughly enjoyed the tour, seeing the different rooms and looking at the paintings by artists of long ago, but she tired of the people around her, not seeing one that she would want to spend time with, or even have as a snack later, so she walked out and ambled down to the jail, where a group was waiting to take its tour.

After she seated herself on a bench outside, she looked around, noticing a very handsome man. He was dressed in jeans, a blue and white plaid shirt, and on his head rested a cap with the logo US NAVY SEALS, to which lots of little pins were attached. She knew that every pin had major significance to the wearer, and she also knew that Navy Seals were a special breed of men, strong and intelligent, the best of the best. The man looked younger than his years, his pins showing that he was a Vietnam veteran, putting him in the near or over fifty range, yet his neatly trimmed black beard and hair made him look a few years shy of forty, she thought. She had heard of the term wannabes, and wondered if this man was a fake vet. He appeared to be alone and that fact had her drooling for both his companionship and his blood. Perhaps she could strike up a conversation with him, she thought as a smile crossed her lips. The man had just glanced at her, making eye contact and returning her smile with one of his own and a nod. Her fantasies were running rampant, wanting to take him here and now: sex than the kill!

A woman dressed in period costume brought her out of her thoughts by saying, "Good morning, everyone, I am Marge Cummings of the Williamsburg Foundation and it is my pleasure to welcome you to the Public Gaol. Please come inside for a brief introduction to what you will see here."

As Lani made her way inside through the narrow door, Marge said, "Children, please sit on the floor and woman you may be seated on the chairs. I ask the men to please stand along the walls.

The Navy Seal said, though not very loudly, "Two hundred years ago, women knew their place and would stand, allowing the men to be seated."

A few of the women, and two or three of the men, also heard the comment. One of these men was also a veteran, since he was wearing a jacket sporting the patches of Vietnam Veterans of America and Veterans of the Vietnam War. He also wore the patch of the 25th Infantry Division below the embroidered name Dale followed by Chu Lai '68. Lani also liked the looks of him. He definitely appeared his age, sporting a full salt and pepper beard, and his long graying hair was tied back in a ponytail, topped off by a black baseball type cap, bearing the words VIETNAM VETERAN. His diminutive eyes danced in the firelight, small lips pursed in a frown as he stared at the Navy Seal, mouthing the word, "Asshole," causing Lani to chuckle a bit. Unfortunately, he appeared to be with his wife and a younger couple, perhaps his daughter and her boyfriend, since she had many of his facial characteristics. They were a fine looking family and Lani suddenly yearned for a family of her own, knowing it would never happen. She saw him glance toward her and she mouthed the words, "You are a lucky man, sir, having your family here." The man nodded at her, though his eyes suddenly appeared sad, and went back to staring at the other veteran *wannabe?*

The Seal looked around and found Lani. He offered a smile, which she returned. She wanted to meet him and have some fun before he died.

After Marge gave her introductory speech, everyone filed out into the courtyard to visit the cells. Lani recalled what the woman had said about why we call the toilet a throne in today's vernacular because when she saw one, it did indeed resemble a throne, the prisoner having to climb several steps to be seated. That definitely amused Lani and caused her to laugh, something she did very little of, it seemed.

Lani climbed the steps and sat on the toilet when the dark-haired veteran stepped inside, the two of them now alone, as others in the group visited the other cells. He looked up at her and laughed, saying, "Miss, you really look funny sitting on the throne."

When Lani stepped down, he offered his hand in assistance, which she took, feeling his heat, replying, "Yeah, I guess that was quite a project back in the good, old days. The prisoners must have really suffered big time in places like this."

"You're probably right, Miss...?"

"Jamison, Joyce Jamison."

"Fred Diehl. Nice to meet you. I guess the standard line would be what is a nice girl like you doing in a place like this, alone?"

"Well, Fred. I am just passing through and I decided to stop here to take in the historic area before heading north again."

"Heading anywhere in particular?"

"As a matter of fact, I'm going to Allentown, Pennsylvania, which is about fifty miles north of Philadelphia. Ever hear of it?"

"Is that the place that Billy Joel sang about a few years back?"

Lani nodded her head and said, "Absolutely!"

"So what will a nice girl like you be doing in a place like Allentown?"

She laughed again and answered, "I hope to get a job with the newspaper I applied to. I'm a photojournalist and writing a story about the historic area."

He scrutinized her and asked, "Where's your camera, Joyce?"

"Back in my van. I took all the pictures I needed yesterday and now I'm just playing tourist for a few hours. However, I must really run. I have an appointment I must get to very soon."

"If I'm not being too forward, I'd like to offer you an invitation to dinner at the Williamsburg Inn, if you'd care to go?"

"That'd be great, Fred. How about I meet you here just before dusk?"

"Super! I'll see you later, then." They shook hands and he gave her a peck on the cheek, stirring her hunger again. After she walked away, Fred immediately thought that if he played his cards right, he'd be taking off her panties before nine o'clock.

⁂

David had stepped into the Governor's Palace a few moments after the group before had gone above stairs to see the bed chambers of the governor and his wife. He was impressed by the display of power and wealth revealed in the vestibule. Along the walls and around the ceiling were hung weapons: pistols, rifles and swords. They were in magnificent condition, many of them reproductions, yet to the naked eye, they all looked like they were from the period. After listening to the historical patter, David's group looked at the two rooms off to the side and then walked up the steps to the second floor, viewing the bedchambers.

After touring the grounds, David walked through the wrought iron gates, noticing a figure in historical dress standing on a platform talking to a large gathering of people. He looked at his brochure and saw that the man was portraying George Washington and David decided it would be worth a listen. He walked over to the crowd, trying to find a spot to stand where his less than good hearing would allow him to pick up the words the man was saying.

Finally finding a spot, he was truly enjoying the banter between George Washington and the crowd as he answered all their questions. David heard a question posed by a man wearing a black veteran's jacket, a black cap embroidered VIETNAM VETERAN was perched on his head at a jaunty angle. "Mr. President, if you could change one thing you have ever done, what would it be?"

"My friend, how can we change anything that has already happened? To even indulge in a fantasy like that could prove harmful, not allowing us to live to our full measure, second-guessing our ideals and values in light of the possibility that something could go differently than we planned. Perhaps you should not go forth with any of your endeavors until you have completely studied what you wish to do, wondering if you are right or wrong. Formulate your plan and do it to the best of your ability."

The veteran kept nodding his head, understanding the words of the president and it even gave David food for thought in his pursuit of Lani. Perhaps he could not save the world, but if he were fortunate enough to destroy her, he would save many lives, one that might be the next president, or the person to discover a cure for cancer. His pursuit would continue. He couldn't change what had already happened, but he could change the future.

As he was lost in his thoughts, several people in front of him moved and with an ashen face he moved closer to the platform. When he was directly behind her, he said, "Hello, Lani!"

Without turning to face him, perturbed that she couldn't feel his presence until he was nearly on top of her, she replied, "Hello, David. I was hoping to see you here after Harrison told me that you were at the lecture last night." She turned and stared up into his face and said, "Perhaps we should get away from this crowd so we can talk..."

"Or you can kill me!" He interrupted, talking a bit loudly, drawing the glances of a few tourists as Lani hooked her arm into his and led him to a bench away from the throng.

She sat down, pulling him down alongside her, kissing him passionately, as he fought off her advances, not quite able to pull away. She was so strong and perhaps even still had a hypnotic attachment to him.

"David, you know you are the only person I could never kill. I love you too much."

"If you love me, you'd allow me to destroy you to end our torment."

She laughed, haughtily and replied, "Don't misunderstand me, David. I would never kill you, but I certainly cannot allow you to destroy me, for I am not tormented. I enjoy this life of mine, even if it means killing to live. Life is precious, perhaps even more so to an immortal because of what I will live to witness throughout eternity.

He stood up, agitated, walking in a circle in front of her, finally facing her and stating, "How can you do this, Lani? You were human one time. Don't you understand what you are doing to your own kind? So many of the people you have killed could have gone on to make major changes in the way we live, perhaps eradicating disease and war for all time. How long will it continue before God destroys you?"

She stood up and grabbed his coat, breathing her horrible breath in his face, causing him to become nauseous, nearly throwing up all over her, which probably would have made him feel better. "God! Don't you dare speak that name in my presence? He has allowed creatures like myself to roam the earth, destroying what He made? His own fucking children, David! He allows me to kill his own fucking children! What kind of God is that?" She released her hold on him.

Speaking in a more gentile tone she said, "Remember what Washington just said to the crowd over there a few minutes ago. Nothing can be changed that has already happened. Let it go, David and allow me to suffer my eternal damnation without interference. I am going to leave now and I suggest you don't follow me or I swear I will change my mind and kill you, horribly, I might add. Hell, I may even let you live like I do for a few hundred years. Give it up, man!"

As she walked away, David began to ponder what he could do, always believing that a vampire could be killed by a stake. Those novelists and screenwriters had to have some knowledge of what they were talking about, but no, vampires did not exist to them, it was pure folly. *How does one deal with a real vampire?* As he sat there deep in thought he heard footfalls over the oyster shells strewn about the area and looked up into the face of a former Navy Seal. David thought him rather young to be a SEAL, especially with Vietnam Veterans pins on his cap. He figured the guy was a wannabe, but he let it go.

"Yo, pal. I saw you trying to get it on with that girl and I need to tell you you're out of luck. She's meeting me later and with a little luck, I'll be banging her while an old fart like you beats off in front of the HBO movie of the night."

David literally jumped up from the bench and grabbed the man's open jacket, getting into his face, saying, "If you keep your date with her, you will wind up in the morgue before the evening's over. She's a vampire!"

"Yeah, right, bozo, and I'm fucking Santa Claus. Don't spout your delusions to me because she wants a younger guy. I saw how she blew you off and you're pissed as hell, aren't you?" He pushed David away, nearly knocking him off his feet when he fell back against the bench.

Look, friend, I'm not lying. I'm trying to save your life, for Christ's sake! Listen to me, please."

The man laughed at David, and sauntered away, both hands stuck in his coat pockets, whistling the Navy hymn.

All David could think of doing was to follow him where ever he went to in the historic area, hoping that his meeting with Lani would be somewhere in Colonial Williamsburg. The guy must never have realized that David was shadowing him, because he never looked back. David thought, *The guy probably is a wannabe, or else he would have known he was being tailed.*

Dusk was approaching and David was beginning to think that the man had been full of shit and wasn't going to meet Lani and that all he wanted to do was hassle an older guy. The man walked toward the Public Gaol and that's when David saw Lani standing by the gate to the courtyard. He could see that by using her incredible strength she had broken the lock. David assumed she did this to lure the man inside and probably kill him in one of the cells; however, that would draw attention to her identity and perhaps David was wrong. Maybe she was just going to play with him and allow him to live.

The man walked up to Lani. She smiled and said, "Hello, Fred. I was hoping you would keep our date, but I have been standing here for some time now and I kept searching for you."

"Joyce, how could I not keep a date with a woman as incredibly beautiful as you are."

"Fred, look what I found. They forgot to lock the gate to the courtyard. Want to go in one of the cells and fool around."

A leer crossed Fred's face and he replied, "Sure, Joyce. Sounds like fun. I bet nobody has ever christened any of these cells. We could be the first couple to have sex in the Public Gaol." He didn't know how she'd react to the word sex, but he hoped that's what she had in mind when she mentioned fooling around.

He received his answer by a nod of her head and they strolled into the courtyard and went into the cell in which there was a coffin. Earlier in the day Marge told them that if a person had enough money and was waiting for the hangman to come, he or she could have a coffin built and placed in the cell, ready to receive the body after death.

After Lani led him to the coffin they sat down on the lid and began kissing passionately, neither of them hearing the footfalls outside the cell. She was breathing hard and Fred had already unbuttoned her jacket and was squeezing her right breast as Lani was focusing in on his neck, moving her head to the right and downward, her fangs extended to full length as she squeezed his penis, feeling it grow. She began to lick his neck, tasting his salt, whetting her appetite for his essence, when David walked in, surprising them.

"Lani, no!" He shouted, startling Fred, who wondered what the hell was going on. Here he was ready to bang this babe on a coffin in a jail cell and the old fart was rushing toward them, pulling him away from Joyce, but the dude called her Lani.

When Fred fell to the floor, he looked in horror, seeing what Joyce, or was it Lani, had become. *What has she become?* Her eyes were completely red and her teeth were so long. She was snarling like an animal.

She pounced on Fred, saying, as her wicked breath nearly gagged him, "Fred, you are one lucky man, tonight. Because of his interference, you will live, but you will not remember what happened here, only that he found you unconscious here in the cell. For you see, Fred, I am a vampire and I was prepared to kill you and drink you dry for what you said earlier today."

"Wha—wha—what did I say? I don't understand any of this. Vampires are not real."

"I'll tell you what pissed me off enough to want to destroy you. When we were ushered into the house for orientation, Marge told the women sit down on the chairs and you said, 'Two hundred years ago, women knew their place and men would be the ones sitting. I am almost two hundred years old, Fred, and I knew where my place was, but today is much different and I don't like men that belittle woman. So feel very lucky, friend, because I'm going to spare you, but in a moment you will not remember any of this."

Lani hypnotized Fred, then stood up and looked deeply into David's eyes.

"This is your last warning, David. Leave me be and I will let you live. If you ever interfere again, you will know what it is to be immortal because I will turn you into a vampire and we will go out and kill in tandem. Wouldn't that be fun?"

She kissed him hard, her breath even more nefarious now, and he fainted.

When he recovered, untold minutes later, she was gone and Fred was beginning to come to. David elected not to tell the man what really happened, but he vowed that no matter what, he would meet up with Lani again, and this time destroy her.

Memories

Momentarily forgetting her strength, Lani's hand hit the steering wheel so hard she nearly cracked it. She muttered out loud, "Fucking David! Why must you still be alive, *because you love him, is why*, spoiling my plans and keeping up with your constant, relentless pursuit? Her head began to throb and she knew it was starting in again, but she didn't know why.

Sometimes it was a face, sometimes a place, but lately, it seemed, Lani's memories were flowing like the blood she took from her victims, flooding her with happy thoughts at times, regrets at others. *Could my life be nearing an end?* The advent of the Internet allowed David more liberty in his hunting, even though it was probably a stroke of luck that he had caught up with her in Williamsburg. It was soon time to get out of America and head to Europe where she wasn't known and she was sure that David would not follow, for he was becoming to old to play this game with her indefinitely.

As she crossed the Potomac River, she looked to her left and saw the Washington monument, recalling the last time she visited the city in 1992, for the tenth anniversary of the National Vietnam Veteran's Memorial. It was to be her first and only visit to this black shrine, immediately thinking about the fun she would have that week. There were thousands of veterans in town, some here for the first time, and she would have a field day, getting laid every day and killing them with sadness and remorse, because of what had befallen them during the war. She would only take those who appeared extremely ill with the affects of Agent Orange, the herbicide, which put them one foot in the grave already. Lani would take them out of their misery, so they could at least die with some dignity, instead of wasting away, plus if they appeared to have been murdered, their beneficiaries would collect more money that way then if the death was caused by the horrible disease infesting their bodies.

❧

She approached The Wall for the first time ever and saw him. He was horribly disfigured from the war, yet he wore his jungle fatigues with pride. His two rows of ribbons, including the purple heart with two clusters, showing he had been wounded three times, and the silver star and a bronze star gracing the top row were on both his faded jungle jacket and his boonie hat. Lani knew that this man had seen some terrible conditions: *worse then what I witnessed during the Civil War?* Chances are he probably risked his life more than once in Vietnam. His hair was long, but not tied back, like many of the other veterans strolling The Mall today. A heavy moustache covered his upper lip and his brown eyes appeared so tired. She didn't notice a wedding ring on his finger so she decided to approach him.

She was within a step of the man when he nearly fell. His cane found a deep hole in the grass, but Lani quickly reached out and grabbed his arm before he tumbled.

He turned to face her and doffed his hat, saying, "Thank you, ma'am for helping out an old man and not letting me fall down. I don't get around as well as I used to, you know." *He is probably in his mid forties, yet he appears twenty years older, I think.*

Lani offered a smile and replied, "You're welcome, Sir. I don't like to see anything happen to you guys, with all the shit you have gone through already." She pointed to his ribbons in a knowing fashion.

"You got someone on The Wall, Miss?"

"Jorgenson, Lani Jorgenson. Everyone has somebody on The Wall, I guess, because you were all called to do something so I can live my life pretty much the way I please, and for that I say thank you."

The veteran placed his hat back on his head, the angle jauntier than it had been before he had seen Lani and she immediately knew what he was thinking. His eyes became so bright and alert, and he smiled warmly at her. *He still wanted to get it on with a young chick!*

"My name is Austin Numbers."

A silence followed as they both walked toward the black granite memorial bearing the names of over fifty eight thousand men, killed and missing from the war. As the structure came in view, Numbers gasped, the enormity of it setting in. He closed his eyes and tears began to form, ultimately flowing down his cheeks at a rapid rate.

"Lani," he said, looking toward her, "If it wouldn't be any trouble, would you walk The Wall with me. There's three names I need to see and touch."

"Yes, Austin, I will walk with you. Do you want to talk about it?"

He covered her hand with his and said, "After I see the names, if I don't fall apart, I'll tell you my story. Okay?"

She nodded and answered, "Whatever you need to do, I'll be right beside you, Austin."

They walked The Wall, starting at the east end, glancing at the reflections of the people they passed. At the base of nearly every panel were little American flags, unopened beer cans, packs of cigarettes, and letters and pictures of loved ones left behind to go on without the person they were paying tribute to. Austin clutched Lani's hand so hard, his grip probably would have broken a few bones in a human, but it did nothing to her, although seeing all those names stirred something inside. She was actually surprised by his strength, given the rest of his condition. Looking at this memorial, seeing not only the names etched in the granite, but also seeing faces of those she had killed over the years, insuring her survival, caused her to shiver with the thoughts and visions she was now experiencing.

Austin felt her shudder, her hand turning colder, and asked, "Are you okay, Lani?"

She nodded her head and responded, "Yeah. I'm all right. I guess all these names get to everyone who has walked by here these past ten years."

He gave her a hug, something she didn't expect, and she was able to feel his pain and suffering pass into her body along with his warmth. His scent was wonderful and she could almost taste him while her head was buried into his chest. She was so hungry, but she could not take him here with all these people around, but after sunset, he would become part of her. The authorities would find his bloodless corpse and they would be mystified as to what kind of murderer would drain the body. It would definitely become an FBI X-File.

After viewing the trio of names on the wall, and giving them a hand salute, Austin began to cry, unabashedly; unashamed of his outpouring of grief and it was Lani's turn to do the hugging. *Why am I doing this? He is only another tortured human who will satisfy my raging hunger.* His tears poured out the anguish that had been building up inside him for twenty five years. It was almost as though his heart was bleeding through his eyes. He finally let out a few final sobs and without another look at the names, took Lani by the hand and walked away, as passersby parted the way for them, allowing them space leave the memorial, their curious eyes following them as they passed by.

They strolled to the Lincoln Memorial and climbed the steps, gazing upon the huge statue of the nation's sixteenth president, and the only one that Lani had met in her long life: she thought back to that day almost one hundred an thirty years ago when she and Mr. Lincoln shared a table together at a restaurant near the White House, where both of them had sought shelter from an unannounced thunderstorm.

⁂

She remembered the president was extremely courteous, pulling the chair out for her and pushing it in toward the table when she was seated. They shared small talk about the city, the state of the war, especially the recent carnage at Gettysburg, and of course, the intolerable weather conditions that prevailed every summer. Lani, the vampire, and Lincoln, the emancipator, drank coffee and conversed for the better part of a half hour, the storm finally passing. Lincoln stood, took Lani's hand and kissed it, tenderly, almost fatherly, and said, "Young lady, it was a pleasure for an old man like me to have the opportunity to share some time with one of our nation's greatest assets, its youth." He nodded his head and bowed, walking out into the street before Lani had a chance to thank him for freeing the slaves. Of course, she could not tell him that free slaves were easier to slaughter then kept ones, and their disappearances didn't trigger much concern, except for their immediate families. She saw him through the window, engaged in lively conversation and laughter with several townspeople who saw him come out from the restaurant.

<hr />

She and Austin sat down on the top step and looked across the reflecting pool to the Washington Monument and directly behind that, the Capitol. "So much has changed," she said, not realizing she was talking out loud.

"Excuse me?"

"I'm sorry. I was just thinking how much this city has changed since it was first conceived. There is so much to see here, with all the museums and monuments."

"You almost give the impression that you know quite a bit about the history of Washington, almost like you lived it."

"That would make me almost two hundred, Austin. Do I look that old?"

He laughed, saying, "No, you don't look a day over a hundred, Lani."

When they stopped laughing, Lani said, "Would you like to talk about your guys, now?"

Austin perceptibly stiffened and his eyes took on a far away look as he gathered his thoughts, once again clutching her hand in his, turning toward her.

"It was summer, Sixty-seven, and hot as hell, but then again 'Nam was always hot. It was hot and dry or hot and wet, except at night, sometimes it got downright cold over there. Dirtbag, Needledick, G-Man, and I were on ambush about two hundred meters out from our overnight position, what we called a night laager, the platoon had set up." He saw her smile when he told her the nicknames of his buddies.

She said, "Needledick I can pretty much figure out for myself, but as for the other two, I'm clueless, and I assume you had a name, too?"

"Yeah, I did, Lani. I was known as Stiff, because no matter where we were, I always managed to get a boner every night. Used to think about pussy every time we set in and I crawled in my hole; that sucker would just pop up and make a tent in my fatigues, 'specially since we didn't wear underwear.

The humidity would just do a number on your groin area, so to avoid crotch rot, no skivvies. Dirtbag got his name because he had this bag of dirt from his home in Iowa, and he carried it with him wherever he went in the 'Nam. Told us that he felt better carrying a little piece of home with him. G-Man got the name because he wanted to become an FBI agent, but he wasn't smart enough, so Sammy drafted his ass and he became a G-man anyway, sort of, a GI is the name for Government Issue, so the name G-Man kinda worked.

"Anyway, we were on this ambush and it was dark, black as three day old coffee, and it was so quiet we could almost hear each other breathe. Figured the dinks could hear us, too. For over a week we were humping, smelling gooks all over the place, but never makin' contact. Seemed like they were a half a klick ahead of us no matter where we went. We'd find fire pits that were still warm, tracks that were still soft. It was almost like they were leading us somewhere, and most of us wanted to get the fuck out of there and go back to the firebase, but LT Minnich kept pushing and prodding us to keep going. He wanted to find them and kill them all, even though we had no idea how many were out there.

"So here we are sitting in this ambush and it starts to rain, coming down so hard that it was impossible to hear anything, but we got lucky. A gook, probably a fuckin' new guy VC, Viet Cong, tripped a wire to a frag grenade we had set out, and we opened up on them, sprayed the shit out of the jungle with M-16s and grenades. Back at the laager, the platoon started sending out flares, and mortar rounds were dropping all around us. Fuckers were so close we could hear the shrapnel hitting the trees a few feet from where we laid."

Austin got up and started looking around as though he was back in Vietnam, but he finally sat back down and after lighting a cigarette and taking a huge drag, he ran his hand through his hair, sighed and spoke again.

"My rifle had jammed and as I was trying to clear it, somehow I accidentally pulled the pin on a grenade. I yelled, 'Grenade,' and we all were feeling around on the wet jungle floor trying to find the frag before it exploded and killed us all. G-Man found it and went to flip it away, but it exploded in his hand. The shrapnel flew all over the place and Needledick caught a piece in the heart, killing him instantly. Dirtbag and G-Man were fucked up bad and I took a load in the face. Lani, it was so hot and I tried to scratch the fire red, burning pieces of metal from my face and I tore myself to shreds.

"Seeing the flash from the frag I dropped, the gooks flipped another grenade in our midst, but fortunately Needledick's body absorbed most of the shrapnel, but a few pieces hit Dirtbag and G-Man, and they bought the farm, too." Austin stood up and watched two helicopters fly overhead. He heard them long before he saw them. When they were directly overhead, he raised his right arm skyward, hand balled into a fist and he pumped his arm up and down a few times in tribute to the workhorses of the Vietnam War. Then after he could neither see nor hear them anymore he sat down again and began to softly speak, as the tears flowed freely.

"By this time, the dinks broke it off because our guys were coming out toward our position and I guess there were a lot more of us then them and I made it out okay. I got evacuated to a rear hospital and then I was sent home for rehab, but I've been living with this guilt for twenty-five years and I can't stand it anymore. Lani, you can't believe how much I want to die, and be with my buddies. If I wouldn't have fucked up, they might still be alive."

He started to cry and Lani said, "Let's go somewhere more private and I can help you ease your suffering, if you'd like me to, Austin?"

Austin just nodded, and as the sky began to blacken, Lani led him down the steps and they walked toward the tidal basin.

When they arrived, the sky was more dark then light now, and the area was devoid of people. Austin lit a cigarette and in the glow of the match, Lani saw him looking at her, strangely, and his eyes were totally devoid of life. After taking a drag and blowing out the smoke, he said, "Before you kill me, will you let me make love to you, here on the grass, Lani?"

She was taken aback, but replied, "Why would you think I brought you here to kill you, Austin?"

Even in the darkness, she could see his face clearly as he said, "Because I know what you are!"

"And what am I? Do you think I am some kind of axe murderer or something," she asked, laughingly.

He took her cold hand in his and replied, "Lani, I know you are a vampire, knew it as soon as you told me your name."

"Yeah, right, Austin. Vampires are creatures of legend. They don't exist."

Austin rubbed her cold hand between his, drawing her coldness into him, his cigarette hanging from his lips and said, "A long time ago, an older friend of mine told me about a beautiful, blonde woman he was dating, said she was a knockout. He said, and you gotta understand, that this was a year or so later, he got hypnotized and found out that a vampire had bitten him, yet he survived. Her last words were to the effect that she could not kill him because she loved him so much. My friend's name is David Forrester, Lani.

"All I ask is that when you feed on me, you do not turn me into an immortal because I want to die. I can't live with the memories of my friends any longer, but I don't have the nerve to do myself in.

"Since I told you about David, I know you have to kill me because you cannot allow anyone to live who knows your secret, except for him, can you?"

Lani was totally absorbed in his conversation, knowing he would have to die, yet having so many questions she wanted to ask him. "Have you seen David, recently, Austin?"

"Yeah, as a matter of fact, I saw him a few weeks ago and he told me he was still going to find you and kill you someday. That's why I squeezed your hand so hard earlier, to see if you would feel any pain, to see if you were human or not."

"Why didn't you reveal who I was back at The Wall, with all those people around. You know I could not have done anything there, and you would have had the opportunity to live longer?"

"Lani, I told you, I don't want to live anymore and I don't mind what you're going to do to me, as long as I don't become like you."

Without saying another word, Lani took his face in her hands and kissed him, quickly and savagely. Austin responded by fondling her breasts, after which they both took their clothes off, he braving the cold November air, and they enjoyed each other, both of them climaxing at the same time. Fiercely she grabbed his head and brought his neck down to her mouth. Just before biting him she said, "You are right, Austin, I am a vampire and David is the only man I ever loved, but I will never forget you. Be at peace, my friend." In less than a minute he lay dead upon her naked body, his blood coursing through her, warming her and giving her new life again, until the next time she would feed.

She gently rolled his body on to the grass, took out her blade and slashed his neck obliterating her teeth marks. She quickly dressed him and left him lie there to be found by the police the next morning, victim of a murder. They would be totally confused by the smile upon his face. Lani stood up and saluted one of the bravest men she had ever met and left Washington that very night.

⚜

Her mind once again back in the present, she continued her drive up I-95. She was closing in on Baltimore, but when she saw signs for Gettysburg, more memories caught up with her and she was so shaken she had to pull off to the side of the road. The pain in her head and the voices she could hear were becoming stronger and as she exited her minivan to deal with this foreign mental condition, she flashed back to the two days in July of 1863, seeing the faces of many more men she helped cross over to the land of the dead.

⚜

The company was set up just outside the city, waiting for the rest of the battalion to catch up with them. A nurse was traveling with them, tending to the sick and those who had been wounded in combat in the past week, but were able to continue on in the struggle against the Blue Bellies.

Corporal Milt Weathers, a two-year veteran of the army of Northern Virginia, sat against a tree, rubbing his back up and down against the bark which was helping to relieve the itch that he could not reach to scratch. After a few minutes of rubbing against the trunk, the itch was gone and Weathers smiled, even though there was not too much to smile about. He saw the nurse working on a private who had suffered a sprained ankle, wrapping it tightly with a long, dirty bandage and then wiping his brow, offering him some water to drink.

After she finished with him, she stood up and began to walk to the tent set up as an infirmary, but Milt caught her eye and with a movement of his head, motioned her to come to him.

"Why, Miss Jorgenson, I do believe you are not only the best nurse in the Confederacy, but also the prettiest one."

She smiled and with an accent born out of living in Virginia since 1860 and traveling with the army for two years, her words flowing soft and smooth as gravy over cornbread, she drawled, "Why, Corporal Weathers, sir, if I did not know any better, I would believe you are trying to make a pass at me?"

"If I ever get you alone, you will truly know what a pass is, my dear. How is Jenkins' ankle? Will he be able to press on against the enemy?" He pointed a bloodstained finger toward the soldier she had just tended to.

Nodding her head, she replied, "He'll be fine, Milt. He just needs a little rest right now and then later he'll be able to march. Do you think we'll mix it up with the Yanks soon?"

"I do believe that indeed, Lani. A body can damn near smell them when they are nearby, even though I don't for the life of me know why they would smell much different than us. Hell, we all used to be one country."

She teased him, saying, "Maybe they smell different because they bathe more than y'all do. Smell like rose water them Yankees, while y'all smell like swamp rats." She pinched her nose with her fingers and made a gagging noise.

They both laughed and Lani said, "Milt, I really have to get about my duties now. So many of our boys are hurting bad and I do my best to ease their pain."

"I know you do, Lani, but you need to take care of yourself too. Seems sometimes like you go about your business twenty-four hours a day and get no sleep. A body can wear itself down in a hurry putting in the time that you put in every day. Do you ever sleep?"

She offered a wry smile and replied, "You men don't get too much rest either. I get by on whatever sleep I can manage."

"Well, you try to get some sleep so you can keep patching us up. I think we are really gonna get into some heavy contact soon. I kin smell them fuckin' Yankees as we sit here talkin'. It's gonna be bad, Lani, real bad."

"Oh, Milt, you are always smelling Yankees. If you'd wash your clothes and get all that Blue Belly blood off'n em, you'd smell you'self. Come to think of it, maybe smellin' Yanks is better, 'cause you reek, Milt." She laughed, heartily and slapped him on the shoulder as he feigned hurt, clutching his chest.

"You are right, though, Lani, I do need a bath. Wanna wash my back for me?"

She got up to walk back to the infirmary and responded, "I swear, Milt, you are the most incorrigible man I have ever met in my life." She turned and walked away, hearing him say, "Yeah, that I am, and you love it."

A rider came in hard and fast; his horse was lathered up, having been pushed to its limit. He was yelling, "Yankees are less'n a day's march away and it seems like theys coming here. Where's the colonel?"

Milt rose from his seat and ran over to the private, saying, "How many of them are there, Private?"

"I can't say for sure, Corporal, but I think there could have been a regiment, maybe two. They was thick as flies on the corpses we left behind so far. I saw a few cannons, too. I need to see the colonel and find out where he wants me to go next."

"Colonels not here right now, Private..?"

"Atkins, Will Atkins, Corporal."

"Okay, Will, go over to the fire and get yourself something to eat and drink: I think there is still some hot coffee and hardtack left over from breakfast. I'll find someone to go fetch the colonel and then you can tell him exactly what you saw. It might be a while, so grab some shuteye, if you can. I have a feeling you're going to be riding hard later on. General Lee is only about a day behind us and he's bringing a lot of men with him."

Later that night, after the colonel had been informed of the situation, and Atkins was sent out to find General Lee, Lani made sure that everyone was asleep before she went hunting. She was starving, having been denied a human to feed on for almost thirty-six hours. She had managed to drink some blood from a few of the wounded, who were sleeping, biting them in places that would not be seen, and only taking as much as she could without weakening them even more, but she couldn't stand it anymore. When a battle was in progress, the aftermath was a perfect place for her to scavenge from the dying, helping them succumb instead of suffering too much. Between battles was a different matter, though, since sometimes she had to kill a sentry and drag his body to the nearest river, lake or pond to dispose of, making it appear that the sentry had run away, which was not uncommon in the

Confederacy after two years of war.

As she silently strolled through the woods, she heard footfalls, but they were not human, meaning she'd have to settle for an animal, hoping it was a deer, since deer had nearly enough blood to get her through another day. Her acute hearing picked up the snorting of a Pennsylvania whitetail deer, and after scanning the area, she saw her, a doe, getting ready to bed down for the night.

Stealthily she approached the exhausted deer, but the animal picked up Lani's strange scent before the vampire had time to pounce upon her. The doe quickly stood up and began to run deeper into the woods. Lani vaulted over a fallen tree and caught up with the frightened animal, jumping on her back and riding her like a horse, sinking her fangs into the beast's neck and sucking for all she was worth until the doe weakened, her legs collapsing from under her, most of her blood already gone. The animal expelled a great snort and as Lani drank the last dregs from her, she died, filling the vampire with life fluid. Lani dismounted the dead deer, slit its throat, and licked her fingers clean, ambling back to camp, bloated and warm.

After the battle of Gettysburg began in earnest, Lani was extremely busy tending to the wounded and the dying, even to the point of going out into the killing fields at night, searching for soldiers she knew would not make it, easing their suffering by killing them quickly, sometimes with her teeth, sometimes with a knife or a straight razor. She took no sides in her slaughter, ending the lives of both Union and Confederate soldiers, yet those who could be saved to live and fight another day, she got back behind Confederate lines, occasionally even bringing back a prisoner.

On the evening of the second day, just after dark, and the company had been routed by the Yankees, retreating through The Wheatfield, Lani went out in search of her comrades, As she ended the lives of some, and saved others, she heard a familiar voice in the distance. Seeing Milt's shattered body lying in a pool of blood, she went over to him, hoping to comfort him and maybe get him back to the hospital tent.

Lani lifted his head and gave him some water saying, "Milt, hang on. I'm going to carry you back to the line and the doctors will be able to fix you up."

He grabbed her hand, weakly, his strength ebbing and said in little more than a hoarse whisper, "I'm finished, Lani. I caught a few mini balls and my stomach is torn up real bad from cannon shrapnel." He coughed, great gobs of black blood spraying from his mouth, his breathing ragged. Make it stop hurting, Lani! Please do this for me." He handed her a pistol he had carried with him at all times, a gift from his father before he went off to war. He nodded his head in the darkness and said, "Do it, now!"

Not wanting to risk any noise, she bit him in the neck as she covered his mouth to stop any kind of a scream he might let out, and as she was draining him, he stroked her face, whispering, "Thank you, Lani," and he died. After cutting his neck, she wondered if he somehow knew what she was, because when she changed, there was absolutely no fear or wonderment in his eyes, as all her other victims had expressed, but she had no time to ponder on it now with much more work to do.

After everyone had gone to sleep, Lani packed her meager belongings and slipped away from the camp, heading north to New York.

Once the images faded and she felt she could drive again, she hopped into the minivan and continued on the road north. She entered the Harbor Tunnel, not liking being under that much water, feeling a bit claustrophobic, but she knew it would only be for a minute or so, and when she exited the tube, she felt much better. Baltimore was spread out before her, and she wondered why she had never spent any time in that city in her lifetime. She recalled reading about the city in Captain Lambert's journals, glad that Marcus had saved them before setting the ship on fire.

She stopped for gasoline at the last service area in Maryland, and she went inside to grab a cup of coffee, overwhelmed by the scent of so much blood in one place. The food court was filled with people from so many different states and it would have been so easy to take one, a female, drain her and leave her in a bathroom stall, bloodless, even though questions would have been raised. Lani decided to get her coffee, and get back on the road instead, knowing she'd be in a motel within a few hours anyway.

After a short period of time in Delaware, she crossed the Pennsylvania line, and her head began to throb again, seeing the faces of the eight men, hunters, she killed while traveling from New York to Myrtle Beach, where she had planned on taking up residence for a few years, hopefully. Her mind took her back to that day.

The snow was coming down at a rate of two inches an hour, and she could barely see more than a few feet in front of her, even with her incredible vision. Lani wondered why she decided to take this trip, at this time, especially with the threat of a major snowstorm coming up the east coast, a real nor'easter, the weatherman called it.

She knew she was somewhere in the Wilkes Barre/Scranton corridor, but somehow she had missed a turn off and was on a two lane road in the middle of nowhere, Pennsylvania. The snow, unbelievably, was falling even faster and she didn't see the car until it was too late to stop. Lani turned the wheel and found herself in a deep ditch, from which she could not extract her car, even with the strength she possessed. Grabbing her overnight bag and a few bags of blood to tide her over, she began to walk, hoping to find a house from which she could call for assistance. Her cell phone had died last week and she forgot to charge the battery. She had to laugh to herself, remembering what one of her older acquaintances said about forgetfulness. "Ever since I turned fifty, I've been having these damn senior moments." How surprised she would have been to know that Lani was over three times that age already.

She trudged through the snow for close to an hour, drinking one of the bags of cold blood to keep her strength up, the plasma going down her throat like molasses. Did she remember what molasses tasted like? No, not after all these years! Even the smell of different foods she came in close contact with didn't trigger many memories, but she remembered one thing in particular she had liked to eat when she was a teenager in Maine. Whenever she had New England style clam chowder, she reacted like it was manna from Heaven. The wonderful aroma of the clams and the thick, creamy sauce was almost as delightful as the taste itself. It was a memory she had not had in a long time and she felt so alone for the first time since leaving David.

In the distance she could make out a light source and when she got closer, the house loomed in front of her. Several cars were parked near a barn on the property and she wasn't sure if she wanted to deal with more than one or two people at this moment. She was hungry and angry with herself, and if too many humans were inside, she could be forced to kill them all. A flagpole stood just off the deck and attached to it were the American flag and right below it, the black and white POW-MIA flag. There were definitely veterans inside, probably making this house a hunting camp. It was deer season in Pennsylvania. She let out a sigh and decided to go inside, knowing that even if there was not phone service to the house, one or more of the hunters would certainly have a cell phone.

She knocked on the door and in short order it was opened by a young man, perhaps sixteen or so, who was wearing jogging shorts over a pair of long johns and a Baltimore Orioles baseball cap. He said, "Can I help you, Miss?"

At the mention of the word miss, the card game that had been in progress stopped and seven men scampered to put on some more clothing before she was allowed inside. "Hang on, Junior, while we put on some pants, then you can let her come in?"

The boy who was called Junior said to Lani, "Give my dad and his friends a second, okay. They were sitting around in their skivvies playing cards and I guess older guys don't like young ladies to see them in their undies."

Lani nodded her head and in less then two minutes she was ushered inside.

The house was warm and toasty, the heat sources being a roaring fire and warm air flowing from baseboard heat. Lani stepped inside and took off her coat and removed her boots, placing them in a box by the door containing several pair of boots and shoes. Lani could feel their hungry eyes looking her up and down when she was bent over, as she was wearing skin hugging jeans, white tee shirt and a brown leather vest. She walked over to the fireplace and warmed her hands and face, then turned to the men of various ages, and said, "Thanks. I was freezing out there."

One of the older men, a leather faced man with white hair and beard spoke first. "Miss, what are you doing outside on a night like this? You could have caught your death of cold out there." She looked at him and marveled at how his physical appearance matched that of the description she had read of Captain Lambert in Marcus's journal. She had run across things like that over these many years, even seeing the spitting image of herself once, about twenty years ago, thinking of killing her, yet allowing her 'twin' to live. She had smiled, viciously, wondering if David had ever run into her back then and tried to take her head.

Lani said, "My car is stuck in a ditch a couple of miles from here and I've been walking, hoping to find someplace from where I could make a call. My cell phone died last week and I forgot to charge it. A blonde moment, I guess."

That elicited a roar of laughter from the hunters, putting them at ease. They sat down at the table again and resumed their game, while the older gentleman offered Lani some coffee, which she readily accepted, although the scent of blood was making her head spin and she wanted to eat, soon.

After handing her a cup of steaming black coffee, the old man offered her a seat on a somewhat threadbare sofa, which could have had a few springs replaced, but she sat on it anyway and sipped her drink. She smiled because the old man had added a bit of brandy. "This tastes wonderful, Mister. Thank you so much."

"He raised his cup to her and said, "You're welcome. My name is Lester Crawford and this is our hunting camp." He introduced her to all the card players, one of which was wearing a baseball cap bearing the logo Desert Storm Veteran And Proud Of It. She said, "Welcome home, and thanks for your service." He merely nodded his head after reading her lips. She lifted her cup and he responded in kind, never saying a word.

"Hank doesn't talk, Miss...?"

"Lani Jorgenson."

"Lani. Like I said, Hank doesn't talk. An Iraqi bayonet severed his vocal cords and he ain't been able to say a word since, but he sure can read lips, can't you Hank, you sorry sonofabitch." Hank had been looking toward Lester and flipped him the bird, which had the assemblage in stitches again. Even

Lani managed a chuckle.

After finishing her laced coffee and asking if she could have another, she asked if anyone had a phone she could use to call for a tow truck.

One of the other men, Slim, she remembered him being called, offered, "Lani, ain't no tow truck in the world going to come out here tonight for any reason. I'm afraid you're stuck here until the snow stops and we can go check out your car ourselves. Problem is," he said, as he walked to the window and looked out, "it might not be until late tomorrow afternoon before we can get out of here. Snow's really piling up out there."

"I guess I'm stuck here for the night, then. Do you mind if I sack out somewhere? I'm really beat from my ordeal."

Junior, who was really named Peter Parsons, Junior, son of the owner of the house, who had unfortunately passed away in spring, said, "Lani, you can take my room and I'll sleep out here on the sofa. At least you'll be away from these guys and their farting and snoring all night."

"Know why they call him Junior, Lani?" This from Tiny, a man of thirty something, who would probably never see forty since he stood about five eight and weighed about two sixty. She could sense how slowly his blood flowed and figured he had about a year, at best, even if he dieted and exercised every day. Killing him would be the best way for him to go out, instead of the pain he was going to experience when he had his first heart attack.

"No, Tiny, why do the call him Junior?"

"'Cause he didn't want to be known as little Peter, or even worse, PP."

A pillow hit Tiny in the side of the head and Junior yelled out, "Fuck you, Lardass."

Everyone laughed, including Lani.

After an hour or so of small talk, Lani said, "If you all don't mind, I'm going to call it a night, and thanks for your hospitality." She stepped into Junior's room, closed the door and ripped open a bag of blood, gulping it down as quickly as she could, finally feeling a little better. Even though she needed no sleep, she lay down on the bed and listened to the animated conversation going on fifteen feet away. Mostly they were bragging to each other about their kills and the size of their penises, probably because there was a young woman in their midst and their glands had begun to act up, seeing Lani in her tight blue jeans and a tee shirt that didn't hide the size of her breasts.

She heard one of them, who was more than a bit drunk whisper, "Junior, why don't you go and check on her, man. She's not too much older than you. Maybe you could get your first piece of ass tonight." Lani smiled, hoping he would go through with it and come in. He'd get laid and die a happy young man.

"Fuck you, Jason," he said, "I got laid already. Mary Jane and I did it this summer, down by the lake on dad's old army blanket." He grinned and chuckled, "Told me it scratched the shit out of her ass, but she sure liked it while I fucked her."

"Yeah, well, you don't have a hair on that skinny ass of yours if you don't at least go and see if she is comfortable. I know she was giving you the eye all evening, kid," said Billy Jenkins, twenty-seven and only married eight months. "If I would still be single, I know I'd be in there trying my best to get some. Hell, why would she have picked a hunting camp? You heard that she said she was from New York. She's probably a hooker, praying on unsuspecting men like ourselves." The alcohol was really talking, now, since a few of the men mumbled in agreement. Lester was asleep in a lounge chair and had no idea what was going on, as he dreamed of his late wife, Martha and what she used to do to him after a hard day's work at Bethlehem Steel. A smile crossed his face and his hand wandered down to his crotch, which he started to fondle in his sleep.

"Yeah, right, Billy. You'd go in there and check on her if you weren't married! Cheryl would have cut your balls off if you would have even looked at another woman since you guys got out of high school."

"It's gospel, kid. I'd go in there in a minute. Lani is a fox. Did you check out how her tits stood out in that tee. Oh, man!"

Everyone at the table began to needle Junior until he finally acceded to their wishes and knocked on Lani's door."

"Yeah," he heard from inside. "Is it morning yet?"

"No Lani, I just need to come in to get something from my dresser. Are you decent?"

"Sure, Junior, come on in. I'm under the covers."

He came in and closed the door behind him, checking her out as she lay in his bed, covered up to her neck, her jeans and tee shirt draped across a chair, her panties and bra lying on the floor beside the bed. Junior's eyebrows rose. She was buck naked in his bed and he began to get an erection, which she couldn't help noticing.

She said, "Is that a banana in your shorts, or are you happy to see me?" She chuckled and he was ready to walk out when she said, "Junior, come here please."

He looked over toward the bed and Lani threw back the sheet and blanket, revealing her absolutely stunning, creamy white body. A catch caught in his throat as he strode toward the bed, removing his long john top before sitting down beside her, kissing her, wondering if he could get past her awful breath, and fondling her breasts as she massaged him through his shorts and long john bottoms, which were quickly removed. Junior mounted her and their passion could be heard in the next room, as the hunters shared high fives. She screamed as she climaxed, followed a short time later by Junior as he emptied himself inside her.

She kissed him and said, "How was I, Junior?"

"You were absolutely amazing, Lani."

"Even better than Mary Jane?"

"How did you know about her?" He began to get dressed, looking at her tits and wondering if he should go back out there, or stay in here for the rest of the night.

"The walls aren't very thick, and guys, when they drink, talk louder than they think they are talking. I heard Billy say he thought I might be a New York hooker. Well, he was right and since you are all going to help me get my car unstuck, you can tell them out there that whoever wants a free ride should come on in here and I'll take care of them."

Junior went out and relayed the message and Jason was in there in a shot, returning in fifteen minutes with a huge smile on his face.

Lani serviced four of the men, and when nobody else took up her offer, she had sex with Junior one more time. As they were screwing each other's brains out, daylight began to flood through the bedroom window. When Lani came, her fangs extended and she tore into his neck, savagely. Her hunger had augmented and she couldn't wait any longer. As she was feeding, the door opened and Billy saw what was happening to his younger friend. He screamed, causing Lani to stop and glare at him as blood spurted from Junior's neck, covering her and saturating into the furniture and carpeting.

He raced to the gun rack and grabbed a thirty eight caliber pistol, turned and fired point blank into Lani who was now all over him, biting into his neck, killing him in moments, as all the others, in their drunken stupors focused in on this formerly beautiful woman, now the epitome of evil, drenched in the blood of two young men, fangs bared.

Tiny waddled toward the door, hoping to escape the horror and carnage, but Lani got there first and said to him, "Tiny, you're going to be a lucky man, because now you won't have to worry about the heart attack you were going to soon have."

His chest heaved as she kicked his legs out from under him. Tiny landed on his huge stomach and he felt the pain as her teeth sank deep into his neck; his carotid artery finally breeched and his blood flowed into her mouth, slowly, at first, but she sucked harder and just before he died, his eyes popped right from their sockets.

The rest of the men were dispatched as quickly as mercifully as was possible, as she left Lester and Hank for last.

Lester cried out, "What in God's name are you, Lani?"

"Trust me Lester, I am nothing in God's name and thanks for your hospitality." His heart gave out as she drank from an artery in his right arm, leaving Hank for last.

Since he was deaf, and drunk as a skunk, he never heard, nor saw the carnage that had taken place in the past ten minutes. All of his friends were dead and she shook him awake, allowing him one last nightmare before they would be stopped forever. Her fangs found the tunnel holding his life's essence and it flowed freely into her, killing him in a few minutes.

Lani looked over her killing field, and after a moment or two, went to her bag and extracted her razor knife, slashing eight throats, not concerned with obliterating her fang marks, because the bodies would be burned beyond all recognition when she was through. She picked each corpse up and placed them in their sleeping positions. Satisfied that the scene looked normal, she dressed and started a few fires, using pieces of the burning logs, having it seem that an untended fireplace was the cause of the fire.

After walking from the house, watching it go up in flame and smoke, she strolled back to her car, hoping to await someone to help her out. When she found the road, and ultimately the car, she looked in the direction of the house and saw a black cloud rise from where the house had once stood. Less than an hour later, an eighteen-wheeler stopped after seeing her signal for help and with the driver's help, her car was ready to travel once again.

※※

Lani's head still throbbed, after recalling all the incidents that had exploded in her consciousness today, hoping that there would be no more, for the images were quite troubling

Continuing her drive up the Pennsylvania turnpike, she was looking forward to living in the Lehigh Valley for a few weeks or a month, and then it was off to Europe and another new life. She grew excited with the prospect of learning new languages and furthering her education of new cultures, for she would experience life more than any other living soul could, except perhaps for Marcus, but his experiences were in an age where there was absolutely nothing to compare to today's world. Lani was looking forward to her first airplane flight, knowing that she would be able to control herself for the time it would take to cross the Atlantic and arrive in England. From there she would travel to a new country every few months or so, until she grew tired and would return to America in five or ten years. With any amount of luck, David would be dead by the time she returned.

She saw the sign for Allentown and a few minutes later pulled up to the tollbooth.

Allentown

After exiting the Pennsylvania turnpike, she stopped at the tollbooth to pay her fare, handing him a twenty, the smallest bill she had. The toll taker was really cute. He was over six feet tall, with sandy hair hanging slightly over his shirt collar, hazel eyes and a killer smile. As he was counting her change, she struck up a conversation with the young man.

"Excuse me, but I am new to the area and I really need some directions to the Red Roof Inn on..." She looked at a notebook on the passenger seat, "Catasauqua Road." Looking back up into his eyes, she was distracted by that gnawing feeling deep inside her, the one she always had when she found a victim. It upset her knowing that she couldn't take this man here, because of the traffic stacking up behind her.

Ron Gerancher looked at the face of the most beautiful woman he had ever seen in his nearly twenty years, and he had seen a lot of faces working this job for the past three years since he graduated from Emmaus High School. He just didn't have the grades to go to college, but he was taking some courses at Lehigh Carbon Community College. He was working hard to earn enough credits in journalism classes to transfer to Kutztown University in a year or two.

"Miss, I happen to live near the Red Roof, and if you could wait ten minutes, when I get off duty, you can follow me there, if you'd like."

"Yeah, that would be great, then I wouldn't get lost and have a blonde moment." They both laughed, for totally different reasons."

"Cool, just pull over to the right and when I punch off, I'll pull up in front of your van and we'll be off."

"Listen, Ron," she had read his nametag, "if you wouldn't mind, would you be able to help me take my stuff into my room when we get to the Inn. I hurt my arm yesterday and I can't carry my bags too easily. A gentleman helped me load my van when I left Virginia and I will pay you for your time. My name is Lani Jorgenson and I would really appreciate your help. I'll buy you a cup of coffee as well because you will surely know where I will have to go tomorrow morning for an employment interview."

"No problem, Lani, I'll help you out, but you can't pay me since I'm a chauvinist at heart and rescuing beautiful women is something I do really well."

She smiled warmly and said, "Great, Ron. I'll wait for you over there and you'll at least allow me to buy you a cup of coffee or something, for your trouble."

"Okay, Lani. I can go for that. It's been a long night out here."

Lani pulled the van off the road and watched as several cars and trucks passed through the toll booths, always curious about the humans inside the vehicles: What were they like? Did they have families? How quickly would she be able to drain them and satisfy her growing hunger for another day? She thought back to that last day in Williamsburg and how David, her relentless pursuer, saved Fred's life. David was able to quickly search online newspapers and websites for unusual happenstances and it seemed like he was beginning to figure out where she was going to move to next. *Will I be able to kill him when we meet again?* She was sure it would be sooner then she would care for, especially since she was considering leaving the country to travel to Europe for a while. With luck, when she would decide to return, he would be long dead and buried.

From the corner of her eye, she saw Ron hop into his Jeep and in a few moments he had pulled up in front of her van, leading her to the eastbound entrance ramp for US Route 22. The four lane highway was clogged with traffic, but she kept her eye on Ron's Jeep, even when a car, a small, red, foreign job nearly wiped out her left front side, cutting in front of her, then immediately exiting onto route 309 South. Lani was really pissed, having to slam on the brakes, sliding on some black ice. As she slid, her one hand came off the steering wheel and she hit the left inside dome light, causing it to go on. It took her a moment or two to regain control and when a car in the inside lane slowed down to avoid hitting her, Lani's fangs were bared and her eyes reddened, frightening a young red haired boy in the other vehicle. With her acute vision, she saw him tap his mother on the shoulder, and she read his lips. He was telling his mother about the vampire in the minivan. By the time the mother looked toward Lani, she was back to normal again and smiled at the woman and child. The mother swiveled her head back to look out the windshield, but the child kept looking at Lani until she showed her fangs again, licked her lips, and laughed at him. He pulled away from the window and started jabbering to his mother again, who totally ignored him as the car gathered speed and pulled away from Lani's van.

Two exits later, Ron eased onto the ramp, crossed Airport Road, and after a short journey on Catasauqua Road, turned into the parking lot of the Red Roof Inn. Lani pulled up beside him and said, "Give me a minute to check in and get my room key, then we'll unload my stuff and head over to the diner. After that asshole cut me off, I could really use a cup of coffee."

"Yeah, Lani. I know what you mean. That road is one of the worst in Pennsylvania and people are always cutting me off. I hope you at least flipped him the finger, even if he didn't see it."

She laughed heartily, replying, "Ron, you would never believe how I reacted to him and to the people in the car beside me. Trust me, it was better than flipping the finger." *Why did I say that? I don't need him to wonder what could be worse than giving the guy the guy the finger. I shouldn't have bared my fangs to that kid on the highway a second time, either.*

Ron scratched his head, not knowing what she meant, but not really caring either. He just wanted to help her with her stuff, grab a coffee and head home to try to get in a little studying before calling it a night. He looked at his watch, which showed 11:30 in the green glow of the internal light. Maybe he'd get to bed by one o'clock and get seven hours sleep before heading to classes. As he stood there thinking about the assignment that was given this morning, a two thousand-word short story about the most remarkable person you know, Lani approached the cars with a room key in her hand. Fortunately she was on the first floor and with Ron's help they were able to put her four bags inside her room in no time. She would not allow him to carry the small cooler he had spotted in the back of the van after she raised the tailgate to get her luggage out. Ron noticed some smoke escaping from the cooler, immediately knowing that she had something in there on dry ice and his curiosity was getting the better of him. To his knowledge, the only things requiring dry ice were refrigerated medical supplies and blood plasma, yet she didn't look old enough to be a doctor. Perhaps he'd feel her out over coffee and satisfy his inquisitiveness.

The diner was nice and warm and they removed their jackets, Ron taking Lani's off and hanging it on the hooks placed on the side of the booth. As she sat down, he noticed her figure for the first time, seeing she was built really well, firm breasts pushing outward inside a red turtle neck sweater, long legs covered by stone washed jeans. She wore white Nikes, probably a size seven, he thought. Her blonde hair was tied back in a ponytail, and even without makeup, her porcelain face was incredible. As she sipped her coffee, color came into her cheeks, intensifying her beauty.

"So what brings you to our fair city, Lani?"

"I have a job offer in Allentown and I figured this would be a good place to stay until I get settled. The price was right and it's outside the city where there are fewer people to deal with."

"What kind of work do you do?"

"I'm a physical therapist and after a review of my application, Lehigh Valley Hospital hired me to work at their facility on Cedar Crest Boulevard. I need to go there tomorrow morning for my indoctrination. Is that close to here?" She remembered seeing a billboard advertising the facility, which made the lie come out easily.

"Actually, Lani, you should have gotten a motel on the other side of town. Do you recall seeing Cedar Crest Boulevard on the way here, because it was the exit after that guy cut you off."

"No, Ron, I must have missed it with everything that was going on at the time. Guess I did have that blonde moment after all." They both laughed. *Why am I laughing so much? First the headaches and the flashbacks and lately so much laughter. I should be an emotionless killer yet I am feeling so human. I remember a few weeks ago seeing two people on the street that looked so much like my parents, but after blinking my eyes, they were gone. What is happening to me?*

After taking another sip of coffee, the warmth spreading throughout her body, not satisfying her like blood, but making her feel better anyway, she looked into Ron's eyes saying, "So, like what do you do with your time when you aren't in that Godforsaken toll booth, Ron?"

Ron stared back at her nearly hypnotic smile and replied, "I'm a journalism major at a small community college north of the other side of town."

Lani's eyebrows rose a bit, a barely perceptible movement, yet she was sure Ron caught it and she thought she better be careful what she said to him, or she would definitely have to kill him and that would be a bad start in a new town; taking someone out who had a family in the area. "Journalism, huh? Do you want to be a writer or a reporter after you graduate?"

"I'd like to write the great American novel, but there are so many starving novelists out there: I guess I had better get a real job to pay my expenses and write fiction on the side. I know of one guy for sure in this area who has had a few books published already and he still hasn't got the big break yet. I met him once at a local writer's conference after reading his first mystery and he is really a good writer: he even won an Edgar for best new paperback original for his third book. After talking with him, I realize that it takes more than talent to make it in that arena. He said, 'You are at the mercy of the agents and publishers. If they don't like the material, it will never rate being put between covers and placed on bookstore shelves,' but, I still want to give it a shot, no matter what the odds are."

She said, "What do you like to write, Ron?" She began to sip her coffee again.

"Don't laugh, but I really like vampire stories, Lani."

When Lani coughed into her coffee cup, Ron asked, "Are you okay?"

"Yeah, I'm fine, Just swallowed too much," she responded, coughing spasmodically from both the coffee and his answer. She would really have to be careful, but she thought it might be fun to share a few of her exploits with him, just before ending his existence; but no, she could not kill him and have people asking questions already. Too many people had seen them together, and if she wanted to kill him, she would have to wait until a later date. Perhaps she could have other kinds of fun with him, a young guy with a healthy sexual appetite. She didn't think he was gay, but she'd find out soon.

"Ron, what do your family and friends think about your journalistic aspirations?"

"Well, mom and dad support me, but my younger sister thinks I'm a dork. I don't have many friends, but they like to ridicule me, too, telling me that vampire stories suck, except they like to watch Buffy kill them on TV."

"How about your girlfriend? What does she think about vampires?"

"Well, to tell you the truth, Lani, I don't have a girlfriend right now. I was going with a cheerleader when we were in high school, but she went to a real college and she's now dating a senior. I heard they were going to get married after she graduates. He is a law student and has a job lined up already through his old man's contacts."

"Sorry to hear that, but since you aren't going out with anyone right now, maybe you could show me the town, if I'm not to old for you."

"How much older could you be, Lani. I'd guess you were maybe twenty one or twenty two at the most."

"Yeah, I'm twenty one, but some of my old friends think I act like a much older woman at times."

"It seems like when you say older friends, you act like you're a hundred years old or something, like you have the weight of the world on your shoulders."

Lani stirred her black coffee with her finger, staring at a spot on her napkin, absorbing what Ron had just said. This young man was seemingly able to read things about her that no one else ever had before, and in such a short time. She looked up from the napkin into his eyes and replied, "I know, Ron. I have not had a very perfect life so far and sometimes I think it is downhill from here. All my family is gone and I am the only one left and it hurts to know that I have nobody left in my lineage. It's not the weight of the world, but it is a heavy burden to bear." She took his hand in hers and said, "You are so perceptive and that will probably go a long way toward making you a great writer. So tell me about vampires: an interesting subject."

Ron smiled as she kept his hand in hers and offered, "Well, I guess the only things I know are what I read already and the movies I saw, plus watching Buffy, but I think that if vampires did exist, they wouldn't be as easy to kill as they are in print or on film. I'm not even sure if a vampire could be killed by being pierced by a wooden stake, since a vampire's heart supposedly doesn't beat, so what would a piece of wood do?'

Lani studied him as he spoke, wondering what she should actually tell him, if anything. If she agreed with him he might become more aroused and he would ask more questions or bring up more points to ponder. It was an interesting, unique situation and she wanted to allow it to last as long as possible, but not to the point where he would begin to believe in such creatures. She lived for a long time with humans having suspicions about immortals, but nothing to confirm her existence as a vampire, save for David, but to her knowledge, the only one who believed him, Austin Numbers, was long dead.

"You may be right, Ron. I have not seen many vampire movies, nor read the books, because they are just too frightening, but I guess the only true way a vampire could be destroyed would be by a beheading, or perhaps being burned or drowned. But a stake to the heart? I don't think so either."

She asked him a few more things about school and home, which prompted him to look at his watch. "I'm sorry, Lani, but I have to run. I have an early class tomorrow and I need to get some sleep. When can we get together again?"

"What's your schedule like, Ron? Mine is going to be pretty flexible, at least for a few days, so perhaps we better go by yours."

"I'm free tomorrow night. Would you like to go to dinner and to a movie?"

"Dinner is not good, but I sure would like to go to a movie. How about anytime after 6:30?"

"Great. The Carmike Theater is just around the corner. I could meet you there about 6:30 and we'll just catch whatever is playing, if that's okay with you?"

"Sounds good, Ron. I'll meet you outside the theater."

They stood up and Ron helped her into her coat and then put his on. They strolled out of the restaurant together and went their separate ways with Lani wondering why she was doing this, knowing it could only lead to trouble and, quite possibly, his demise.

She unlocked the door to her room, noticing a musky smell that she hadn't noticed before, and went to the bathroom to relieve herself, cleaning the bowl afterward, so as not to give the maid something to see that she need not see at all. Lani sat down on the bed and opened the lid to the cooler, removing several bags of blood, warming them by running hot water over them as she was taking a shower, hoping to get the blood to at least body temperature before she drank. After ripping open the top of the bag, she held it over her mouth and let the life fluid of an unknown donor drain from it into her throat, not wanting to have the plastic in her mouth. Although the essence was now coursing through her, warming her and making her feel whole again, she was unhappy that she had to dine in this manner. *This method of eating is almost like a human cooking a meal in a bag—it gave the nourishment, but none of the pleasure associated with eating 'real food'.* Lani placed the empty bag inside a suitcase. She sat down at the table, opened up her laptop and began to write in her journal.

For years, before laptops became popular, she had kept handwritten journals, but they had become too cumbersome to haul with her everywhere she went. Since she needed no sleep, Lani would spend hours at a time transcribing her life stories to disk, knowing that someday people would read about her, and also how the vampire population had been eliminated, courtesy of the writings from Marcus's journals, but she knew it would not be soon. There were times, as she wrote, that she would take a few moments to read words she had originally written in the past one hundred and fifty nine years, thinking it would make a hell of a book someday, then she smiled, thinking about Ron's inability to write a true vampire story, using only the information that writers had made up about these 'fictitious' creatures of the night. She laughed to herself, wondering how people could invent things about a non-existent creature that really existed. Lani typed in the events from the past few days and considered going hunting, since she was still hungry, *or do I just want to kill someone or something?* She lay down on the bed, not even getting under the covers, since the room was so warm, the musky smell still emanating from the baseboard heaters, plus she had just drank. She reached for the remote control and began flipping through the channels.

When Ron returned home, still smelling the scents of perfume and breath mints, plus another odor he could not quite manage to sort out, he opened the refrigerator and took out a carton of milk, swallowing several ounces right from the container. His mother hated that, but what the hell, she'd never know. Opening a jar of Skippy, he ran his finger through the peanut butter and inserted it into his mouth, sucking his finger clean after forcing the sticky mass down his throat. He closed the lid and returned the jar to its place in the pantry.

He took the stairs two at a time and after entering the bathroom he took a leak, shook his penis off, then squeezed it several times while thinking about Lani and how gorgeous she was. Ron considered whacking off, but he was much too tired and so he went into his room, shucking everything from his body, except for his underpants, crawled under the covers and was asleep in two seconds, even though his mind was working overtime, trying to figure out what was in the cooler that required dry ice.

Lani grew bored with television, and it was still only two in the morning. She got up, dressed and decided to go for a drive to see what this city had to offer her in the way of derelicts. She always looked for the homeless first before killing regular people, if possible, actually doing the cities and towns a favor by destroying those whose only claim in life was to keep the taxes high when they needed to be cared for, which was something they didn't even do themselves. When she headed back out to Airport Road, she noticed a tall building, perhaps thirty floors or so, standing like a sentinel, its upper floors ablaze with lights, in the center of the city. After driving down Seventh Street and onto some of the nearly deserted streets of Allentown, she parked her car in the vacant parking lot of a movie theater across the street from a prison, listening to the sounds of tortured souls screaming obscenities to the guards as they made their rounds. Lani stood there with her hands in the pockets of her black coat, a black beret covering much of her blonde hair, when a car pulled up to the curb and two men wearing suits and topcoats stepped from the vehicle and approached her.

The taller of the two tipped his cap, flashed her a detective shield and said, "Mornin' ma'am. Can I ask what you are doing just standing here in the middle of the night?"

Lani looked him square in the eye and replied, "I couldn't sleep, detective, so I just decided to go for a drive. My car is right here in the parking lot." She pointed to her minivan and continued, "I'm not doing anything illegal, am I?"

As the other detective walked over to her car, shining his light through the windows and writing down her license plate, the one questioning her responded, "No, you aren't doing anything illegal, but we don't really like it when young woman are in this section of town late at night without an escort."

"Thanks for your consideration, detective, but I can take care of myself if anyone puts a move on me."

He smirked at her aloofness and said, "That may well be so, Miss, but I think it would be wise if you got back into your van and went home to...?"

"I'm staying at the Red Roof Inn on Catasauqua Road. I only came into town tonight and tomorrow I am starting a new job." She was beginning to get nervous, giving out all this false information, which they surely would check out. Lani hacked into the computer sites she needed to keep her identity up to date. Out of the corner of her eye she saw the other cop looking under her car, moving the beam from his flashlight to and fro, wondering what the hell he was looking for.

"Jack," the other detective yelled, "I found something here that you need to take a look at."

Lani was more than a bit curious, knowing he could not have found anything under her car, since she never hid anything there in the first place. She walked over to the van with the detective named Jack and when they came around to the other side of the van, the other officer was holding what appeared to be a bag of marijuana in his hand, an obvious plant. *What do these bastards want? Money? Sex? Or do they just want to bust me for the hell of it?* She knew that most cops were very civic minded and family men, but there were always one or two in a city of this size or larger who were on the take or just fuck-offs, and she had just found Allentown's, she figured.

Jack told her to face the van, put her hands up on the roof and spread her legs. He patted her down, spending way too much time rubbing over the back pockets of her jeans and when his hand came around the front, he rubbed her crotch, several times. After he finished there, he checked out her coat and reached around the front, bringing his hands up under her jacket and squeezing her breasts. She said, "Are you having fun, yet? We could all go back to my place and I'll fuck both of your brains out if you forget about the grass you found?"

"What do you think, Al, should we take her up on her offer? She sure has great tits and I bet she'd be a hell of a ride?"

"Sounds good to me, Jack." He grabbed his crotch and said, "It's been a couple of weeks since the old lady and I had sex. I could sure go for some young stuff like this one. Let's do it, since she's more than willing."

Lani hopped into the car with Al while Jack drove her minivan back to the motel. Nobody saw them enter her room and nobody saw her drag them back out to the car, unconscious and bitten, but not drained nor dead. She drove back to the city and parked the car in an alley, rearranged them in their correct seats and sliced their jugulars with her razor knife, obliterating her teeth marks, allowing blood to splash and soak everywhere, making it look like a double murder of two policemen. She smiled, wondering how long it would take the force to figure this one out, or even if any information would be released. And the poor guys never got to have sex anyway. She also took a few minutes to scatter the marijuana around the passenger compartment, adding another element to the mystery, before removing their weapons and taking four hundred dollars from their wallets.

She drove back to the Red Roof and immediately after cleaning up, entered this episode in her electronic journal, spending great care to make it sound as messy as it was.

꽃

On Tuesday night, just before six thirty, Lani pulled into the parking lot of the Carmike Theater, exited her car and after walking less than the half the length of a city block, she entered the lobby, seeing Ron smiling at her as she approached. *God, he looks great! Wait a minute; did I really think His name? Ron looks so good and I am really so hungry for blood. Sex? Both? Lani, this isn't going to work, girl.* "Hi, Ron. Have you been waiting long?"

Lani looked great in a blue mini skirt and a white blouse, her hair down and her face having more color than it did the other night. "No, I've only been here for a few minutes. What would you like to see tonight?"

Thinking she'd like to see the expression on his face after she bit into him, she immediately shrugged it off saying, "Doesn't matter, Ron. I haven't seen any of these movies, yet. I don't go to movies too often. I think I have claustrophobic tendencies, sometimes."

Ron selected a movie and they went into theater number six, walking all the way to the front of the theater, then walking up the stairs to the top row of the stadium style seating theater. After sitting down, Ron started chomping on his popcorn and sipping his Pepsi, Lani having refused his offer for either snack. He was a bit concerned, since she refused an invitation to dinner, popcorn and Pepsi, and two nights ago had only black coffee, not wanting to see a menu. Ron wondered what she liked to eat and when, figuring they might go for a pizza after the movie.

Two and a half hours later they left the theater, both feeling a bit dissatisfied with the film they had seen. Ron had seen the trailers last week and the movie looked very promising, yet almost all of the good stuff was shown in a two-minute snippet of 'adverteasing'. Ron threw his trash into the large container and as he was helping Lani into her coat, said, "Would you like to go for some pizza, Lani?"

She replied, "No thanks, Ron. I'm trying to watch my weight all the time and I rarely eat anything after lunch. Sometimes I only have a big breakfast and I'm good for the day, but I'd like to have a good, hot cup of coffee again, because I'm feeling a little chilled."

He took her hand in his, and she definitely was freezing, even though the temperature inside the building was quite comfortable. "Wow, you sure are cold, Lani!"

She offered a weak smile and said, "Cold hands, warm heart." An image of David, in 1965, popped into her head almost every time she said those words.

They both drove to the diner, ordering coffee and just sat for a few minutes in silence, wondering what to say to another, when Ron broke the uncomfortable silence. "You know, Lani, you are really a gorgeous woman, and I'm sure you'll make a great physical therapist, but I don't think you and I could become a couple. I hope you won't take offense to this, but I just don't feel much for you as a possible girlfriend, but I sure would like to have you as a girl friend, if that's okay."

Lani almost burst out laughing. She was off the hook, and Ron would keep on living to write his stories about vampires and whatever else his mind could dream up, but she didn't want to sound too pleased when she answered. She had been looking down at her coffee cup, absently stirring the hot, black liquid with her finger, stifling her feelings as she listened to him talk. She looked deep into his eyes and replied, "It's not easy being dumped on a first date, but to be honest, I really couldn't see a relationship blossoming either. Maybe we are too far apart in age, even though I'm only a year older. *Yeah, right!* I would like to be a girl friend, though, and an e-mail buddy, too. Who knows, we might want to try this again sometime and, well, perhaps the two words could become one."

"You never know, Lani. I'm just so happy that you aren't mad and that we will still be in touch with one another. Just send me an e-mail when you need to talk to someone or if you need to know anything about the area, and I'll get back to you right away."

They exchanged e-mail addresses, finished their coffee, kissed like brother and sister and went their separate ways. *Why did I give him my e-mail address? Why do I even have one, when all I receive is junk mail, since I have no one to correspond with?*

Lani hurried back to the motel, warming up her last three bags of blood in a tub full of hot water, and drinking like her life depended upon it. She was actually happy to be out of a situation that could have led to a fine, young man's death. Even though many people would die while she lived in the Lehigh Valley, Ron Gerancher would not be one of them.

❧❦

On the way back to his house, Ron's goose bumps rose and his breathing became erratic, flashing back to the one point in the movie, where Lani seemed to be paying particular attention to the scene. He recalled looking over at her and saw her teeth grow. A reddish tint burned in her eyes. He was staring at a vampire and he was frightened nearly out of his wits, wanting to run, yet not wanting her to know that he knew what she was, even if it was impossible. He also recalled her swirling her finger in coffee so hot that he needed to put in several small ice cubes from his water glass to cool it sufficiently to drink; yet she felt nothing doing this.

❧❦

On Thursday morning, as David Forrester was perusing online newspapers, still staying at the Williamsburg Inn, an article caught his eye.

The story, written by Kathleen Hammond of The Morning Call, in Allentown, Pennsylvania told of the murders of two men, posing as detectives, who were found in an alley by a local resident. He read that the phony cops were found sitting in their car, their necks horribly slashed. That was all he had to read to know that Lani murdered the two men after drinking them nearly dry. David cringed at the thought and absentmindedly rubbed his neck, the wounds of thirty-five years ago only phantoms in his mind, yet he could still feel the punctures.

David closed his laptop and began to pack. He had to get to Allentown as quickly as possible, even though she warned him that she would kill him the next time he interfered in her life.

Late that afternoon, he checked into the Hilton on Hamilton Street where he placed a phone call to the newspaper to get in contact with Kathleen Hammond, who he was told had left for the day approximately ten minutes before he called and she was not scheduled to come into the office until tomorrow morning around nine. "Would you like to leave a message on her voice mail, Mr. Forrester?"

"Yes, I would like that. Thank you."

"Hold on while I connect you sir."

After four rings, the answering machine kicked in. "Hi, this is Kathleen Hammond. I am not at my desk right now, but if you leave your name, number, and a brief message, I'll get back to you as soon as I can. Have a great day."

"Hello, Miss Hammond. My name is David Forrester and I am staying at the Hilton. Please call me at your earliest convenience. The number here is 555-6397. This is in regard to your story about the two men who were killed. I may have information that could lead to the arrest of the murderer, but I would rather talk to you before calling the police.

Just about the time David was making this call, Lani Jorgenson was on the other side of town having a glass of wine in a local bar called The Firebase.

JASON

Jason Weber lifted his glass, drawing the eye of the bartender, who was busy serving three men in business suits. Following a nearly imperceptible nod, Weber placed the glass squarely upon the center of a coaster bearing the logo of the St. Louis Cardinals, which happened to be his favorite team. As he looked up and down the length of the bar, he noticed an empty stool next to a willowy blonde who was absently stirring her drink. She had a vacant, lost look in her blue eyes; her mouth turned downward, her brow furrowed as in deep thought. As he continued his study of the woman in the strapless, black gown, somewhat early in the day for that type of dress, especially here, he noticed a very old looking necklace gracing her long, thin neck. The bartender had finally arrived with a fresh glass of Yuengling Lager, in Jason's mind, the best beer ever brewed.

"Harry," he said to the tall, young server, dressed in Levis and a T-shirt bearing the logo of the Lehigh Northampton Vietnam Veterans Memorial, "get a drink for the lady down at the end of the bar. She really looks like she could use one about now. Any idea who she is?"

Harry Jamison, son of Jason's best friend, Marty, along with Jason were two of the three owners of The Firebase. The bar was a hang out for veterans, cops and government workers, on the south side of Allentown. Harry looked toward the woman as she continued to swirl the nearly melted ice cubes in her otherwise empty glass. She was staring at a jar of Slim Jims, which was directly in front of her on the bar, and he thought he had never seen anyone so sad in his whole life. It was apparent to Jason that Harry was turning the wheel of his mental rolodex, searching for a name to go with the beautiful face he had served fifteen minutes ago. She smiled warmly when Harry approached her, yet he detected that the smile was merely a cover, hiding some inner turmoil. Bartenders had a knack for somehow knowing that stuff. If you came into the bar on a semi-regular basis, say at least twice a week, Harry would most likely know your name, and what you drank. As Harry continued to research his mental file, Weber lit another Winston, crushed the empty pack and laid it beside the ashtray containing the last seven cigarettes he had smoked, down to the filter, in the course of the past ninety minutes. Three packs a day and counting, Jason mused.

"Sorry, Jay. I just don't recall ever seeing her in here before. Maybe she's a new girl in town. I heard that Jane has recruited some fresh meat for her house up on South Mountain." Jane was Jane Beitler; the city's most protected madam. She had been under the watchful eye of local veterans for nearly thirty-one years, ever since her son was blown into about a hundred pieces in Tay Ninh province. Three other kids were sent home in bags after Art Beitler, nineteen years old, and only in 'Nam for sixteen days, stepped on the buried, pressure detonated 105 round.

As Harry sauntered toward the shelf holding a variety of wine and whiskey, the mention of Jane's name inflicted a chill on Jay's spine, fortunate that he and Marty were still alive with their memories. Along with Art, Jay and Marty enlisted one day after an all night booze party, their manhood at stake. Two returnees told them, "You guys don't have the fuckin' balls to go in the army and kick some serious VC ass." Three hours later, their minds and bodies fortified with the strength of several dozen drinks, the trio reported to the army recruiter at 7th and Hamilton streets. Signing on the dotted line, they requested to enlist under the buddy system, which would keep them together for their three-year obligation. After basic training at Fort Dix and infantry AIT, advanced individual training, at Fort Benning, Georgia, they were shipped to the 25th Infantry Division. Weber remembered that day as if it had just occurred. They were on a sweep, having just walked through a filthy, leech infested rice paddy, preparing to enter some dense jungle, when Art stepped on the buried round. Jason and Marty were well back near the middle of the platoon, but they both saw pieces of their friend, along with the other two guys, flying high in the air, bits of flesh and bone raining down upon them, carried on a massive spray of blood and gore. Jay shivered at the thought, not having relived it for several years now, and he was suddenly soaked in sweat.

Harry walked back to Jason, having given the drink to the woman. He noticed that Jason was acting rather strange, his eyes darting back and forth as he hunched down over the counter, nearly spilling his beer and burning his fingers with his cigarette. Harry had seen that look many times on the vets that frequented The Firebase and he perceived he needed to give his godfather a moment to collect himself. When Jason closed his eyes and sighed, Jamison knew he could now approach his father's friend and associate.

"Jay, the lady thanks you for your thoughtfulness and would like if you would come sit beside her. I think she wants to get laid. This could be your lucky night, man."

"Thanks, Harry. I think I'll take a stroll and see what happens. She's pretty hot looking for sure and I haven't had much action since Susan left me three months ago."

Jason had been married to Susan Appleby for nearly seven years, his second marriage, her third, and things were really great until he started having nightmares several times a week, the last straw coming when Jay came out of it, straddling her nearly limp body, trying to choke the life out of the Viet Cong he saw in the bed. After he released her neck, the marks of his thumbs visibly showing on her throat, and she began once again taking normal breaths, he apologized, but to no avail. Sue couldn't handle it anymore and she left, lock stock and barrel, not even giving him a forwarding address. He had met Sue on his mail route and after being her carrier for a couple of months, eating lunch there on occasion, they began going out and lived together for a year and a half before marrying. She was 12 years younger than him and had just come off a bitter divorce. Her first husband had died two years after they wed, shot in the chest, the victim of a burglary at their home. Jay's first wife had also died, from pancreatic cancer at the age of thirty-nine, eleven years ago next week. Sue's second marriage only lasted six months. He was convicted of wife beating and was going to be in prison for a long time.

Lani studied him as he rose from his seat, gathering his money and stuffing it all in his right hand pants pocket, throwing down the last of his beer and crushing out his cigarette. He was very tall, about six feet four inches, with a salt and pepper beard and hair, tied back in a rather long ponytail. He was dressed in Dockers and a black T-shirt emblazoned with the electric strawberry, the insignia of the 25th Infantry Division. His black ball cap bore the words Vietnam Veteran and Proud of It. On his way to her side, he stopped briefly to talk to another man about the same age, and reading his lips, she knew he was telling the man a dirty joke about a priest and a nun. She smiled when she saw his mouth utter the punch line. It was one she had never heard before in her many dealings with veterans. When he laughed and gave his buddy the interlocking thumbs handshake, his nearly black eyes shone with delight, crow's feet etching the sides of his eyes.

Jason was trying to play a little hard to get, not wanting to show this woman that he was over anxious to meet her. He blew too many attempts to get laid over the years by moving too quickly, lessening his chances. Jay had seen her observing him with his peripheral vision, even to the point where he saw her smile when he told the punch line to the joke. He was intrigued that she was able to read lips. If she could read his mind right now, they could cut to the chase and book on out of here to his favorite motel for what he assumed would be really great sex.

When he rounded the corner of the bar and got to the empty seat, she had turned and offered him a smile, so wide and so bright, it momentarily stunned him. There was a fire glowing in those eyes of hers that was burning into his very soul. He was almost frightened by her poise, suggestive, yet inwardly Victorian, as though she had done this many times before tonight. If she were indeed one of Jane's new girls, it would cost him a fortune.

He returned her smile saying, "Hi. I'm Jason Weber," offering his hand. His voice was gruff, from too many cigarettes and lagers, yet it was also a gentle voice.

She placed hers in his palm, turning it upward, offering him the back of her hand, as she replied, "Lani Jorgenson." Jason kissed her hand lightly, noticing it was cool to his touch, but he said nothing and, kept her dainty hand in his grasp as he seated himself beside her, His leg touched hers with some pressure, which was the first signal of what was to hopefully come. If she backed away, he knew this night would be conversation and drinks, which would be okay, too. To his surprise and delight, she pressed closer to him. He could smell the different scents emanating from her—a very exotic perfume, the oral bouquet of mouthwash and wine when she spoke, and something he could not put his finger on. It was not a bad fragrance, albeit a bit musky, and it slightly overpowered the redolence of the other two scents.

"For the lack of a better opening line, Lani, What's a girl like you doing in a place like this?"

"A very good question, but what do you mean a girl like me?" He liked the sound of her voice, soft and syrupy. It had a trace of an accent that had gone by the wayside early in her youth, he surmised. She sipped her wine as he formulated his answer, lighting a cigarette from the fresh pack he had opened. He needed a few precious seconds to make sure he said the right words, still not knowing if she was a high priced hooker.

"Well, you're in a bar on the south side, dressed like you're ready to go to a formal dinner, while many of the patrons are dressed in jeans and tees, except for the three dudes in suits. They, however have an excuse, since they are employed at the bank next door, having come here after work…"

"So I have no excuse for wanting to look my best," she interrupted, teasing him with a quick smile as she took another sip of wine. Her eyes danced and she seemed to be plying him for a quick answer.

"No, I'm not saying that at all. I merely was stating a fact that you seem to be dressed for something else other than The Firebase."

"Actually, Jay, you are right. I was on my way to a party at the Hilton and the directions I was given had me driving right by here. I was intrigued by the name of the bar and its exterior blew me away, so I thought I'd stop here for a drink or two. I noticed you almost immediately and something told me I had to meet you, but since I just don't throw myself on a man, I needed a little time to see if you'd buy me a drink or if I'd leave, wondering what I may have missed out on."

He was beginning to believe that Lani wasn't a hooker and that would be more than great. Free pussy was a boon to people his age. "Well, I sure am glad you decided to stop by. So, I can gather you haven't eaten dinner yet. We could go somewhere else to get something to eat, if you'd like?"

"Thanks for the offer, Jay, but I had a bite earlier and I usually try to eat only once a day, sometimes twice, but that's rare for me." She smiled playfully at the double entendre.

"Would you consider dancing? I know a club on the other side of town where we could have some fun. What do you say to that?"

She smiled again and replied, "I think I'd like that. I don't believe I'll miss anything at the party I was supposed to attend anyway, but we'll have to drive separately, since I need to find a place to stay for the night. I have to leave in the morning to attend a meeting in Harrisburg."

"What do you do for a living, Lani?"

"I work for the government in a classified capacity. If I tell you what I really do, I'm afraid I'd have to kill you."

He laughed heartily, saying, "Would I die happy?"

"I don't know about you, but I'd be ecstatic." She laughed in kind as he wondered what the hell they were talking about.

After finishing their drinks, they left The Firebase: Jay walked Lani to her car. "Follow me and if I don't see you behind me anymore, I'll pull over till you catch up.

"Yeah, Jay. It sure got dark since I arrived. I'll keep my eyes peeled for you and I won't get lost."

Driving north on South Fourth Street, Jay fondled his crotch with one hand, absentmindedly wondering what she would be like in bed. A blue sixty-six Mustang pulled out in front of him from the K-Mart parking lot, and Jay had to slam on the brakes to avoid a collision. Lani had to do the same, thinking back to the night she came into town when she almost got wiped out. She wondered if the kid's heartbeat ever got back to normal after looking into the eyes of the world's only vampire. Lani laughed out loud as she saw Jay stick his arm out from the open window and flip the guy the finger.

"Fuckin' asshole," Jason muttered as he flipped the bird, "Nearly spoil my night with an accident. I don't think so." He looked in his rear view mirror and saw Lani was still behind him, as they turned left. After two more turns, Jay turned right onto South Tenth Street, passing the old Mack Truck facility on his right. He had worked there when he was younger, losing his job after fifteen years of employment. Fortunately he passed the Postal exam and was rewarded with a fairly high paying job, even though he was now earning one hundred and sixty dollars a week less than what he had made at Mack, plus working about five times as hard. People always thought that letter carriers had an easy job, not knowing that they spent two hours in the office, sorting mail and fending off supervisors, before beginning six and a half hours on the street, including a half hour lunch and two ten minute breaks. Jason turned left onto Martin Luther King Boulevard, and passed the old baseball field where he used to sometimes hit golf balls after work, sharpening up a game he no longer played because of his bad knees.

Fifteen minutes later they pulled into the parking lot of Triple Play, a fairly new club, located just on the fringe of a brand new housing development a few minutes from the western edge of the city. Triple Play consisted of three separate clubs housed in the same building, each club featuring a different type of music—popular, oldies and country, each area having a different decorative motif.

"What kind of music do you like to dance to, Lani?"

"It doesn't really matter, Jason, as long as we have a good time. That's all I'm interested in tonight."

He escorted her inside and they first went into the oldies section of the club. As they walked in, a limbo contest was in progress, and Jason asked Lani if she'd like to try it. Lani nodded and got into line, hiked her dress up and slithered under the bar, which was at a height of only thirty inches from the floor. Considering she did it wearing an evening gown was even more impressive and the crowd applauded wildly. Lani curtsied and waved to the crowd as Jason laughed for all he was worth.

They sat at a table for about an hour, drinking, talking and occasionally dancing, especially slow dances, where Jason could hold her close and breathe in her wonderfully exotic perfume. She felt a little cold, but while they danced, he could feel her warm up significantly, as though she were drawing from his body heat, since he was beginning to feel a bit chilled, as well.

Later they went into the country music club and did some line dancing. Jason even displayed a hidden talent by singing karaoke, Friends In Low Places, by Garth Brooks, stirring up the crowd by adding the infamous third verse, acappella.

After he returned to the table, Lani said, "Jason, that was wonderful. You have a really great voice, and I'd love to stay here for hours, but I really need to get to a motel and get some rest before I head to Harrisburg. Is there any place close by where I can get a room this late at night?"

"Yeah, I guess you need to call it a night, and my chances of seeing you again are probably slim, aren't they?"

Unfortunately, you don't know how right you are, since you will be dead before the sun comes up. "So, do you know where I can stay tonight?"

"Actually, there is a place nearby, and I'm sure they will have a room for you."

They walked out to the parking lot, both of them noticing her four flat tires. She cried out, "Oh, shit, Jason! What am I going to do now? One flat I could have handled, but all four, that's ridiculous."

Jason checked them all out and said, "It was vandals, Lani. They're all slashed and I don't know of any place open this late to get new tires put on your car."

"Well, I guess I gotta try to get someone over here as early as possible tomorrow so I don't miss my meeting. Will you drive me to the motel, Jay? At least I can get some sleep tonight."

"Sure, Lani. I can do that."

She threw some things into the back seat of his car and they were on their way.

The Hideaway Motel had long been known as a haven for one-night stands. Many times the trysts would only last one or two hours as a businessman and his secretary would have a short, steamy round of sex before returning to the office and their respective spouses, if having any to go home to that is. Since it was not a crime for two consenting adults to share a room, if only for a brief period of time, the owners, a husband and wife team of Puerto Rican descent, looked the other way after checking in a couple who were merely there to fuck their brains out. Although these affairs went against their own beliefs, they were in this game for the money, and besides, this was America, not San Juan.

Jason pulled his 1986 blue Plymouth Reliant up against the concrete stop in front of room 17. His high beams washed light on a door that was desperately in need of a coat or two of paint. A small bed of dead flowers lay beneath the long, narrow window. One of the panes was held in place with duct tape, and he could see that the glass had not been cleaned in some time.

Lani opened the passenger side door to an audible cracking sound, caused by a misaligned door hinge, shattering the still, night air. As she turned to step out, the slit in her gown revealing pasty, white legs, she placed her feet upon the macadam, which was quite badly broken up, the right heel of her shoe catching the edge of one of the small holes. She closed the door, eliciting another groan from the metal touching metal. In the distance Lani could hear the sounds of a heavy volume of traffic moving in a northerly direction on the Pennsylvania turnpike.

She strode to the door, just as Jay was turning the key in the lock. He was aware of her presence beside him, her scent betraying her, glad that they had left the club and come here. What a break he got with her having four flat tires and now she was going to get the best fuck of her life. He smiled at her, and was rewarded with one in return.

They entered the darkened room and Jay immediately flicked the switch, turning on the lights on the nightstands on both sides of the queen size bed. The pale blue walls were starkly bare, save for a print of a well-known painting. Jay could not recall the title, although he had seen the print in a number of places he had visited over the years. A multi-colored bedspread reached down over three sides of he bed, touching the apparently clean, yet well-worn stone gray carpeting. Jay was pleased to see that the room had been vacuumed recently, possibly today.

Lani kissed him and said, "Get ready for bed while I go to the bathroom."

As he sat down on the dark blue, Early American style chair to remove his shoes, Lani retired to the bathroom to freshen up and take a pee. He watched her walk in, marveling at one of the nicest butts he had ever seen. Moments after he had pulled back the spread and crawled between the deep blue sheets, his head dropping onto the large, soft pillow, his neck touching its refreshing coolness, she came out, stark naked, both of them knowing what they wanted, and not wanting to waste time. He stared at her as she walked toward the bed, her nearly perfect; yet pale looking body was seemingly translucent in the diffused light. She climbed in beside him, sliding into his arms.

"Hold me, Jay," she whispered in his ear, "I'm so cold and I need your warm body against me."

He held her, his hardness brushing against her as they kissed. The scent of her mouthwash was covering a smell he had been familiar with at one time, but he had forgotten what it was. It was a sweet, yet slightly unpleasant odor, but he was so horny, he just dismissed it. She reached down and gave his penis a squeeze, kissing him harder, her tongue sliding into his receptive mouth. Lani moaned slightly when Jay fondled her breasts, her nipples stiffening with his touch.

As she rubbed his back, she felt a long scar, running from his right shoulder blade to nearly the tip of his spine. He winced a bit as she kept running her fingers over it, finally throwing off the covers and standing up on the carpet. He went to the bathroom and took a leak, returning to the chair he had sat in before. Jason lit up a smoke and inhaled deeply.

Lani came over to him and sat on his lap, saying, "Did I do something wrong, honey?"

She took his cigarette from him and took a long pull, keeping most of the smoke in her lungs as he responded, "I'm sorry, Lani, but whenever someone touches my scar, I go back nearly thirty years to a little piece of jungle bordering a small ville in 'Nam."

"Do you want to talk about it, Jay?" She stroked his face and kissed his cheek, nuzzling her head into his neck, her fangs fully extended, wanting him now, yet not before they had some fun.

"We were making a sweep of the ville, checking for gooks and war materials and afterward, on the way out we took some sniper fire from the far side of the ville and hustled into the jungle for some protection, getting out of the open.

"Unbeknownst to us, we landed smack in the middle of a squad of VC and it was hand-to-hand combat from that point until we were all killed, or they died. I was on top of one of them, choking the life from him when this other gook, slashed me with a bayonet, giving me that wound just before one of my buddies greased him with a handful of rounds from his M-16."

He lifted Lani's head from his neck, just after her fangs retracted, and continued, "The dude saved my hide that day, even gave me some of his blood later on. He bought it a week later, though." He picked up the dog tags lying on the end table and said, "I always wear these in case I get into an accident. Paramedics will know what kind of blood to give me. I'm sorry for bailing out of bed like that, Lani. I just get antsy when someone touches that scar because it brings everything back, you know."

"Come back to bed and after I'm through with you, I promise you will never feel this way again."

Lani pushed him onto his back, squeezing and rubbing him back to full, erect status and then mounted him, her sexual hunger growing as they made love fiercely, thoughts of David dancing in her head. She almost hated what she was about to do because it had been a long time since she had felt something for a man beside pure lust, followed by the thrill of the kill. As she writhed and moaned, eagerly accepting each of his thrusts, she continued to think about the man who had been hunting her for thirty-five years, not knowing he was in a deep sleep less than five miles from this place. After they climaxed, screaming like teenagers having sex for the first time, Jason laid his head back on the nearly sweat drenched pillow, releasing a great sigh of satisfaction. He smiled at her, incredibly content.

He could feel her hot breath, the underlying odor beginning to register in his brain, as she licked his neck, tasting his salt, Jay's eyes shot wide open when she sank her fangs into his neck, his blood exploding into her throat as she began to suck the life from him. He knew the scent now; it was the scent of death that he had smelled many times in Vietnam.

As he struggled, Lani held his arms down, her strength astounding him. Jason thrashed and turned, his life quickly ebbing, with each and every movement he made acting like a pump, allowing her to drink from him even more quickly. Mercifully, he fell into a catatonic like state as she drank, only wanting to take enough to keep her warm through the night, wondering if she could spend eternity with him; but no, David was still her only love and it might take her a long time to get over him. *What is happening to me? I am being betrayed by human emotions that should not befall an immortal. Is my life truly nearing an end?* She shook off the thought and got back to doing what she had to do. Her eyes began watering.

After looking at him for a long period of time, struggling to regain her composure, she let go of his limp arms and hopped from the bed. Lani withdrew a razor blade from her purse and began to slash his neck repeatedly, severing the jugular, his heart still beating, pumping blood through the incisions, and spraying the area. All evidence of her fangs was eliminated, making her gruesome act appear as a murder. Of the two bags of blood she had in her purse, one matched his and she poured it all over the bed sheets. She surveyed the scene, satisfied that it appeared the work of a killer and not a vampire. Her job was finished, a murder had occurred here.

After cleaning herself off, by virtue of a luxurious hot shower, her skin glowed with warmth from within and without. She then removed all evidence of her visit, left the room, checking to make sure that no one would see her and she began walking back to her car, less than a mile away, hoping to find someone to fix her four flats. She thought that by slashing her tires, after excusing herself to go to the bathroom while at the club, Jason would have to take her to the motel and hopefully stay with her. Since she hated changing tires, Lani flipped open her cell phone and called the car club. As she waited, she realized that she forgot to clean the toilet bowl, a mistake she rarely made, but going back to the motel was out of the question at this point.

KATHLEEN

The incessant buzzing of the alarm clock finally registered in her brain, yet she threw the pillow over her head to shut out the unpleasant noise. The drone continued to filter through the material and foam, finally causing her to feel her way up the nightstand to turn off the first miserable sound of morning. Kathleen Hammond disliked many things, but her alarm clock was number one on the list, since it signified having to put another day in on the J-O-B, even though she loved writing the stories she reported on, from the insignificant to the spectacular. Reporting was a good way to earn a living. Someday, though, when her first novel would be published, life would be even better because then she could become one of the world's premier novelists. "Yeah, right!" She muttered aloud as she finally found the annoying source of the noise in her ear, turning it off as the clock fell to the floor.

Her back tightened up again, so she kicked her sheet and blanket to the floor and started working the muscles by grabbing her right knee with both hands and pulling back toward her chin. Bones cracked as she released her grip, allowing her leg straighten and fall back to the mattress. Twice with each knee and twice holding both knees had her feeling much better in less than two minutes. Kathleen rotated her neck a few times. It was terrible to feel this bad in the morning, but the ski accident in '91 when she was 21 really did her in and she'd been having problems ever since. Of course, she was lucky to be alive. You don't often get that opportunity when you fall ass over tin can halfway down a mountain slope. Luckily she landed in a pile of soft snow, which cushioned her fall and probably saved her from a broken back. Unfortunately, her knee popped, but it had been going out occasionally since her fall down the mountain, and she knew how to stretch it out and pop it back into place.

Although she knew she would be late for work, Kathleen still took time for her morning regimen. She hopped from the bed and stepped on to the treadmill. After turning on the police scanner, she turned on the machine and reached into the cradle for the remote control, flipping on channel 2, hitting the mute button. While watching the weather scroll across the bottom of the community bulletin board, she cranked up the speed to four miles per hour, a good jog, and decided what she would wear today.

Ten minutes into her thirty-minute workout, her knee popped out again and she tumbled from the side of the machine. She grabbed the handlebar and nearly wrenched her back in the process. Kathleen headed to the bathroom for a shower, pulling off her tee shirt in the process, depositing it on the bathroom floor. She muttered, "Christ, getting older really sucks." She had celebrated her 29th birthday five months ago, but on days like this, she felt fifty.

A good hot shower increased the blood flow to her aching muscles and she began to feel much better. She toweled herself dry and looked at her reflection in the full-length mirror. "Not bad, Kate, not bad," she said to herself. Kathleen had been having a weight problem since her accident, but she finally tired of carrying that excess twenty-five pounds and eleven months ago had gone on a Weight Watchers program, losing all that plus six more. Her waist size was now 25 and her body really looked great. All her muscle tone had returned with her constant exercising but she was still displeased that she lost some of her bust size. She had gone from a 37D to a 34C and she wished she were just a little bigger. Kate liked to wear low cut clothing and when she wore a sports bra her breasts flattened out to the point where she looked like she had nothing, and she thought:

"Let's face it girl, guys like to see some tits when they're shopping around." Kathleen had split up with her beau of four years, *it should have only lasted four months,* and since moving to Allentown she had only been on two dates.

After dressing in a pair of khaki Dockers and a white button down shirt, she slipped into a pair of Reeboks. Throwing a jeans jacket over her arm, she grabbed her purse, briefcase and camera, bounded down the two flights of stairs, and stepped outside into the morning sun. The warmth felt good and she thought perhaps the jacket would not be needed, but the weatherman was predicting cooler afternoon temperatures and some wind. She threw it in the trunk of her completely restored 1967 Camaro, a car she had always wanted to have. Her dad had one, but he had sold it after he got married. Hers was red with black vinyl interior, bucket seats and the tires were wrapped around chrome wheels. The engine was a 327 cubic inch, 350 horsepower, powered by a four speed standard transmission, same as her dad had. She laughed about how he used to say, "Great car, the Camaro. Four on the floor and a six-pack in the trunk. Women love it, Katie."

Five minutes later, she stopped at the mini-mart on Tilghman Street for a cup of coffee and a cheese Danish. "Fuck the calories, I earned them, today," she muttered softly to herself. A store patron put his hand on her shoulder and asked, "Excuse me, Miss, did you say something to me?"

"No, I'm sorry, I was just talking to myself and I guess I was a bit loud."

He smiled and said, "That's okay, I guess we all do that at some time or another. Have a good day."

She laughed and replied, "You too." *Cute buns for an older guy,* she thought as he hopped into his dark green Plymouth Voyager and fired it up. As he turned toward the rear window, while proceeding to back out of the parking space, she noticed his thick, graying hair rested comfortably on top of the collar of his dark blue shirt. He also had a neatly trimmed salt and pepper goatee Dressed in slate gray slacks and a gray herringbone jacket, he looked like a college professor. As he was driving away, she noticed a POW-MIA sticker on his rear window, plus one of the unit he served with, probably in Vietnam. It looked like two yellow axes on a green field. She made a mental note to find out what unit he served in, and maybe by checking out the local Vietnam vets groups… "Stop fantasizing, Kate. There's someone out there you'll hook up with." She realized she was talking out loud again and shook her head in resignation of one of her worst habits.

After pouring a cup of coffee, French vanilla creamer and two packets of Sweet and Low, added to satisfy her sweet tooth, she picked up a Danish and strolled to the counter.

"Mornin' Kate. How are you today?"

"I'm great, Jack. Wassup?"

"Not much, girl. Just biding my time here until the band starts getting more gigs. It's a bitch having to work a job you hate just to make ends meet until you can do what you really want to do. How's the book coming?"

"The plot is coming along fine, as are the settings, but the characters are giving me crap, man. They just don't want to talk to me and my dialogue is really sucky, but in time it'll come around. I hope to finish it before the end of the year and then the search for an agent will begin in earnest. Do you guys have anything coming up in the future?"

"One gig, next Friday at The Firebase."

"That bar on the south side where all the vets hang out?"

"Yeah, that's the place. We gotta work in some more tunes from the sixties for the old farts. That's the shit they eat up and then the place gets packed. More bucks for me and the dudes that way."

"I'll pencil that in on my calendar. Try to get down there and see you guys. Maybe I'll help you out and do a piece for the paper."

"That'd be cool. Dudes'd like to see their names in print. Want to get some Super Six tix before you split. Pot's up to 40 million?"

"Yeah, Jack. Give me five, cash option. When I hit I'll give you a mil. How'd that be?"

"Great! I'll count on you winning, then." He flashed her a smile and threw the piece sign at her back as she walked out to the car, sipping her coffee.

Kathleen ripped open the Danish and ravenously bit into the flavorful pastry. She was hungrier than she thought and gobbled it down in four huge bites, barely chewing them, following each bite with a long pull of now warm coffee. After she finished, she threw the trash on the back floor, meaning to clean out the growing pile in the next day or two. Neatness was not one of her strong suits.

She checked herself in the rearview mirror, brushing wisps of her auburn hair back over her ears, and adding a bit more lipstick. She wiped her tired hazel eyes with a tissue and was just ready to pull out onto Tilghman Street and head to the office when she saw two police cars heading west, followed by a car with two detectives. The newswoman decided that there may be a story waiting at the end of that cop convoy and she pulled out behind them.

~~*

They turned a few blocks up and pulled into the Hideaway Motel.

She took her Morning Call identification badge from her purse and clipped it on to her shirt pocket, grabbed her camera and micro cassette recorder and ambled over to the motel office after seeing the entourage step inside.

Allen Perkins had seen her car pull up and he waited by the door for her to step inside.

"Mornin' Kathleen. How did you know to be here this morning? Psychic powers? We didn't even put this out over the radio."

"Stroke of luck, Allen. I just happened to be pulling out from the gas station when I saw you guys drive by and I figured there just might be a story waiting for me. What have you got?"

"Not sure yet. Owner called," he motioned to the Hispanic gentleman and lady behind the counter, " and said his wife found a dead guy in room 17 and told us to get out here quickly. He didn't elaborate, but he said there was something really strange about the body."

"Are you ready to go in?"

"Yeah. You coming?"

"Absolutely, Allen. And yes, I know the rules. I can only give the people what you let me have. You've given me a lot of good stuff, and you know I won't screw you, but I am going to take some pictures to download in my computer for later."

"I have no problem with that, Kate. I know you'll be straight with us. Shall we go?"

Kate nodded and followed the cops to the room. She noticed a car in the lot, possibly the dead guy's, but a brief glance offered nothing of value there. She'd take a longer look later.

They entered the room: the sweet, sickly smell of blood permeated the air. The body was lying on the bed. Its bone white color looked stark against the blue sheets and Allen had never seen a body in that condition. Blood was splattered about and a large pool of it had grown from the man's throat deep into the sheets and mattress. As he took a close look at the body, his partner, Norman N. Nothstein, TripleN, as he was known at the station, along with the two uniformed cops, was checking out the rest of the place, dusting for prints and taking pictures of the scene and the body.

When Kate finished taking pictures of the room, she walked over to Allen, who was still inspecting the cuts on the neck of the body. Triple N had joined the two of them and said, "Allen, the guy's name is Jason Weber, fifty, lives at 2137 South Hall Street in town. Some of his other cards show that he was a member of Vietnam Veterans of America, the VFW, American Legion, and National Association of Letter Carriers. No indication whether or not he has a wife. No pictures in his wallet. The guy was flush though; had about four hundred in his wallet, plus a signed check for two thousand made out by a Vincent Harkins, address 375 Mockingbird Lane, Sarasota, Florida. It's dated eight days ago. That's about it."

"Okay, Norm, see what you can dig up about his spouse, if there is one and give Harkins a call. Use the cell phone. I want to know about that guy in a hurry. It's pretty unusual for someone to be carrying around a check that large for several days. I guess the perp who whacked him wasn't interested in money but must have been pissed off to cut him up like he or she did."

"I'll get right on it, Allen. Oh, by the way, the uniforms found something strange in the john. Come on in and see what you make of this."

Kathleen and Allen shuffled into the bathroom and they were summoned to the toilet. The toilet had been flushed, but spots of what appeared to be blood stained the sides of the bowl, almost as if blood had been dumped inside and quickly flushed away."

Kate had a thought about something similar happening a long time ago and she made a verbal note on the recorder to check her files later.

Allen had gone back to the body and was really looking hard at the cuts on his neck and the pattern of bloodstains.

"What do you think happened here, Allen?" Kathleen had actually startled him because he was so into his investigation.

"I don't know, Kate, but something doesn't seem right here. It just seems that there should be more blood. I know that there are stains in the toilet, meaning the murderer could have spilled some away, but why? Plus, a severed jugular would have sprayed a much wider pattern then we have here, unless he was sliced later, maybe after he died, but that doesn't make much sense, either. I guess we need to get these cuts checked out at an autopsy to see what kind of a story they tell us."

"Shit!" She uttered.

"What?"

"I forgot to call in that I'm on a story. I better phone in real quick like before they send a team out to look for me."

She flipped open her cell phone and told her boss where she was while Allen, still puzzled, continued to look at the cuts on Weber's neck. "Marv, I'm not going to be in until later. I happened upon a murder investigation and I'm gonna stick with it until I have enough to write the prelim for tomorrow's edition. I'll get back to you when I have more to give you."

Kate listened for a short time, writing down a phone number on a piece of paper and then put her phone back into her purse.

"Allen, is it okay for me to talk to the owners yet?"

"Yeah, go ahead. Just remember the rules, Katie."

She strolled over to the office where she found Mr. And Mrs. Hector Rodriguez sitting on a sofa behind the counter. "Excuse me folks, can I ask you a few questions?"

Mr. Rodriguez stood up and walked to the counter, staring at the reporter, thinking how nice it would be to be young again and have someone like her by his side.

"When did Mr. Weber check in and was he alone?"

"He came into the office and asked for a room for him and his wife."

"Did you see his wife?"

"Si. I did. After the man pulled his car up in front of the room, she was getting out of the passenger side and I got a look at her before she went inside. I don't think it was his wife because she was very young, probably even much younger than you are, ma'am. She was very well dressed, as though she could have been a hooker, but what do I know."

He shrugged his shoulders and closed his eyes as though trying to remember something. "I remember that she almost broke a heel off her shoe when she stepped from the car. I heard her say, 'Shit!' She looked up at me and smiled. Her teeth looked really strange, almost as if were growing and I turned my head away at the sight." He had been pointing to the upper canines, the two sharp teeth used to bite into food.

"Did you tell the police any of what you just told me about her and her teeth?"

He shook his head and replied, "No, because they didn't ask me."

"That's okay. I'll tell them what you said, later." She knew she was going to break a rule by holding information back from Allen, but she needed to do some research before giving her friend this tidbit.

"Did the police ask you to come to the station to have a sketch artist draw the woman for you?"

"No, they haven't. Not yet anyway, but the one detective is coming this way now."

Allen walked in and also asked Mr. Rodriguez about whom Weber was with and what she looked like. He was ready to tell the detective about the teeth, because he was ready to point to his mouth, but Kate interrupted him asking, "How was she dressed, Mr. Rodriguez?"

"She was wearing a black evening gown and looked like she was dressed for a formal dinner or a nightclub." As he continued to talk about how nice she looked and how she almost broke a heel, Allen walked to the window of the office and looked toward the motel room. He was still puzzled about what happened to all the blood and if the slash wounds were covering something else. *What though?*

"Mr. Rodriguez, I'd like you and your wife to come to the station to see what our sketch artist can come up with."

"Do you need us to come there now?"

"Yes, I'm afraid so."

"Okay, sir. I will call my son and he can run the office while we are gone. We can probably be there in about a half hour or so."

"Fine. I'll have the patrol officers stay here until your son comes and you and your wife can go down with them and a patrol will bring you both back."

Hector Rodriguez turned to tell his wife what they had to do. She didn't speak any English and so he had to translate Allen's words. As they were talking, Allen took an incoming call on his cell phone, then turned to Kathleen, and said, "Want to follow the meat wagon to the coroner's office to find out what the autopsy shows. He said he had nothing going right now and they could do Weber's corpse as soon as it was brought to the office?"

"Yeah, I sure would, Allen. Something is bugging me about this murder and later I want to search my computer files. I think something like this happened before and I downloaded the information."

The detectives followed the ambulance to the coroner's office, followed by Kathleen who was deep in thought about what could have happened in the motel. All she knew was that something wasn't right.

Harold Smoyer, the coroner, cut away some of the tissue around the neck wound and placed it in a plastic bag, handing it to an assistant to get it analyzed for any foreign matter and then he continued slicing narrow pieces of flesh and muscle until he was down to the vascular system. "I see something here that is very interesting. I'm cutting the remainder of this area out to put under the microscope."

After placing the section of the artery he removed on a glass slide, he went to the microscope and placed the slide under the objective lens. The coroner looked through the ocular lens and found something that startled him. He stared at it for a few seconds, just to be sure.

"Before he was sliced, he was bitten by something, perhaps a small animal or a bat, gauging by the width of the holes in his carotid artery."

While Kathleen spoke of their find into her recorder, Allen phoned headquarters to have them ask Mr. Rodriguez if he had ever observed any animals or bats in any of his rooms. After a few minutes Allen's phone rang and he answered. Basically a one sided conversation ensued with Allen hanging up after saying, "Thanks, Gene. Have a good day and give my love to Melissa." He snapped the phone closed and placed it in the inside pocket of his suit coat.

"Rodriguez said he has never seen any kind of animal or bat in any of the rooms. So what else could we have here Harry?"

"I don't know, Allen. I have seen many bites in the past twenty years, but this one is so clean and perfect, almost as though the teeth sank into the artery and were pulled straight back out. That is not the sign of an animal, but it didn't hit me right away. Perhaps he was injected with something, which should show up in the tissue."

Fifteen minutes later, a fax came through the machine and Harold walked over to see what it was.

After reading for a minute or so, he said, more to himself than anyone else, "Unbelievable."

Allen and Kathleen looked at one another and then at Harold, who said, "Traces of thymol, eucalyptol, methyl salicylate, menthol, alcohol, benzoic acid, citric acid, and sorbitol solution were found in the skin. Those are all the ingredients found in a household product. Whatever bit our friend here," pointing to the corpse of Jason Weber, "had recently used mouthwash."

The three individuals looked at the body and then back at each other, wondering what this startling revelation could mean.

⁂

Forty minutes later, she parked her car in the lot across the street from the Morning Call, grabbed her stuff and was ready to race across the street when a 1976 green and yellow Ford Pinto nearly struck her. Kathleen had looked to her right, it being a one-way street and, seeing no traffic, stepped off the curb. The car must have just turned the corner and she never saw it. A greasy looking white guy had looked away from his line of travel and was staring at a daytime hooker, dressed in a red mini skirt and halter-top. He obviously didn't see Kathleen standing on the street. Fortunately she saw him in time and just avoided his left front bumper as he sped past her, never seeing Kate flipping him the finger yelling, "Fucking asshole!" As she watched the car moving away, spewing a great cloud of burning oil, the hooker looked at her and said, "Driver's like him should be put away, don't you think? Are you okay?"

"Yeah, I'm alright, but he nearly got me. I must say though, any guy spotting you would definitely look away from where he was going. That is a great outfit." She was a brunette, about five feet eight inches tall, weighed about one thirty or so, and had the greatest brown, almond shaped eyes Kate had ever seen. Her eyelashes and brows were perfectly formed and colored, accentuating her pale pink lips and beautifully tanned skin.

She smiled and replied, "Well, you know how it is, sweetie, we working girls gotta dress like a honey so they show us the money."

"Rita, are you doing okay? Eddie isn't slapping you around again, is he?"

"Naw, Kate. He's been treating me real nice lately, since I've been bringing home a lot of cash from the Johns driving down the street."

"You could do a lot better working at Jane's place. She won't beat you up and you'll always have a place to stay. I worry about you girls on the street. Two ladies got whacked the other night down at 5th and Gordon by a couple of out of towners. Both girls are at Lehigh Valley Hospital, Cedar Crest, with broken ribs. Guys got their cash, too. Ain't safe on the street anymore, Rita."

"I know; that's why I work mainly days. There are plenty of men in this town in need of our services and I do a lot of guys during their lunches and breaks. Lots of construction and destruction going on in this city and those workers are making big bucks in OT. Their wives have no clue that their husbands are having more for lunch then sandwiches and fruit. Plus sometimes I go over to The Firebase and fuck a few of the lonely hearts who are really in need. So, I'm doing okay, baby. Don't worry about me."

"Rita, you know of any new girls in town?"

She gave some thought to the question and replied, "Yeah, I seen some new meat over at The Firebase. I don't think she's a working girl, but I know I saw her yesterday afternoon. Blonde chick, young, early twenties. Dressed to the nines when I saw her, but she didn't seem to be going after anyone. I remember she just sat at the bar drinking wine. Seemed like a real space cadet to me."

"Okay, Rita, you take care of yourself, and if Eddie ever starts in on you again, you give me a call. Do you still have my card?"

She nodded her head and patted her purse, strolling down the street where a car had pulled over after honking his horn to her. "There's Eddie now, Kate. I gotta run."

Kathleen watched her get into the car, throwing her arms around her pimp, before he pulled away, tires squealing.

The newsroom was not very busy, as most reporters were out on assignments. Two columnists were hard at work, typing on their keyboards, summoning up enough intelligible words to put in tomorrow's edition. Kate laid her laptop on top of her desk and unlocked a drawer, placing her purse and camera in the bottom right hand drawer.

She turned on her computer and went to her document file, scrolling down to the one marked Vampire Sightings.

After reading for a few moments, she clicked on to the website for the National Scanner, scrolling down to archives and pulling up a story about a sighting back in '83.

Kokomo, Indiana-September 17, 1983

Today I interviewed a woman, Mrs. Randall Heberle, 32, who lives at 555 Northrop Street, Kokomo, who swears she saw a vampire in her house preparing to attack her husband.

Mrs. Heberle, a known alcoholic, stated that the vampire was young, blonde, and very attractive. When she saw the creature ready to bite her husband's neck, her fangs appearing to grow before her very eyes, she screamed, immediately gaining the attention of the beautiful, undead female, who snarled and jumped away from her husband who had appeared to be in a catatonic state.

Mr. Heberle, 37, a heavy drinker, who had just come home from work as I was conducting my interview said he had seen her several times in the past few weeks, hanging out at the bar across the street from where he worked. He had spoken to her a few times and noticed that she had the strangest breath he had ever smelled—a combination of mouthwash and a musky, underlying odor he could not identify.

He also said that he didn't believe she could be a vampire, if vampires did exist, because she had walked in the daylight, and myth stated that vampires could only move about at night, that they'd disintegrate in the light of the sun.

Kate looked up from her computer screen, not really believing what she just read, but knowing that if it was true, she could be on the verge of the biggest story since the resurrection of Christ.

It was time to begin writing her story for tomorrow's edition.

Vampires and Highlanders

With Allen's help, Kathleen was finally able to procure the sketch of the blonde woman seen at the Hideaway, and now, in her apartment, she scanned it onto her website, adding some background information from what she had dug up over the past several days from her vampire files, files she thought she would never really use, since vampires did not exist.

She had set up the site about six months ago, mostly for the Highlander part, as she was in the process of writing a novel about the Scottish Highlander Clans of the 14th Century. Kate had received a number of hits from people wanting to help her with her research, but she also wanted to have a vampire site just for fun. She had always been fascinated with the concept of undead creatures that sucked blood to stay alive.

As she began to write, she noticed that she had incoming mail and jumped back on to hotmail to read it, blinking her eyes several times to make certain that she read the message correctly.

From: Mark Hughes<Mark576@juno.com >
To: Kathleen Hammond<Highlander4@hotmail.com>
Subject: The Blonde Woman
Miss Hammond,

A few nights ago, as me and my mom and dad were coming home from visiting my Grammy in Harrisburg, we were driving next to a minivan that was a little out of control. A car cut off the minivan and I saw it slide on some black ice. When our car was next to the minivan, I saw that the inside light was on and a young woman, who looked a lot like the one the sketch showed was driving, but she was scary looking when I first saw her. She looked like she was snarling and when she turned her head toward us; I saw fangs in her mouth! I swear, Miss Hammond, that I think this woman is a vampire! I tapped my mom on the shoulder to show her, but when my mom looked at the lady vampire, her face was normal again and her long teeth had disappeared. When my mom turned her head to face the front again, the woman opened her mouth and I saw the fangs grow again! Her eyes turned red and she licked her lips and smiled at me! I was really scared, Miss

Hammond, and I didn't know whom to tell, but I decided I had to tell you. Even though I am only twelve, going on thirteen, I don't tell lies, ma'am. Please send me an e-mail as soon as possible. Could there be a vampire in Allentown, Miss Hammond?

Mark

Kathleen honestly did not know how to respond to Mark, even though she also believed that the woman in the sketch was a vampire. She had to remain cool and treat Mark's e-mail in a professional manner, but she needed time to think, and suddenly her throat was dry. She got up from her chair and walked into the kitchen, grabbed a cold can of Old Milwaukee, popped the top and took a deep drink. The beer hit her empty stomach like a right hand from Larry Holmes, and the infusion of alcohol made her head spin a little. "Kate, you have to remember not to drink until you have eaten something. You just can't handle it." Her voice seemed twice as loud as usual, and it sounded quite tinny to her ear. As she held the can, she noticed her hand was trembling some, so she set the beer down on the counter and opened the cabinet next to the sink, hoping to find something to eat. She found a half full bag of Gibbles potato chips and downed a handful of the greasy goodies, chewing them briefly before swallowing, just to get something into that empty pit, before finishing her beer.

After consuming the can of beer and the remainder of the chips, she opened another can and went to the bathroom to pee. She sat for a while, tipping cold golden liquid into her throat and feeling warm yellow liquid flow from her body into the toilet bowl. She had to smile, thinking of that old adage: in one end, out the other. She flushed and washed her hands, seeing the reflection of a totally overworked woman in the mirror.

Hoping to lift her spirits some, she turned on the radio, which was usually tuned in to an oldies station. She loved that kind of music, finding the songs relaxed her. The DJ was just finishing up a blurb for a local auto dealer and as she sat back down in front of her computer, the opening strains of Soldier Boy, by The Shirelles, began to flood the room. It was one of Kate's favorite oldies, and hearing it, after the murder of a veteran, *by a vampire draining him of all his blood,* made it even more poignant.

Kathleen opened her inbox to find two more e-mails had just appeared in the past few minutes, the subject being The Blonde Woman. She could hardly believe that this was happening. One e-mail shortly after putting the sketch on the website was pure coincidence, but three in a matter of less than a half hour was unbelievable, but she had to know what the computer mail had to say. She opened the first one.

From: Ron Gerancher<Geronimo@aol.com>

To: Kathleen Hammond<Highlander4@hotmail.com>
Subject: The Blonde Woman
Miss Hammond,

Several nights ago I met the woman in the sketch. Her name is Lani Jorgenson, and I know for a fact that she is a vampire, because I saw her fangs grow when we were on a date at the Carmike. After the movie, we went for coffee, and I told her I couldn't see her again because I didn't think that she was right for me. I think she killed those two phony cops they found, and I'd bet that she killed that poor guy who was found in the motel. I would like to meet with you and tell you everything I know.

Ron

Her hands were more than trembling now, as she opened the next e-mail.

From: Marty Walsh<WalshLTD@aol.com>
To: Kathleen Hammond<Highlander4@hotmail.com>
Subject: The Blonde Woman
Dear Miss Hammond,

I am in Allentown on business and I happened to read the article about Jason Weber, on mcall.com, seeing your byline. I called the newspaper, but you had already left for the day, and then I got very busy with some clients and truly forgot to get back to you until seeing the sketch on your website. I am certain that this woman, her name is Lani Jorgenson, is the woman who was involved with my ex-wife recently. Jordan has been missing for some time now, and shortly after her disappearance, Lani Jorgenson also disappeared. Although I was due to go back to Myrtle Beach by the end of the week, I have decided to stay here to see if I can help you find this woman. I must admit, though, I certainly didn't expect to find her picture on a vampire website. This you must explain to me. Please get back to me at your earliest convenience.

Sincerely,
Marty Walsh

Kate let out a gasp, and raced to the bathroom to vomit the bile that was building up in her stomach. After retching for a few minutes, she opened the medicine cabinet and took a huge gulp of Lavoris, gargling it and swishing it around in her mouth to rid herself of the awful taste that lingered after she threw up. She spit the residue into the sink and gargled one more time, staring at the bottle and thinking back to the autopsy. *Traces of mouthwash in the wound!*

Her mind raced. What should she do? This story could be huge, but she didn't want Lani Jorgenson to know that she was being pursued. She called the newspaper and got the night editor.

"Sam, this is Kathleen. I need a big favor from you and I can't explain why right now."

"What is it, Kate? You know I'll do anything for you if it's within my power."

Yeah right, she thought. *All you've been trying to do since I came to this paper is to see if you could figure out a way to get in my pants.* "Great, Sam! The sketch I had sent in to run with my article. I want it scratched until another day. I'm working on something and I think if the sketch is run, I'll blow an even bigger story. I know the cops would like the picture out there, but I'm going to call in a few favors on this one. Sam, you gotta do this for me, if you never do anything else again. Please, man, I am begging you."

Sam Tolliver knew that the reporter really wanted the picture scrubbed, bad, though he couldn't figure out why, since it might shed some light on this murder, but she seemed petrified that if the picture ran, something bad would happen to her.

"Okay, Kate. You got it, but you're going to owe me big time for this one."

"Yeah, Sam. I know I'll owe you, but if what I am working on is the real deal, we'll all be in for a big payday, and I might even buy you dinner, sometime."

"I'll hold you to that. Can you give me any clue about what you are working on?"

"Not yet, Sam, but I guess I can tell you that this story might be the biggest story of the century. Look, Sam, I really got to run. I need to make a shitload of calls tonight and still try to get in on time tomorrow, which reminds me, I haven't checked my voice mail. Will you patch me through, Sam?"

"Can do, and I look forward to that dinner sometime."

After a few rings, her voice mail came on and she entered her password to retrieve her messages. She had five, but the only one that got to her was the message from a David Forrester. She jotted down his number, planning to call him within the next few minutes.

❦

David had arrived in Allentown two days before the police discovered Jason's body.

Prior to checking in at the Hilton, he took a side trip to his former home, Macungie, in order to check out the memorial that had been built and dedicated over two years ago. After turning onto Lehigh Street, he drove approximately three hundred yards. Looking to his right, seeing the black POW-MIA flag flying directly beneath Old Glory, he knew this is where he would find the site. David pulled into the parking lot of the Macungie Veterans Association Home, VFW Post 9264, shut down the engine and stepped onto the macadam. He walked to the front yard, which was surrounded by a wooden fence, with four inch by six-inch American flags placed every few feet around the top of the fencing. As he stepped up and onto the brick walkway, he looked down at the bricks, inscribed with names of businesses, churches, schools and individuals. He paused briefly at one brick, that of a high school chum he didn't know had passed away and he was suddenly saddened. The man was only forty-nine when he died and David wondered if he had died as a result of the war. He knew that Art's skin tone was very pallid in his teens, and he may have had a bad heart then, but he'd never know for sure unless he checked it out further.

David stepped from the bricks and ambled over to look at the restored one zero five howitzer, which was mounted upon a concrete slab. The big gun, which he assumed had seen action in Vietnam, was painted OD green and was kept in immaculate condition. A white plastic chain link fence protected it, hopefully to keep people from sitting or climbing on the gun. He walked completely around the gun, again stepping onto the bricks leading to the flagpole. David looked down at the base of the pole, which was surrounded by tiny white stones. A five-pointed black granite star formed the base and each point had a 20th century war inscribed upon it. WWI, WWII, KOREA, VIETNAM, PERSIAN GULF.

He then went to the memorials. The Vietnam memorial was in the form of an obelisk. Built from black granite, it stood about five feet tall from base to top. It was shaped like an elongated V lying on its side; the base was inscribed with the words SOME GAVE ALL, on one side and ALL GAVE SOME on the other. Each side of the memorial was inscribed with the names of those who died in the war; one side had the names from Lehigh County and the other side from Northampton County. The top of the obelisk was etched with a scene depicting soldiers stepping from a helicopter into a rice paddy. David immediately experienced a flashback and sat down on one of the two granite benches. He cried for those who were lost in that war and he was so engrossed in his thoughts that he never even heard the man sit down beside him until he felt a hand on his shoulder, startling him.

The man, a veteran, wearing a black satin jacket bearing the logo of Veterans of the Vietnam War, Post Pa-75, asked, "Are you okay?"

David wiped the tears from his eyes and nodded. "Yeah, I'm okay, but seeing that etching on top of the memorial really brought back some memories."

The silver haired veteran patted David on the shoulder and said, "Yeah, it does the same to me every time I see it, and I've been coming here every week for over two years. My dad's name is back there on the Wall of Honor."

"Wall of Honor?"

"Yes. We built that wall as a place for loved ones to inscribe the names of deceased veterans from the two counties, Lehigh and Northampton. You from around here, man?"

David smiled for the first time since coming here and said, "I lived here when I was a kid, then I moved away. Right now I really have no home, since I have been traveling for some time This is really a nice memorial, and I have seen a few over the years."

"You a 'Nam vet?"

David shook his head and replied, "I was a journalist over there for a year."

The man and David stood up and the man gave David a hug. "Anyone who was there is a vet as far as I am concerned, man." He shook hands with David, placed a small wreath between the obelisk and a bronze replica of a helmet resting over a pair of jungle boots, touched a name on the wall and walked away without saying another word.

David watched him walk to his car; head slumped onto his chest. After he drove away, David walked behind the obelisk and looked at all the names on the Wall of Honor. It was a wall about six feet high and also V shaped. The wall consisted of four panels, each one about four feet wide and almost a foot thick. On each end of the wall was etched a prisoner of war in a bamboo cell and an American flag. David turned around and saw the rear of the obelisk. He read the inscription, knelt and placed his hand in the hand print that was blasted into the black granite and recited the Pledge of Allegiance, the tears once again beginning to flow even as he spoke those words that so many people have forgotten over the years. It was a disgraceful when he read stories about students refusing to stand and recite the words that men like these died for. He hoped that his visit here would help to give him strength in his upcoming battle with Lani.

In his relentless pursuit to find and kill Lani Jorgenson, he had learned many things about his opponent. The fact that her trail of victims seemed to be littered with sexual conquests, and when she killed her lover of the day, week, month or whatever, she had to make it look like a murder, removing all evidence of her fangs, and she was very good at it. He had read of a number of cases involving waterlogged bodies pulled from lakes, rivers and the ocean, all with numerous slashes on their necks. He had posed as a police detective, a news reporter and a grieving, long lost member of the decedent's family to obtain information not available to the general public. Lani made very few mistakes, which attributed to her longevity.

He remembered the time he had caught up with her at the cemetery and she had threatened to kill him the next time they met, but that didn't happen. She allowed him to live because of her professed love for him. She taunted him by saying, "How many stories have you read over the years about my kind that have been proven false? How many ludicrous movies and horrible novels have you seen and read that show vampires hunting in packs and roaming the world? Although I am the only one, David, I want to live and in order to do that I must have blood. Whatever you tell people, they will not believe a word you say, so give it up and let me be!"

On the morning after the murder, he had just returned from breakfast, his heart was beating rapidly after reading the story in The Morning Call.

Man Murdered At Local Motel
By Kathleen Hammond
Of the Morning Call

Yesterday tragedy struck as a local letter carrier, Jason Weber, 50, who resided at 2137 South Hall Street, was found dead in Room 17 of the Hideaway Motel on the western edge of the city limits. His nude, bloodless, ghostly white body was in pristine condition, save for several wounds carved into the left side of his neck by a razor blade or an extremely sharp instrument.

Investigation, led by detectives Allen Perkins, and Norman N. Nothstein, revealed that a yet unknown, young woman accompanied the deceased to the room. Owners of the motel, Hector and Julia Rodriguez have been working with the police department sketch artist to come up with a picture of the woman. At this time, she is not a suspect in the murder, but merely a possible witness. The Morning Call anticipates having the sketch available for tomorrow's edition.

The witness was described as Caucasian, 20 to 22-year-old, blonde, approximately 5'7" and she was elegantly dressed in a black evening gown. If you have seen this woman, please call the Allentown Police Department at 610-555-8567 and ask for extension 753. It is imperative that the police find the woman to determine who could have murdered Mr. Weber.

During the course of the autopsy, it was noted upon skin analysis that components found in common mouthwash were present in the examined tissue, possibly offering that Mr. Weber could have been engaging in sexual activities shortly before his demise.

Kathleen Hammond, The Morning Call, 610-555-9594

❧

David heard the phone ring and picked it up before the second ring was completed.

"David Forrester here, may I help you?"

"Hello, Mr. Forrester. This is Kathleen Hammond and I apologize for not getting back to you sooner."

"Yes, I knew you would be rather busy. Merely believing that a vampire exists is difficult in itself, but being directly involved really puts strain on a person, does it not?"

"I'm not sure that I want to believe in the existence of a vampire, but with what has been happening lately, I cannot discount the possibility that a vampire does indeed exist, though it seems impossible. Where do you fit into this strange puzzle, Mr. Forrester?"

David told her the story of him and Lani, to which she replied, "Mr. Forrester, that is the most amazing story I have ever heard in my life, and I truly believe every word you have said."

"Since we may be spending some time together, Kathleen, please call me David."

"Just this evening, David, I received three e-mails about Lani Jorgenson, and maybe it would be best if the five of us could meet somewhere and lay out everything we know to one another. I would also like to have two of my detective friends in on the powwow, if that's okay with you?"

"That would be fine, Kathleen. Contact the other people and I'll get a meeting room set up here at the Hilton for sevenish tomorrow night, if that time is good for you?"

"Plan on it, David. With the information I have received, I'm sure there will be no problem with tomorrow night. If anything changes, I'll let you know, but for now it is a go."

"Great, I look forward to our meeting. I'm sure you have a lot to do between now and then, but I will tell you something, Kate, I have been pursuing this woman for nearly thirty-five years and I truly believe that we will find her and finally put an end to her existence. Till tomorrow, then."

After she hung up, she took a deep breath, sat down at the computer and replied to the three e-mails she had just received. She logged off and dialed Allen's home phone to tell him what had just transpired, hoping that he and TripleN would be able to join them tomorrow night and to tell him that she squashed the sketch for tomorrow's edition.

Allen said, "You are really serious about this, aren't you, Kate?"

"Yes, I am Allen. There is so much evidence to support the fact that the woman in the sketch is a vampire of undetermined age."

"Well, I have a tape…"

"What tape, Allen?"

"A tape of a phone call that you would certainly be interested in hearing, although no one at the department believed what the man was saying. Triple N and I will be there, Kate, but only because it's you. If anyone else would be laying this shit on me, I'd laugh him or her off. You know that for a fact." He briefly explained to her what the tape contained.

"I know, Allen, but I think you will become a believer before you leave that room tomorrow night, especially in light of the tape."

"Okay, Kate, we'll see you tomorrow, then. Take care. I have to run. Another call is coming in for me."

He hung up without giving her a chance to say goodbye.

※※

The next morning, Kate stopped at the Mobil station to grab a quick, calorie-laden breakfast consisting of a sausage, egg and cheese sandwich, hash browns and a cup of hazelnut coffee. Jack was behind the counter and he was really busy. Seven customers were in line ahead of her, and Kate's patience was wearing thin this morning. She wanted to get to work and see what she could dig up on anyone named Lani Jorgenson.

Her mind was working overtime and she barely heard Jack say, "Mornin' Kate."

She shook herself out of the funk she was in and said, "Sorry, Jack. I was a million miles away this morning. Got a lot on my mind, I guess."

As he rang up her order, Jack said, "Hey, I checked out your website last night and saw the picture of the chick you think might be a vampire. She's a babe, for sure!"

"What do you mean, Jack? Have you seen her around in the past few days?"

"Yeah, I have. She stopped here the other morning and bought a cup of coffee and a pack of Salems. You know how I like to flirt with the girls that come in here, so I gave it my best shot, killer smile and all, but she seemed to be preoccupied about something and really didn't pay too much attention to me.

"I remember when she paid me, her fingers touched my hand, and it was freaky, girl. She was so cold, like she'd been living in a freezer. Pulled her hand away real quick, too. It was really weird, man!"

As customers began to pile up behind her, Kate moved off to the side, allowing them to take care of their business, needing to hear more about this woman.

A few minutes later Jack was able to talk again. "Like I was saying, Kathleen, she pulled her hand away and nearly ran out the store. One thing I noticed about her that didn't seem to fit though was that for as good looking a woman she was, when she spoke, asking for a pack of Salems, I caught a whiff of some of the nastiest breath I ever smelled, even though it was covered up with breath mints. Smelled like she had eaten some bad meat."

"Did you happen to see what she was driving, Jack?"

Jack nodded his head as he made change for a fifty from a customer who had just filled his gas tank. "She was driving a Ford Windstar. It was dark blue, but I'm not real sure of what year. Could have been a ninety-eight or ninety-nine. It's hard to tell these newer cars and vans apart. They all look the same."

"Are you free tonight, Jack?"

"Not sure. Me and the dudes were going to get some practice in for the gig at the Firebase tomorrow night. Why? What's up?"

"Several people are getting together at the Hilton to share information about the chick you saw in here and on my website. If she is a vampire, we have to destroy her before she kills more people, especially on our turf."

"I'll try like hell to get there, Kate. You said the Hilton?"

"Yeah, around seven. I sure hope you can make it. Your input would mean a lot and maybe you can recall the license plate if you think about it today. I know how good you are with remembering numbers. Try to picture what state the plate was issued in, too." She glanced at her watch and said, "Man, I gotta split, or my boss will rip my heart out for being late again. Hope to see you later, Jack."

When she hopped into her car and ripped the sandwich from its aluminum foil bag, it was nearly cold, but that didn't matter; she needed food. She chewed a few bites as she pulled out onto Tilghman Street and headed east. The sandwich and hash browns finished, she tossed the wrappers into the rear passenger compartment and downed her luke-warm coffee in several gulps, feeling heartburn gnawing in her chest. A couple of Rolaids helped to settle her down by the time she arrived at the Morning Call office.

The guard gave her a smile and opened the door for her with a "Mornin' Miss Hammond", to which Kathleen smiled back and replied "Mornin' Dennis."

She entered the building and hopped on the elevator to the second floor and quickly walked to her desk, flipping on her computer before she was barely seated. Out of the corner of her eye, she saw her boss looking at his watch, but he let it pass and went back into his office and sat down at his desk.

Between phone calls and typing up a few paragraphs of follow up information about the Weber murder, she logged onto every site she could think of that might give her a lead on Lani Jorgenson, finally finding a record of a Lani Jorgenson, 21, of Bangor, Maine, having disappeared while on a visit to New York on October 20, 1840. The report stated that she was the daughter of a minister and his wife who had traveled to the city as a birthday present for their daughter. They allowed her to go for a walk with a well-dressed, wonderfully delightful young man, who said he had just arrived in the city a few days ago and knew no one. The minister said, "He seemed like such a nice young man, we felt that Lani would be safe with him, and now she is gone." A search was immediately started, but after several days, yielded no results and the case was filed as unsolved.

Kathleen hit the print button, absolutely glad that Harold Longenbach created a website for 19th century disappearances. She signed his guest book, thanking him for the information he possessed, and that she would fill him in later as to what it could mean.

At six fifty five, she walked into lobby of the Hilton, strode to the information desk and asked, "Mr. David Forrester has reserved a meeting room for seven o'clock. Could you direct me, please?"

The clerk looked at the reservation book and saw that he had reserved The Beck Room for the evening.

Kathleen offered her thanks and found her way to the room, opened the door and went inside.

Seated at the table were three teenagers, plus Allen, Triple N, and a nattily dressed older gentleman who had to be David Forrester. She smiled and nodded at the group and took a seat.

It was a strange alliance, she thought. Led by a sixty-four year old man and her, a twenty-nine year old reporter, the rest of the group sat there, stone faced, the only common denominator being the belief *or was it disbelief* that Lani Jorgenson was a vampire and they would all participate in her destruction.

David spoke first, saying, "Perhaps we better introduce ourselves to one another and let the group know what has brought us together tonight. My name is David Forrester and I am here because I have been hunting this woman," he pointed to the sketches lying on the table by each person, along with a pen and a note pad, "for almost thirty-five years. I know what she is and the destruction she is capable of. We must rid the world of her before she finds out we know she is in the city and leaves. I have come close several times now, the latest being less than two weeks ago, in Williamsburg, Virginia. I will answer any questions you may have, later, but I am quite interested in how all of you are involved with this mission. Kathleen, would you please address the group next, and then we'll go around the table, I guess."

Just then, a man entered the room and said, "Forgive me for being late. I got hung up on the way. I'm Marty Walsh." Everyone introduced themselves to Marty with handshakes and a few words before he seated himself.

Kate stood up and said, "I am Kathleen Hammond, a Morning Call reporter, and I first became aware of Lani Jorgenson a few days ago when I followed the two detectives, seated on the other side of the table, to a crime scene. Jason Weber, a local letter carrier, was found in room 17 of the Hideaway Motel on the western fringe of the city. His bloodless corpse was found to have had its neck slashed, and blood had seeped into the sheets and some was splattered onto the wall, but I'm sure the detectives can add more to this. The owners of the motel said he had entered the room with a blonde woman, the woman on the sketch in front of you, who had disappeared without a trace. I asked my boss, and the detectives, not to run the picture, for fear she would leave Allentown and go somewhere where we would be unable to find her. Last night I found a remarkable piece of information on a website titled Unsolved Disappearances Of The Nineteenth Century, and I printed out the page I found."

She passed the copies around and waited for everyone to read them before continuing.

"With what David has told me, and what you will all hear from Mark, Ron and Marty, plus the two detectives, I think we will all see that Lani Jorgenson is indeed the woman we are searching for, and that she has been a vampire for almost one hundred and sixty years!" Mark, would you please tell everyone here what you saw.

Mark recounted to the group the information he had e-mailed to the reporter, after introducing his brother, Matthew. "Matt believed my story right away, even though mom and dad think that I am making everything up, so he drove me here tonight. We told them we were going to a basketball game at Muhlenberg College."

As Mark spoke, Kate studied the twelve-year-old boy who had probably received the fright of his life, seeing Lani bare her fangs and lick her lips. He was a tad chubby and his face was peppered with acne. Mark had bright, blue eyes and brown hair, which hung out from the bottom of his red Philadelphia Phillies baseball cap. He spoke with the clarity of a much older person, having Kathleen believe that he was probably well read, and a very good student in school. Plus she was really impressed when he wrote that he did not tell lies, quite commendable for a young person. He was wearing a blue t-shirt bearing a Nike logo, blue jeans and sneakers, the basic daily wear of most teens and pre-teens. Mark's brother, Matt, hung on to every word Mark said, and he nodded his head often. Matt, Mark had said, was seventeen, and a senior at Dieruff High School. He had brown hair, green eyes, and pouting lips. His oval face was a bit puffy, probably from being a little on the heavy side in the past few years, and he seemed to not want to say anything, to steal his brother's thunder, although the way his eyes darted around, he needed to know everything that was going to be said.

It was Ron Gerancher's turn and when he told the assemblage that he had gone on a date with Lani, seeing her teeth extend at a movie, they were blown away. Ron said, "I tell you guys, I was scared shitless when I saw those fangs, glad that she hadn't seen me see them, or I would have been toast. It was hard to be cool, but I figured if I pretended that she was just another woman, and not a vampire, I'd at least live through the night."

Ron, Kate thought, was a very handsome young man, and could see why Lani wanted to go out with him, wishing she were a decade younger for a moment, until the sound of the door opening brought her back from her unfolding fantasy.

In stepped five longhaired, young men, wearing the traditional dress of the younger set, jeans, t-shirts and sneakers. One of them spotted Kathleen and yelled, "Yo, Kate! Me'n the dudes are ready to find this Lani chick and kick her ass." He slapped high fives with two of his buddies, as they all laughed.

David startled everyone by standing up and shouting, "Do you people think this is a game? It's not, I assure you. Lani has been killing humans for nearly one hundred and sixty years, and this, by God, is no laughing matter." He pounded the table with his fist, emphasizing his point.

Jack and his four band mates immediately stopped their laughter and he said, "I'm sorry, man. It seemed to me that all you guys were in such a serious mood, I'd try to lighten things up a bit, but it didn't work. We really do want to help because Kate is a great lady and I know she doesn't bullshit anyone. We believe her about this Lani being a vampire, and whatever it takes, we're here for you guys."

David, though still annoyed, said, "Okay, guys. I guess I get a little uptight because we are so close here and I want to live out the rest of my life without having to chase Lani all over creation. She has to be destroyed soon, or all of us are in mortal danger."

Kathleen said, "David, you know more about Lani than anyone here, but how do we kill someone who is already dead?"

Ron spoke up, saying, "Mr. Forrester, I don't mean to interrupt you, but when Lani and I were having coffee, I told her I was considering writing a vampire novel and during the course of our discussion, that issue came up. I remember telling her that I thought a vampire could not be killed by driving a stake through its heart, since a vampire's heart does not beat and she agreed. She told me that she figured the only ways to kill a vampire would be by fire, drowning or beheading, and that makes sense to me. How about the rest of you guys?"

Everyone nodded their heads in agreement but TripleN said, "How do we get her to a place where we can kill her with one of those methods?"

David answered, "That is a good question; however, it is one that really can't be answered, since I don't think Lani will allow us to lead her into a trap where she can be killed. Let's face it, people; she has existed in this fashion for almost one hundred and sixty years. I'm sure that she has taken on smarter people then us."

"What about The Firebase? She hung out there at least once since coming to town. Maybe, with Jack's band playing tomorrow night, she'll come in looking for another victim." Mark offered.

Kathleen responded, "You know you could have something there. It would be at least worth checking out. We know she drives a Ford Windstar with South Carolina plates, and we should be able to check out all the vans in the lot to see if we get our girl."

Marty, after sitting quietly all this time, finally spoke. "I never met the woman, but as I told Kathleen, I believe she killed my ex-wife earlier this year in Myrtle Beach, and I want a piece of her."

David asked, "What do you know about her, Marty?"

"Not much, really, because Jordan and I didn't communicate too often after we were divorced, but the day she disappeared, she called me babbling about her friend being a vampire, but I could tell she had been drinking, and I didn't really give much credence to what she was saying. Her folks told me she had been hanging out with a blonde woman, going to her house and painting her portrait, and I knew the two of them were getting it on. Jordan found out about Lani and unfortunately I guess she was killed possessing that kind of knowledge. That was the last time she was heard from." He also told them about the videotape, the one thing that Lani did not destroy, which he then proceeded to show it to the group, backing it up at points, and pausing on Lani's face. Hers was a face that looked like so many other woman of that age, yet hers could change into pure evil, whenever she wanted to feed.

Allen had been taking in all of the information in and decided he wanted to have the group hear the 911 call that had come through night before last. "Guys, what you are about to hear has to stay in this room because I'm putting my ass on the line letting non-police personnel hear it, but I think it will shed more light on what we are dealing with." He pressed the play button.

"Nine One One. State your emergency, please."

(A fright-filled voice) "Yes, my name is Lawrence Kehl and I think I am seeing a murder in progress. I'm on Liberty Street, just outside an alley between Sixth and Seventh Streets and I see a woman. She's lying on top of a man. His legs are kicking, but she has his hands held down to the street and I swear she is biting his neck." (Mild laughter can be heard in the background of the dispatch office}

"Please send a patrol car immediately. I can hear him screaming and he is struggling to try to fight her off. (A man screaming could be heard on Lawrence's cell phone)

"Sir, are you in any danger. Can she hear you? Can you describe her at all?"

"No, I don't think I'm in danger, but it is hard to describe her from here. I'm going to get a little closer."

Allen pressed the pause button and said, "Do you hear how confident his voice is getting. He is in contact with the police and they are on the way, because you can hear the sirens getting closer as the tape continues." He pressed the button again and the voice sprang back to life.

The sounds of his footsteps could be heard as he approached the mouth of the alley, along with the sound of sirens in the far distance. "I can make out that she is blonde, well built, wearing blue jeans and a black coat. He is wearing a business suit, but I can't make out his face." (Suddenly Lawrence coughs loudly and his voice goes up an octave) "Oh, my God! She heard me cough and now she's looking my way. Her mouth and chin are red. It's blood. She was drinking his blood. I can see his neck is a red mess and just before she heard me, I saw her slash his throat with a knife or a razor."

Allen once again paused the player. "At this point, you will definitely hear that he is running as his voice is coming in gasps and his footfalls are louder and spaced farther apart.

"Oh, Lord! She's a vampire and she is chasing me. I can hear her running. Help me, please!"

The group heard him fall to the pavement, yet he still managed to hang on to his phone, asking for help one more time.

"Help me, please! Oh, God. Her face is so loathsome: Red eyes and the teeth. The teeth are so long. Ohhh!"

Everyone's attention was drawn to the tape player in the middle of the table as they heard the sound of her teeth tearing into his flesh and gurgling noises as she drank from him. When she finished, they heard her pick up the cell phone and the next sound was metal cutting through flesh as she slit his throat, although they didn't know why she was doing that.

There was silence for a few moments, the only exception being the sirens which were obviously getting closer, but then they heard the voice of the vampire, soft and syrupy, say, "Did you enjoy hearing him die as much as I enjoyed killing him. He tasted wonderful, you know?" (A maniacal laugh followed the silence as she broke the connection.)

Allen shut off the tape player and said, "With everything I have heard and seen here tonight, hearing that phone call again made a believer out of me and I know we have to destroy her as soon as possible.

Kathleen said, "I guess we are all in agreement as to what we have to do, so I guess the next thing would be to meet tomorrow night, somewhere near The Firebase and go from there. I guess the K-Mart parking lot would be just as good a place as any."

"What are we going to do for weapons," Marty asked.

"Allen and I will be armed and that should help," TripleN offered.

David responded by saying, "I don't think guns will kill her, but they might slow her down some. We need weapons that will be able to burn her or remove her head. I am bringing my sword. I almost got her back in eighty-six, but she was too fast for me. I think the best thing would be to somehow get her into her van and torch the thing. If she tries to get out, the detectives can slow her with bullets and maybe I can get in there to take her head from her body."

Kate sat there, unbelievingly listening to the nonchalant way that the men were describing how to kill a woman who had once been human, and it was very unsettling to her. Was she getting weak in the knees, knowing what they had to do to destroy the vampire, yet having to kill this woman to complete their mission? Fortunately the vision of Lain as pure evil superimposed itself on her brain so she no longer had absolutely any qualms about the vampire's destruction.

David said, "That's it then. We meet tomorrow night at seven o'clock in the K-Mart parking lot to hopefully end the existence of Lani Jorgenson."

The vampire hunters dispersed, thoughts raging through their brains wondering who would live and who would die before Lani met her destruction.

Preparing For Battle

At seven o'clock, they all gathered in the K-Mart parking lot to finalize their plans. In the event Lani would be inside The Firebase, it was determined that TripleN would stay by her vehicle, if it was in the lot, along with David, Ron and Mark, the three people whom Lani would recognize immediately. Perhaps she wouldn't remember Mark, but the team didn't want to take that chance. Allen's friends would also hang out in the lot; all of them would be carrying weapons and walkie-talkies, hoping to box her in, if she was indeed forced out into the open. Kate, Allen and Marty would go inside the club, hopefully to find their adversary. The only problem was that there were way to many ifs in the scenario.

Before venturing the few blocks to the club, David thought it would be a good idea to go into K-Mart and get some supplies that may help them trap the vampire.

Marty asked, "What do you think we would need, David?"

He replied, "Well, we are all pretty much aware that the only three ways to kill her would be by beheading, drowning, or burning her. Obviously, drowning her is not a realistic possibility, but burning or beheading are both definite means of her destruction. I think we need to get some kind of torches and weapons capable of cutting her head off, simple as that, and we should be able to find what we need here."

"Guys," Kate chimed in, "there is also a hardware store a little ways from here and whatever we can't find here, we should be able to get there."

Allen nodded his head in agreement, followed by the rest of the hunters.

The group strolled up to the doors of the brightly lit, decorated store. Christmas shopping was in full bloom now. A man, standing by a Salvation Army kettle was ringing his bell as shoppers both dropped coins and bills into the mouth of the vessel, while others took a wide birth, desperately clinging on to the few coins that would do nothing to make them richer, but could certainly help the downtrodden. Kathleen was always saddened by those type of people, and she was determined that if they attained victory over Lani tonight, she would write a hard hitting story about the misers she saw every time she shopped.

It was rather warm inside the store, with all the humanity scurrying about, and most of the group unzipped their jackets and stuffed hats and gloves into empty pockets. David had to smile to himself, wondering what the throng inside the store would do if they knew that a battle between the living and the dead could be taking place very soon.

❧❦

The three teenagers walked together, talking in hushed tones, truly frightened by the venture in which they were about to participate. Mark kept seeing Lani's face change in his mind's eye and he was troubled. He slept very fitfully last night, finally asking Matt if he could bunk with him.

"Sure, Mark. I know you're scared, and I am too. And I never even saw her." After Mark crawled under the covers, Matt tousled his brother's hair and lightly punched his chin. "You know, Mark, it's still hard to believe that out there somewhere is a real vampire. When we kill her, imagine what that will do to the book and film industry. Its going to blow them away knowing that a real vampire can't be killed by a stake to the heart, and the fact that she is able to move about in the daylight, without disintegrating, is going to ruffle a few feathers, also. We're going to be heroes, little brother. Maybe our pictures will be in magazines and we'll get to go on talk shows and tell everyone how we helped kill the last vampire on earth."

Matt was getting all excited with the prospect, while Mark had many reservations about going up against an opponent they knew very little about. Matt brought him out of his mental funk by punching him again, smiling, and saying, "That'd be way cool, Mark. You and me on Jerry Springer, Oprah, Montel, and God only knows how many shows." Then another thought struck him, which made his brother smile. "Man, think of how the chicks will dig us." He looked over at Mark and said, "Shit, you may get laid before you're thirteen, kid."

Mark laughed, but said to Matt, "Yeah, that'd all be neat, alright, but I don't think any of that stuff would happen. You know the adults are not going to let us get too close to Lani, for fear that we may get hurt or killed, and then they have to bear the responsibility. Let's just see what happens when we finally catch up with her, and then go from there. Now we better get some sleep so we are ready for tomorrow night, Matt."

"Okay. You may be right, but chicks and Springer would still be neat."

❧❦

Allen and Triple N had spent the better part of the day trying to drum up some support from their closest friends on the force, meeting with seven cops after their shift ended at three o'clock, hoping that along with the others, nine armed cops would be able to destroy her.

The force was gathered in the break room of the department, drinking coffee or soda, or playing grabass when the two detectives ambled in. Triple N passed out information booklets to each cop, which included the sketch of Lani, and all the hard copy information they were able to gather together from Kate and David.

Once everyone had looked over their packets, albeit briefly, Allen got their attention and said, "First of all, thanks for coming and being willing to help take this woman down. I know some of you are skeptical about Lani Jorgenson being a vampire, but it is the God honest truth. I swear this to you. If we don't destroy her, she could keep killing people for centuries. Hell she's almost two hundred years old already, and still looks in her early twenties. Imagine the knowledge she possesses, which will make our jobs even more difficult."

Joe Brannigan, a cop for almost eight years, and a Desert Storm vet, raised his hand with a question.

"Yes, Joe. What's on your mind?"

"How do we kill an immortal, Allen?"

"We figured that there were only three ways, beheading, burning or drowning. This information came straight from the horse's mouth, so to speak. One of the guys in the group, a nineteen year old named Ron Gerancher had a date with her the other night and she told him the ways to kill a vampire."

"Allen! Why would a vampire tell a kid how to kill her?" Emil Lakatosh, a fourteen-year veteran of the force, and a former military policeman who saw duty mostly in Germany, posed this question.

"It came out in the conversation when Ron told her that he was writing a vampire novel." Allen smiled and added; "Ron said that she almost choked on her coffee when he told her that. Of course, at that time, he didn't know she was a real vampire. He found that out two nights later."

Brit Edwards, a detective for seventeen years, and a twenty nine year veteran, with only eighty three days to go until retirement asked, "So how do we get her boxed in, Al?"

Allen shrugged his shoulders and replied, "Your guess is as good as mine, Brit. We can only hope that if she is inside The Firebase, we can get her away from all those people and out in the parking lot and hopefully box her in out there. At least with the place having a barbed wire topped wall around it and only two vehicle openings, we might have a chance. 'Course, she could be able to jump to unknown heights. I know from what I have heard that she is a strong fuckin' bitch, and a few of us may get hurt out there. You guys all know that if you don't want to get into this, all you have to do is walk away and I won't fault you if you do. Frankly, I am scared shitless having to deal with something we know so little about."

Kit DeFranco, a four year veteran, and the only cop in the room who had ever blown a perp away, said, "Al, I don't know about everybody else, but I want a piece of the action. You guys all know I'm a little left of center sometimes, but I don't go off half-cocked. I think we all need to see this mission through and kill this vampire before she splits to who knows where and continues killing human beings. It's still hard to fathom that a creature is among us that survives by drinking blood, but I believe every word of what I heard today and I'm ready to fight."

Everyone around the table nodded in agreement and Allen said, "Thanks, guys. I knew I could count on you. See you at The Firebase. This information has to stay with us in here. Not a word to anyone outside this room. Right?" The cops all nodded their heads before leaving the room to prepare for battle.

As he looked around in the camping supply department, hoping to find some kind of torches, Ron thought back to what had occurred at home earlier in the day.

He was pumping iron, as was his everyday custom, but secretly eager to believe that a few more curls with the twenty pounders would somehow give him the added strength he would need for the mission at hand. He had told his mom what might happen tonight, "*if they were extremely lucky and Lani lets her guard down.*" She was appalled that Ron actually believed that a vampire existed.

Ron's mother, Helen, a hairdresser who worked for a local Holiday Hair, said, "Son, you spend too much time writing your stories about these creatures and you definitely see too many movies about vampires. Now you believe that one actually exists! I wish you would tell me what you really planned to do tonight, instead of making up such a ludicrous tale to tell your father and I." She had just placed some freshly washed clothing on his bed for him to put away when she noticed a sketch lying upon his bed. When she looked at the sketch, her hands began to shake, and she fainted.

Ron heard her fall and he quickly dropped his dumbbells to the floor, hurrying to where she lay, yelling for his dad to come up to his room.

Bill Gerancher, a forty three year old tire salesman, totally out of shape and thirty pounds overweight, climbed the stairs huffing and puffing all the way up. He entered Ron's room in time to see his wife come out of her thirty-second coma. Father and son helped her up and had her sit on Ron's bed until she had all of her bearings.

"What happened, son?"

Shrugging his shoulders, Ron replied, "Don't know, dad. She came in to give me my laundry and as we were talking she fainted."

"Ron, get her a glass of water, please."

When Ron returned from his bathroom with a full glass of water, he handed it to his mother and she gulped it down in seconds.

"Mom, you look like you saw a ghost. You are so pale. What happened?"

She looked back down at the sketch again and then back up to her son and husband. "Is this the woman you all think is a vampire?"

He nodded his head and his father shot both of them an inquisitive look, since he was absolutely clueless. "Vampire? What the hell is this all about, son?"

Ron filled his father in and then they both looked toward Helen, who was just staring at the sketch, shaking like a leaf, hoping to find out what made her flip out like she did. Obviously the sketch played a part, but what part?

When she finally spoke, her voice cracked as she began. "Yesterday, I cut this woman's hair. She came into the shop and sat quietly while waiting for someone to take care of her, and I must admit that I stared at her more than a few times, twice catching her eye and a smile, even though her smile was cheerless. When it was her turn, I was free and as I cut her hair we just engaged in small talk. She was only in my chair for about ten minutes because she only wanted a trim and no wash. While I jabbered like a magpie, like I always do, she remained fairly quiet. I think she only said, 'Could you please take about an inch off and then just comb it out, please.' When I finished her, we went to the cash register and she handed me a twenty for a twelve-dollar cut and said, 'Keep the change.' I put the eight bucks in my purse and she was gone. But, I remember that when she handed me the bill, her hands were very cold to the touch, and her breath was simply awful. I felt so bad for her."

They helped her to her feet and went downstairs to the living room. Bill brought his wife a brandy and got himself and Ron each a beer. Occasionally Bill would allow his son to have a beer at home, and he knew that now was definitely a time when a little alcohol would be okay.

Bill Gerancher handed his son a Budweiser and said, "I'm going with you tonight."

Ron looked at his father and stated flatly, "Absolutely not, Dad. I don't want to hurt your feelings, but you are too old, too fat, and too out of shape to be chasing vampires. I don't want you to get hurt."

He grabbed his son by the front of his tee shirt and got into his face, saying, "Who the hell do you think you are, boy, that you can say that kind of shit to your old man?"

Doing something he had never done before, Ron grabbed his father's hand and with a grip like a vise, removed it from his shirt, letting his father go before he hurt him. This was something he would never want to do, but he repeated himself, telling his father, "No, dad. You are not going and even though I am only the son, you have to listen to me. She will kill you if she gets a chance and you wouldn't be able to defend yourself."

Helen chimed in, "He's right, Bill. There is no way you would be of any use out there in the kind of condition you are in. The doctor has told you for months to lose all that weight before you have a heart attack. At least you quit smoking, which was a good thing. I love you, dear, but listen to your son for a change. I still find it hard to believe that Lani, little as she is, could harm anyone, but none of us know how strong she really is, Bill. For Christ's sake, she is a vampire! I don't want Ron to go either, but I know that everyone involved is depending on one another and he will be okay" She had gotten up from where she had been sitting and walked over to hold her husband's hand.

They walked hand in hand out to the kitchen, leaving Ron alone with his thoughts. He was ready to do battle.

David was beginning to feel the pressure. As much as he wanted to kill Lani, he was becoming very afraid that she would kill him before she died, if she was indeed killed by the rest of the group. He had begun to bite his nails again; something he had not done in years, even when he saw her in Williamsburg. *Would the nightmare finally end, here in Allentown, Pennsylvania?*

He sat on his bed in the Hilton, sharpening his sword, knowing he would probably only get one chance to behead her and the blade had to be razor sharp. Each stroke he made with the sharpening tool ground off a minute amount of metal, which fell onto a towel on his lap. With each pass, he felt the weapon's edge becoming finer and finer. Finally he was able to slit a piece of paper like a hot knife going through butter.

The tool of her destruction was ready and David gently wrapped it inside the old flannel shirt he had kept it in since that day in 1986 when he wore it to the cemetery where Lani's father was buried.

David looked at his watch; five hours to go, and he decided he should lie down for a while and get some rest, since he would need all the rest he could get. Hopefully by this time tomorrow, he thought, he might be able to finally get a full night's sleep without dreaming about Lani drinking blood from his neck until he passed out from loss of his most precious body fluid. He lay down and closed his eyes, only to see her face change from that of a beautiful, young woman to the face of pure evil, a creature that should have never been allowed to walk the earth, yet she did. She told him that she was the last of her kind and he believed her, though he didn't know why, *because you still love her, you fool.* With her destruction, vampirism would forever cease to exist.

He had been asleep for only a few minutes, according to the time on his watch, when the phone rang.

Suppressing a yawn, he sleepily answered it. "Hello?" He said, waiting for the voice on the other end to answer.

"David, it's Kathleen. Did I wake you?"

"Yes, but it's okay. I don't think I would have slept much longer anyway," he lied. "What can I do for you, Kate?"

"I've been on the computer all day trying to find out more about our adversary, but I have been coming up with blanks on every search, yet I feel as though we are missing something that will help us fight her and win."

"Kathleen, I honestly don't know what to tell you, since I figure you know as much about her now as I do, with the exception of actually meeting her face to face."

"Well, you are probably right. I guess it's the reporter in me, always thinking there is more to the story if you dig deeper. You know what I mean?"

David laughed and said, "Yes. I think I know what you mean, but I am sure that we aren't missing anything, and if we are fortunate enough to get her in a stranglehold, what else do we need to know. She's going to lose her head and that's that."

"Okay, David. Go back to sleep and I'll see you in a few hours."

After she hung up the phone, she sat back down at the computer to continue a search. *For what?*

While the rest of the vampire hunters were in K-Mart, Marty Walsh walked down to the hardware store and found a fire axe. He paid the extra ten bucks to have it sharpened to the point where it could cut paper. Although he hoped he would never get close enough to use it, he wanted to have the best possible weapon at his disposal. He still found it hard to believe that they were going to try to kill a vampire.

He had watched the video and Lani looked so petite, yet she possessed immeasurable strength, and he tried to picture her and Jordan together, even though he didn't want to, but he needed that vision to give him the strength to do what he might have to do later.

"Here you go, sir. This axe is so sharp that it could split a hair in half. Mind if I ask why you need it honed this fine?"

"You wouldn't believe me if I told you, pal, but you will know tomorrow."

Marty paid his bill and walked from the store, axe in hand, the orange sticker with the word PAID standing out like a sore thumb on the light brown handle, and started walking back to the K-Mart parking lot. The clerk stepped out from the store and watched his customer stride away. He pocketed the ten-dollar tip the guy handed him, scratching his head, confused about Marty's words, wondering if he should call the police. The thought axe murderer came to mind, but he went back into the store to wait on the next customer

As Marty walked, he said a prayer and then he thought about his late ex-wife. Talking to himself in a whisper he said, "Jordan, I know I wasn't always there for you and I miss you dearly, but I vow that we will destroy the fiend who took your life, my dear, sweet Jordan. I miss you so much." He wiped away the tears with the sleeve of his jacket, now knowing that he never really fell out of love with Jordan, just let his business get in the way of their relationship, and now he was extremely depressed.

While all this planning was transpiring, Lani Jorgenson was in her room at the Red Roof Inn, entertaining a young gentleman by the name of Christopher Warren. She knew that since talking into that cell phone after killing that man, she may have put herself in grave danger, but she still had enough confidence to stay in the city a little longer.

She had met Chris last night at the Sheraton Jet Port and was immediately attracted to the young, twenty five year old airplane mechanic.

The place was packed for the Thursday night dance featuring music by Plateau. When Lani walked in at nine forty five, all the tables had been taken and there wasn't even a seat at the bar. She smiled to herself, a bit sardonically perhaps, thinking that all she would have to do is yank someone from his seat and it would be hers.

Lani sallied up to the bar and ordered a glass of wine and then just ambled about the room, seeing what might turn up. She wanted a live one because her blood supply was almost depleted and she hated feeding like that. She figured it was almost like a human, brown bagging it for lunch, rather than having a good, satisfying, nutritious meal during the workday. She remembered seeing construction workers, people who burned up a lot of calories while at their jobs having to go the day on whatever the wife packed for them.

She was halfway across the room, really getting into the music, as they were playing one of her favorite songs. For a moment she felt like a human, like she belonged here, but only for a moment. It was becoming more tortuous being in a room full of humanity, looking like them, talking like them, yet being so different, having to kill them to live; it was becoming more unbearable the longer she survived, and yet she wanted to live forever. A brief vision of her parents, arms held open, beckoning her, passed across her eyes, troubling her immensely, and she nearly stumbled, spilling some of her drink on a young woman who gave her the finger and uttered, "Thanks for ruining a two hundred dollar blouse, blondie." Lani, in a state of bewilderment, apologized and handed her two one hundred dollar bills, with her hands shaking uncontrollably. *What is happening to me?*

Minutes later, composed now as she sipped her wine, she felt someone approach from the rear, probably checking out her butt. She was wearing tight blue jeans and a white tee shirt, with no bra. Lani was wearing two-inch spike heels, which really accentuated her ass: she was flaunting her sexuality at every opportunity. Earlier in the day, she had even had her hair cut and combed out by this mousy looking woman who wouldn't shut up. Lani smiled, wondering if the woman had ever gotten an eight-dollar tip before for a twelve dollar cut. Something about the woman had a familiar ring, but she just couldn't put her finger on it.

The man finally got the nerve to come up beside her and after standing there for a few moments, staring at her from the corner of his eye, he said, "Great band, huh?"

Lani gave him the once over, shot him her killer smile and replied, "Yeah, they are great. They sure play a wide range of music."

After a short, uncomfortable silence, he said, "Have you been in the club long?"

She nodded and said, "'Bout a half hour, now and I still can't find a seat."

He lightly grabbed her wrist and said, "C'mon with me. I have a table, if you don't mind sitting with a few of my friends. I'm Chris Warren."

"Lani Jorgenson, Chris. That would be fine, since I enjoy meeting new people."

They wound up at a table with five people, three guys all about the same ages and two girls, who appeared to be a little younger, but in this day and age it was hard to tell sometimes. Introductions were made after Lani slid onto the bench beside Chris and small talk ensued for the better part of an hour, along with the consumption of mass quantities of alcohol. Lani was even on her third glass of wine, which was unusual for her, but she was really having a good time, not even thinking about killing any of these people, and that bothered her. She needed to feed sometime soon, or she would get cramps and be too weak to react to any emergency. The longer she went without blood, the weaker she felt and that was the one condition of her immortality that she never did understand, and Marcus never alluded to it in any of his journals.

"Earth to Lani!"

"Sorry, Chris. I was thinking about a small problem I have and I guess I was ignoring you. I am so sorry." She put her hand on top of his under the table and squeezed it.

He brushed her cheek with his lips and whispered, "Do you want to get out of here and get some fresh air?"

Under the table, unseen by the others, she gave his dick a squeeze and replied, "Yeah, Chris, some fresh air is what I really need."

When they were in the vestibule, he grabbed her and turned her toward him, kissing her hard on the mouth, taken slightly aback by her less than pleasant breath.

"Sorry, Chris. I'm fighting a cold and my sinuses are acting up. When we get to my place, I'll gargle and it won't smell so bad. Is that okay?"

Just the prospect of going to this woman's place was enough to have him forget a little halitosis. He smiled and said, "Do you live far from here, Lani?"

"No, I'm staying at the Red Roof Inn, just down the road about a mile or so. Why don't you follow me there and we'll have some fun. In case I get there before you, I'm in room 107. Come right in and make yourself comfortable." Then she said, "Shit! I don't have any beer. Would you mind stopping somewhere and getting some for yourself, since we may be there all night?"

"Okay. I can run to a bar and get a couple of six packs. Would you like some wine?"

"No, wine I have, but I know you like beer. Take your time and I'll grab a shower. Maybe it will help me get rid of this cold before you get there."

They hopped into their respective vehicles and took off. As soon as Lani walked into her room, she ripped open two bags of blood, drinking them chilled, because she needed her strength back; she didn't know if she would feed on Chris, but she didn't think so.

After a quick shower, she put on sweats and took off her necklace, placing it in the nightstand drawer, after opening the locket and looking at the faded pictures of her father and herself from all those years ago. The vision of her parents flashed in front of her again, causing her to feel weak in the knees.

Chris arrived at the Red Roof about ten minutes after Lani finished her shower and when he walked in and saw her, he was floored. She looked great, even in a sweat suit. Lani was lying on top of the bed, reading, and she motioned him over. He set the paper bag containing two six packs of beer on the table and slid in beside her.

When she kissed him, it was so much better. She had obviously gargled and had chewed some breath mints and she tasted good, especially when she slipped him the tongue. It didn't take him long to remove her clothing, admiring her perfect body as she removed his.

Lani's eyes traversed his body. He was in fantastic shape, which she figured since he had told her that in high school he was a wrestler, and ran the four forty in track. He was also into the martial arts, attaining his black belt at the age of nineteen. He was lean and mean and when her eyes moved down to that place between his legs, her smile got even brighter. He was larger than any man she had ever been with, with the exception of Heywood, the black slave she killed in the last century. Sex with him had almost destroyed her and she knew that a man would never overwhelm her again, although it would be a challenge to stay in control when he was inside her.

He watched her watch him and was he was pleased when she said, "Oh, my God, Chris. I've heard the phrase being hung like a horse before, but I never saw a horse as big as you." She wiggled her finger in a come hither manner and he mounted her, making her eyes bulge as they made love. When he climaxed inside her, she felt strange; it was a feeling she had never had before with any partner, and although the feeling ebbed, she was frightened a bit. *Lani, you can't be afraid of a human; they can't hurt you.* She held him close but her mind focused on David. *I still love him very much.*

❧

By the time David was ready to get up and head to K-Mart, Chris and Lani had made love seven times since they met the night before. Lani was feeling a little weak but she just couldn't get enough of him and went hungry longer than she cared to. As he slept between the fifth and sixth time, she watched him sleep. His breathing was shallow and he smiled a lot. She did too, wondering if Chris would be the person that she would turn into a vampire and walk with through eternity. For a few moments she bared her fangs and lowered her head toward his neck, his scent deliciously wonderful, but she couldn't bring herself to do it and she knew they had to get out of there and go where there were more people. Tonight, though, Christopher Warren would become the second vampire on earth. *Why wait? Will sex with a vampire be as good as sex with a human?*

He awakened shortly after she sat back up. She was running her fingers through his chest hair and said, "Do you feel like going out, Chris?"

Chris sat up and walked to the bathroom as Lani stared at his naked butt. "Yeah. I do. I know they are having a band at The Firebase. A friend of mine is the drummer. How does that sound?"

He didn't see her smile as she remembered Jason Weber from a few nights ago and how delicious he was. She had seen the headlines written about the case, enjoying the style of Kathleen Hammond, and how the mysterious blonde woman who had accompanied him to the Hideaway Motel baffled the police. She had been quite impressed that the medical examiner deduced that he had mouthwash inside his wound, although it only led them to believe that he had possibly had sex with the woman *Did he ever! He was really good for an older guy, but thinking about older guys makes me think about David. Where was he? Hopefully I gave him a hell of a scare in Williamsburg and that should have been enough to have him stop pursuing her, but I really doubt it. I can't believe I am still in love with him, when all he wants to do is kill me.*

The sound of the toilet flushing brought her back from her reverie and she watched Chris walk back to the bed, smiling, holding his hard penis and saying, "Think we have time for one more before we go."

She nodded her head and opened herself to him again.

❦

As they waited in the parking lot for news of Lani's van being spotted, Kate went into McDonald's and purchased enough coffee for everyone, and a hot chocolate for Mark, not knowing whether or not he drank coffee. She paid the cashier and threw packets of artificial sweetener and real sugar into the bags, along with creamers and stirrers.

She came back out into the cold night air, shivers coursing through her body, and not only from the chill of the night, and distributed the hot drinks to everyone. It seemed like forever, but it was probably only a few minutes later that the sound of squelch breaking could be heard on Allen's walkie-talkie.

"Allen, this is Joe. Do you read me?"

"Yes, Joe. You are coming through loud and clear."

"A blue Windstar with South Carolina plates just pulled in a couple of minutes ago. A blonde woman fitting Lani's description got out, but she wasn't alone. A young guy was with her and they went inside, hand in hand, laughing like star crossed lovers."

David heard that bit of news and was distraught over the fact that she was not alone. Their jobs would be a little tougher now. *Star crossed lovers. Like she and I were so many years ago. I certainly hope I can take her head before she turns him into the vile creature she is.* David had a look of resolve etched into his face. Lani would not leave this place alive, no matter what it took, even if it meant his own death.

The Last Vampire

They walked the few blocks to The Firebase and as they waited across the street for the light to change, Marty gave the place a good look. Although he had never been in the service, he had seen some movies showing firebases and the club certainly did look like a miniature of one to some degree. The entire place was completely surrounded by a five foot high 'wall' of concertina wire, with sandbagged bunkers cut into it at forty-foot intervals. The two man bunkers were not roofed, as they would have been in Vietnam, they were merely replicated to a height of five feet. Mannequins, dressed in combat fatigues of the Vietnam era were placed in the bunkers facing the road, to add a jolt of realism. At each of the four corners, a wooden guard tower had been built. Each one was only a few feet higher than the wire, but they were impressive additions. The club itself was a large building, low slung from front to back and covered with weathered clapboards. Everything was painted in the military's favorite color, olive drab green. At the one entrance was a signboard, hanging between wooden poles, eight feet high. Painted on the sign were two words—THE FIREBASE.

When the group crossed the street and walked up to the entrance, they momentarily stopped, allowing Marty to read the black granite plaque that was set into the pavement by the entrance. It read: THIS CLUB IS DEDICATED IN HONOR OF THE MEN AND WOMEN WHO SERVED IN THE VIETNAM WAR. Between the pavement and the perimeter wire was a two-foot wide bed of bricks, many of them inscribed with names, unit designations and years of service. Some had also been etched with the words In Memory Of, followed by the name of a deceased veteran. Marty even noticed a brick bearing the name of a sentry dog.

As they walked beneath the sign and into the parking lot, Marty thought that this was definitely a fitting place to slay a vampire. He somehow thought that the spirits of these memorialized men and women would be able to aid them in their quest to destroy Lani Jorgenson.

While the team was gathering outside, getting ready to do battle with her, Lani was inside with Chris having a blast. She had not felt this good in a long time. *Not since I was with David all those years ago, and more recently, Jordan, until she fucked up big time by finding out what I am.* She squeezed his leg as they sat at their table listening to the music of Jack of Clubs, a really hot local band. Their music was tight and the vocals were amazing, even to the point of sounding much like the groups whose songs they were performing.

The din was way up in the decibel range and it was sometimes difficult to talk, which was okay too, because there were times when Lani was lost in thoughts of the past. *Why am I reliving the past so often, when I have such a long future in front of me?* As they sat there with a few of Chris's friends, listening to the band sing 'Here, There and Everywhere', by The Beatles, Lani was looking around at the humanity surrounding her, aching for blood because of the wonderful scent of all these people, with the exception of a group of construction workers who must have come here from the job without showering. Their combined body odors permeated the air several feet from their table, yet no one approached them to let them know how much they reeked. Of course, her sense of smell was more pronounced than that of humans, so perhaps they really weren't as bad as she thought. She was quite ravenous, having gone without blood for over 24 hours.

Halfway through the song, she nearly dropped her glass of wine when she saw a man who looked incredibly like Marcus and she was momentarily taken aback. She knew it might happen someday, but she was never prepared for when it could happen. It had taken him almost two thousand years before he found Theda in the guise of Lani Jorgenson. He caught her staring at him and strode to her table, smiling, hoping perhaps that she was merely with friends and he would be able to wind up taking her away from here.

"Excuse me, Miss. I couldn't help but notice you staring at me and I was wondering why."

She flashed her killer smile and replied, "I'm sorry. It's just that you look so much like someone I knew a long time ago and your face brought a lot of memories back to me. It was a man who affected me more than any other man I have ever known."

He put his hand out and said, "My name is Rich Kendall, and you are?"

"Lani Jorgenson. Please sit down, Rich."

After sitting down and lighting up a cigarette, Rich said, "You said this guy affected you more than any other man you have ever met, yet I wouldn't take you for more than early twenties. How many men have you known, Lani?"

Suddenly, the faces of thousands of men and women flooded through her mine. *What the hell is happening to me?* "Yeah, I guess that made me sound a bit promiscuous, didn't it? I had meant men that I have known as I was growing up, like my father and his friends." At the mention of his name, her hand immediately went to her necklace, having put it back on before coming here from the motel. She fondled it as she stared at the face of a man who looked so much like the man who gave her the life she now led.

She must have been lost in her thoughts for a while because she felt a nudge from Chris and looked away from Rich to him when he said, "So, Lani, who is your new friend?" He had an angry tone to his voice, but Lani ignored it.

"Chris, meet Rich. He looked so much like someone I once knew, I invited him to sit with us."

Chris extended his hand in front of Lani, grasping Rich's and said, "Nice to meet you, Rich." After shaking his hand, he put his arm around Lani, looked Rich square in the eyes and said, "Talk all you want, but don't be putting a move on my girl, okay."

"No sweat, man. I had no intention on moving in on you *Yeah, right! There is no way a punk like you is going to stop me if I want her badly enough.* I just wanted to talk to her."

Chris gave him a hard look, but only briefly and went back to his discussion with a couple of his friends. He had seen them when they walked into the club and fortunately their table had three empty seats.

Rich motioned toward Chris's back and asked, "Jealous boyfriend?"

"Maybe. I only met him last night, but I really like him and I may keep him forever."

"Sounds like it could get serious."

"Yeah, and I hope I am not leading you on, because you are quite the handsome fellow, Rich, and if I wouldn't be with Chris, I could definitely go for you, for sure." *God, I am so hungry I could eat him right here and now. Revenge of what Marcus did to me by taking the life of a person who was Theda's exact double? Probably, but he smells so wonderful and I am getting dizzy with desire.*

"Do you think Chris would be upset if we danced together?"

"Nah. He is so wrapped up in talking with his friends, he probably won't even know that we are gone, but I'm going to let him know."

She got his attention, and with a hypnotic whisper told him, "Rich and I are going to dance, and when I come back to the table alone, you will think that he left the club and you won't ask any questions."

"Have fun, honey. Rich, she is an incredible dancer, but bring her back to me unharmed." They all laughed.

"Don't worry, Chris, she'll be in good hands for awhile," as he thought, *I really want to get my hands on those tits and that ass, Chris. Bet she's a great fuck.* He smiled at Lani's boyfriend as they turned toward the dance floor.

After two dances, Lani said, "Would you like to step out back for some fresh air? It's getting a bit stuffy in here."

"Sure, should we get our jackets?"

"No, we'll only be outside for a few minutes at the most and I don't think we will freeze that quickly."

As soon as they were outside the building, Lani took a quick look around, and seeing no one, she whispered to Rich, "If you want you can kiss me and squeeze my breasts and then I will give you a big surprise." As she said this, she squeezed his penis, rubbing it through his jeans, giving him an erection while he kissed her, not even recoiling at her breath as most of her lovers *victims* had during the past two centuries. He was squeezing her breasts really hard and breathing heavily, hoping that she would unzip him and give him a blowjob right here and now. When she unzipped him and pulled it out, he stopped kissing her and wanted to look into her face and smile. When he saw her teeth, he nearly screamed, but she put her hand over his mouth just before pulling his head down and biting his neck.

When she finished drinking, feeling warm and toasty again, she slit his throat and tossed him into the dumpster, covering his body with some trash that was strewn about. The fucker would really stink up the place in a few hours, she thought, but by then she would be long gone, with Chris as her mate through the upcoming third millennium. Even though he wasn't Marcus, her revenge was sweet. She walked back into the building, never noticing the woman staring at her through binoculars.

❧❦

Kit had seen the attack on the young man, watching Lani slit his throat and toss him into the dumpster, and although she had wanted to get over there and try to save him, she knew that she would never make it and possibly destroy the plan that was set in place.

When Lani went back inside, she got on the radio.

"All units, this is Kit. Lani just killed a man behind the building and tossed him into a dumpster. I gotta tell you she is one wicked bitch and we are going to have our hands full. You can't believe how she picked the dude's body up with one hand and threw him in, like most of us would toss a baseball. She didn't even strain herself with his weight. I tell you guys, I have seen some strong people in my years on the force, but nothing like this. If we are able to take her down, it's going to have to be really quick, or she will kill several of us, for sure."

Kit got off the radio and sat down on the bumper of a car. Her face was flushed and she was breathing heavily. She could not even begin to describe to the team how Lani's face had changed. Kit had never seen anything like it, especially watching her fangs grow while she was playing with the guy's dick. She had nearly shrieked, but she knew that Lani would have been alerted to that.

Even though she had not seen the inside of a church in years, she felt that now was as good a time as any to begin praying to God and reaffirm her religious beliefs, for seeing her was looking into the face of Satan himself. She muttered out loud, "Girl, there are no atheists in a foxhole, and this will be a war, for sure."

⁂

Moments after Lani took Rich outside, Marty, Kathleen and Allen had stepped inside The Firebase, where Marty was once again blown away by the memorabilia he had seen on the walls and hanging from the rafters. Inside a glass case, protected by an alarm, were weapons of all sorts, both American and Communist made. They ranged from handguns to an M-60 machine gun. The case was about three feet deep and stretched the eight feet from floor to rafters. The weapons were lying upon glass shelving, each one labeled with its nomenclature and the name of the donor. A lock box stood beside the case where donations could be placed to defer the expenses of the security needed to have the weapons on the premises. The walls were filled with pictures of veterans and scenes of the Vietnam landscape. From the rafters hung helmets, flack jackets, fatigue jackets, jungle boots and flags of all sorts. Hanging from hooks above the bar were mugs bearing the logos of all the branches of the services and some had names written on the bottom in magic marker, tributes to the living and the dead, since some had wording like, Jake, I'll never forget you. A Shau Valley 1965, among other names and places. As an entrepreneur, Marty would remember this place and someday, after all this was over, approach the owners to see if they would consider going into business with him to open a chain of Firebases all over the country.

While Marty was in the throes of ecstasy with his idea, momentarily forgetting why he was here, Kate and Allen were checking out the crowd, hoping to find Lani before she saw them looking around. Although they were sure that the vampire had no idea that she was being pursued tonight, the pair of vampire hunters didn't want to be too obvious with their searching. Kathleen had caught Jack's eye and he nodded to her, a sign that he had seen the blonde woman, too. She mouthed the word "Where" but Jack shrugged his shoulders as he continued to play guitar, although he used a head motion to show his friend where he had seen her last.

Kate tugged Allen's shirtsleeve and said, Jack just informed me that she had been sitting over in that section, but he doesn't see her there now."

"Do you think she left before we walked in?

She shook her head and replied, "Her van is still out there, but she could have slipped out the back with the mystery man and took off when we came in here."

"Keep your eyes peeled. I'm going to go into the john and get on the horn to see if any of my fellow cops have seen her outside."

"Never mind, Allen. There she is, now." Kate had seen her come inside from the back door, smiling to herself and whistling, too, she thought.

They both watched their adversary walk to the table where Chris was still in animated conversation with his friends and both the hunters were amazed that the beautiful, young woman they were peering at was one hundred and eighty years old. She was dressed in a black mini skirt and a long sleeved, white turtleneck sweater. Her dainty feet were inside a pair of low, black dress shoes. Her blonde hair bounced on her shoulders as she confidently ambled back to her table, the young man now noticing her and smiling that sweet smile of love. The poor bastard didn't know what he was dealing with. Kate almost felt sorry for Lani, a woman who would have the world by the ass this day and age, possibly being a highly paid model with looks like that. The would-be novelist was even storing this information to use as characters in the book she was now ready to write. *As soon as you slay the vampire, Kate.*

Allen was also taken in by her good looks and poise, thinking she could be a model for Victoria's Secret or Frederick's of Hollywood. He had to admit that if she would not have been a vampire and he would be a few years younger, he wouldn't mind taking a shot at that, although the woman beside him really turned him on and after Lani lay dead in the parking lot, he would ask Kathleen to go to dinner on Sunday to rehash all this over lobster and wine. Afterward…He just smiled as he looked from Kate to Lani and then back again.

※

Outside in the parking lot, the group was getting fidgety, wondering when and if a battle between them and the vampire would take place. The night was getting colder and a brisk wind had begun to blow, snow flurries being carried along with the breeze.

The brothers were shivering, wrapping their arms around their bodies to ward off the cold, *FEAR?*, stamping their feet up and down to keep them warm, too.

"Matt, what do you think will happen here, tonight?"

"I don't know, Mark, but I sure hope it happens soon, because my ass is frozen solid already, and we may get some serious snow tonight."

Mark put his hand on his brother's shoulder and asked, "You scared?"

"Fuckin' A, bro. I have no clue what the hell is going to happen tonight and that is enough to scare me shitless. I'm just afraid that more than a few of us could be killed before we destroy her, if we are even able to kill her. Think about it, Mark. We have to either turn her into a crispy critter or cut her head off. Who the hell is going to be able to get that close to her to do that? I did a lot of thinking after our conversation today, and I gotta tell you, kid, I was almost ready to back out of this clusterfuck."

All the while that Matt was talking, staring out into space, like he usually did in stressful situations, Mark wondered why he was here, too. He was a twelve year old, chubby intellectual, when what this team needed was another couple dozen young men, like Ron, strong as bulls and able to get out of their own way if the situation called for a hasty retreat. But remembering what he saw on the thruway that night, and knowing what she had done over all these years to survive, he had to try to help destroy her, even if it meant getting hurt, or, God forbid, even killed. He closed his eyes and tried to wish her away, knowing that would never happen.

Ron too was cold, on both the inside and the outside; cold fear and freezing bodies did not make for good warriors, he thought. Shaking more from the cold fear then from the frigid temperatures, he was not alone. He looked around at the team, scattered around the parking lot, each alone with his and her thoughts, wondering what was happening inside. Had the three hunters met up with the quarry? How were they going to get her out here to the parking lot *killing field?* Who would live and who would die? It was all very disconcerting. He still remembered the night he met her and how he really wanted to become her boyfriend until finding out what she really was. *Will we succeed?* Ron, like Kathleen was also mentally filing information for the novel he would write.

Earlier in the day he performed many isometric exercises to prepare himself for tonight's battle. He was still upset with himself for not allowing his father to come with him, but he and his mom were right: Bill Gerancher would never survive if he were here trying to kill a vampire. None of the group members were even sure if she could be killed, but they had to try or thousands more would die, and she might even create more vampires.

Inside, Lani had taken her seat next to Chris, kissing him and fondling him under the table. She was getting itchy to leave this place and get back to the motel where she would have one more fling at great sex with the human who would then become an immortal. Thoughts of David kept flooding her mind and that was beginning to bother her greatly. Ever since she began having more memories since heading north, she pondered if her demise was at hand.

As Chris began to respond to her touch, he said to his friends, "Guys, it was great talking to you, but we have to go. Something's come up that needs to be taken care of." He winked at his friends and they all caught the message. Elaine Rimert, the only one of the women at the table who had ever had sex with Chris wondered how he was going to hide his erection from everyone after he stood up.

Chris didn't want to be embarrassed, so he pushed her hand away while he was talking, really giving Elaine the eye, wanting her again in the future. He finished his beer, giving his dick time to soften.

They got up from the table, put on their jackets and strode, hand in hand, to the door, passing within two feet of Kathleen and Allen.

As the young couple walked through the door, Allen quickly alerted the team.

When David heard the message over the radio, he took a deep breath and crouched by her van, peering through the side windows of the vehicle, watching her approach. As soon as she came into the center of the circle, he was planning to stand up and let her see him, since she could not feel his presence anymore from a great distance. That he found out in Williamsburg, almost taking her by total surprise.

As he watched them slowly approach, followed at a distance by Kate and Allen, he could hardly believe what he was feeling. Unbelievably, he felt himself getting an erection, something he very seldom experienced anymore. Was he still in love with this woman *killer* who was almost three times his age, yet would always remain in the guise of a twenty one year old? Soon, if God and luck were on his side, he would see her lying dead at his feet, her head separated from her body by his razor edge sword.

Kathleen, Allen and Marty had picked up the torches they had placed behind some shrubbery just outside the door, so as not to be seen by anyone, and they followed the vampire and her boyfriend toward her van. Knowing he was there, Kathleen could see David peering through the side windows of the van, watching their approach, and as she looked around the parking lot, the team was beginning to stealthy encircle Lani, not wanting to draw attention to their movements, also watching for David to make his move.

It was a bold plan, although one that could get him killed, but at this point he didn't care. He wanted to live, but if the annihilation of the last vampire on earth would have to come at the expense of his death, he would die happily knowing that the evil one had been exterminated. That was what he wanted more than anything: a chance to see her die before he drew his last breath.

The closer Lani came to her Windstar, the tighter drew the circle.

When she and Chris were less than five feet from the passenger side of her van, she felt David and hissed his name. "David. Show yourself or this man dies." She grabbed Chris by the neck and lifted him from the macadam. The immortal began to squeeze the life from him as his legs and arms flailed away at empty space.

David stood up and moved toward the front of the van, allowing Lani to see him. "I'm here, Lani. Let him go and you can finally have me and do with me what you wish."

"Come to me, lover and then I will release him." She looked up into Chris's face and said, "He is turning a beautiful shade of violet, David, and if you don't get your ass over here in ten seconds, I will really apply some pressure to his neck."

Even as she spoke, David was on the move, standing two feet in front of her before the ten second deadline was up, and she *was* counting. She tossed Chris to the side and he landed on his elbow, cracking it, but he could not scream for he still had little breath. She had squeezed him so hard. As he shook the cobwebs away, the pain really set in and he moaned loudly. She looked at him lying there, a hurtful look on his face and she said, "Don't whine like a fuckin' baby, Chris, my love. You should be happy this old fart can still move fast or you would be deader 'n hell by now." Her face was in full vampire mode, and when he saw the teeth and red eyes he gasped, saying, "What are you, Lani?"

David answered for her. "My friend, you are looking at the world's only immortal. Lani Jorgenson was born in 1819 and has been a vampire for over one hundred and fifty nine years, during which time she has ended the lives of thousands of men like you and me."

Lani was still looking toward Chris and didn't notice David withdraw the sword from beneath his long coat. He took a desperate swing, but cut through the air several inches from her neck, nearly falling to the ground on the finish of his swing, losing his weapon as it flew from his hand.

The vampire turned toward him and growled, "Why, David, how thoughtful of you to bring a toy along to play with." She grabbed him and to the horror of everyone watching, she bit into his neck and began to drink, taking enough so that he would pass out and no longer be a threat because she felt others watching her. Her mind raced. *You still can't kill him, can you? You are still in love with him.*

As Lani was sucking David's blood, the team, nearly in unison, lit their torches and closed to a tighter circle.

The sight of all the fire gave Lani some cause for concern. She hissed like a snake, but only briefly before she regained control of her faculties. She turned and checked out the men and women who were holding her at bay with their torches, occasionally stabbing out toward her to see what kind of reaction they would get.

Chris had regained his breath and decided that he wanted to fuck her up for what she just did to him. He didn't know about this vampire stuff, but she was so little and he figured if he had the upper hand he could do some damage to her and maybe give the people with the torches a chance to finish her off.

He stood up and lunged at her, grabbing a sleeve of her jacket and spinning her toward him. She grabbed him by the top of the head and drew him toward her, saying, "Chris, you gave me great sex and now your blood is going to give me great warmth. It's been a pleasure knowing you. She drained him before the horrified looks of a now large crowd of spectators, some of whom had their cell phones out and were dialing 911. They really went crazy when, after drinking his blood, she slit his throat and tossed his bloodless corpse into the crowd. The late Chris Warren landed on top of a couple of old hippies, knocking them both to the parking lot macadam. The man had gray hair tied back in a ponytail and a long gray beard, and when the body hit him, his glasses flew off, not allowing him to see more than two feet in front of him. The woman, whose long hair was still brown, though, witnessed the madness through olive green eyes. The man said, "Brenda, honey, are you okay?" She simply nodded her head as the body was removed from on top of her.

In the distance, sirens could be heard; the police were on their way, but long before a cruiser car arrived, the media was on the scene. A TV pulled in to the entrance of the parking lot, blocking it off completely. The crew climbed up to the roof, cameras and tripods in hand, to film the ongoing drama. A reporter, Shauna Wilkinson, and her technician, carrying a hand held camera, worked their way through the crowd, showing the TV audience a live picture of Lani Jorgenson, the vampire, as she held at bay about a hundred people, a few of which she knew were police officers and detectives. She saw the vampire becoming more anxious looking as the throng grew and the bright light from the TV camera danced on her horrible face, enhancing the redness in her eyes. Lani snarled and cried out like a wounded animal, and everyone knew you should never get near a wounded animal.

⁓⁂⁓

While all this was going on, Kate gave her torch to another person who was willing to take her place in the ever growing circle of humanity, as she circled around, finding the sword and breaking through the inner circle, hiding behind Lani's van waiting to make a move on her. As she was doing this, she noticed David, lying a few feet away, looking pale, but she could see him breathing, and hopefully he would be okay until the vampire was dead.

Just outside the periphery of the group, Bill Gerancher slowly made his way to the circle, looking for a place to burst through and kill the evil thing that he had seen as he began working around to her blind side. He was going to kill her and make his family proud of him.

After their earlier conversation, he had begun to recount the times that he let his son down. While Ron was growing up, Bill missed a number of his baseball games, and, later in high school, his wrestling meets because he was after the all mighty buck. He wanted his family to have everything that money could buy, unfortunately, at the expense of not seeing his son grow up.

Bill thought about the old song, "Cats In The Cradle", by Harry Chapin, and he realized he never wanted his son to grow up just like him, missing out on life. Destroying the vampire would make him a hero to his wife and son. Tomorrow he would start dieting and working out, making himself strong again, helping to promote a long, healthy life. That thought helped boost his courage to a dangerous level.

When he found a small gap in the circle, he burst through the ring of would be slayers. Lani spun on her heels, facing her new adversary whom she heard approach. He was now only three feet away, and she was laughing her ass off at him.

After regaining control, Bill saw the pure evil etched into her face, and her red eyes were mesmerizing. He could not look away, even if he had wanted to. He stopped cold, wondering if he had just made the biggest mistake of his life, but he made a silent vow that he would complete his mission. He raised both of his hands, each one holding a wooden stake fashioned from the maple legs of a broken coffee table that was in his workroom. How could he have known that you can't kill a vampire by driving a wooden stake through her heart? This is the way they were killed in all the movies he had seen. *This is the real deal, Bill. No movie here.*

Lani stared at him, incredulous at who had been sent in to face her. The assemblage all heard Ron scream, "Dad, no! Get away from her before she kills you!" He also worked his way inside the ring of humans bent on her destruction.

She laughed and said, "The boy is right, old man. I will kill you!" Then her face softened and her teeth retracted, giving Bill an opportunity to look at her human form, that of one of the most gorgeous women he had ever seen; a woman he would love to have found twenty years ago. Not that Helen wasn't attractive when he married her, but Lani was...

He snapped out of it when he heard his son gurgling as she had him by the throat, She said, "C'mon, pop. Stick those stakes into me and save the kid's life. It will be so easy. She held both of her arms out to her sides, still holding on to Ron, slowing choking him to death as Bill rushed her and pushed both stakes deep into her chest, causing…absolutely nothing.

Lani dropped Ron to the parking lot; just as she had Chris, and fortunately he wound up unhurt. He uttered a weak, "Dad, get away from her, now," but Bill couldn't move. He watched her remove the stakes, followed by two spouts of fresh blood, the wounds closing up, as he stood there, dumbfounded.

"Nice try, sport, but I guess you watch Buffy too much, thinking that stakes would work on a real live vampire. She is hot, though, isn't she?"

Lani grabbed Bill and drew him toward her. Her breath nearly knocked him out when she spoke right into his face. "You know, pal. You put that wood into me and I lost half of the last snack I had and I'm getting cold, so guess what is going to happen now." She looked down at Ron and said, "Kid, say goodbye to daddy because I need something he has." Her fangs drove into his neck and as she slurped, she let some spurt out to land on his son's face, mixing with Ron's tears as he watched his father die.

He stood up and charged her, once again being throttled and as she was ready to drink from him she heard David say, "No, Lani. Enough!"

She looked down at her one time lover and said, "You are right, David." She smiled coyly and added; "One family member a day is enough, so I guess I have to finish you, now. She bent down and pierced his neck with her teeth, drinking slowly, savoring the blood of the man she loved, as the crowd pressed closer, still not believing anything they were witnessing.

❧❧

As David began to slip away, Kathleen had made her move from around the rear of the van, closing to less than two feet before Lani was alerted to this new presence. Lani stopped what she was doing, and for reasons that may never be uncovered, sat straight up as Kate swung the razor sharp sword, removing her head from her body, killing the vampire at last.

The last vampire had been slain, at great cost, but her kind would never walk the earth again.

Everyone there wanted to see the slain vampire, her head lying a few feet from her body. The media pressed in with the TV camera and microphones, hoping to grab a quick interview with the brave woman who took the life of Lani Jorgenson.

Kathleen was kneeling on the macadam, holding David in her arms, and wishing him not to be dead as the crowd parted for two paramedics to rush to her side. She continued to cradle him as one of the paramedics begged her to let go of him so they could check his vitals. Finally, she let go and it was found that David had a pulse, albeit weak, but if they could get him to the hospital in a hurry, he might make it.

A stretcher was brought in and David was placed upon it and rushed to the waiting ambulance, while a few of the onlookers comforted Kathleen.

⁂

Several feet away, Ron cradled the body of his father, crying, tears falling onto Bill Gerancher's face. As Ron continued to sob for his dead father, his dad's eyes opened and he looked up to his son's closed eyes and said, "Son, daddy's hungry!" Bill Gerancher, vampire, pulled his son's head closer to his mouth, his teeth growing and his face becoming a hideous replica of what it was. He was just ready to kill his first born when Ron was pulled from his grip and a crashing blow from David's sword separated his head from his body. Allen tossed the sword aside and threw his arms around Ron, saying, "I'm so sorry, Ron. You know I had to do it?"

Ron simply nodded and took a last look at his father before disappearing into the crowd.

Epilogue

Lani Jorgenson, vampire, was dead. Born on October 20, 1819, she died for the first time on October 21, 1840, only to live in death for one hundred and fifty nine years, finally dying again on December 16, 1999. With that line, Kathleen had finished her story. She clicked send, and now she desperately needed a beer. The Morning Call stopped the presses waiting for her story. The Saturday, December 13th issue would be delivered as an afternoon edition.

She got up from her computer desk, stretched and yawned and strode purposefully into the kitchen. After opening the fridge and scanning its contents, she selected a bottle of Sam Adams wheat beer, a half eaten hoagie and some potato salad she had picked up at the market a few days ago. Kate didn't remember the last time she had eaten and she was suddenly famished. The hoagie was overly wet and pretty much tasteless, but it didn't matter at this point; food was food, plus, the beer washed it down pretty easily.

She opened the utensil drawer and pulled out a fork. After adding a dash of salt and pepper to the potato salad and stirring it around, she hefted an overloaded forkful of the store bought fare to her lips and with only a couple of chews, wolfed that down, as well. Five minutes later, she had finished her meal, and popped the lid of another beer, taking it with her back to the computer.

The Slayer, as the media was now calling her, knew that David was recovering nicely. After being bitten by Lani, moments before Kathleen lopped off her head, he was so weak, taken out of the combat with the woman he vowed he would kill, but he never got the chance. He was rushed to Lehigh Valley Hospital where he was given a transfusion and was now resting comfortably in a guarded room. The media was having a field day with this story so far, and like vultures, the reporters hovered around the group responsible for killing the vampire.

Kate sat down at the computer, popped one of Lani's disks in, and continued to work on finding her password.

After the battle had ended, and David had been taken to the hospital, Kate and Allen drove to the Red Roof Inn, hoping to find out that she was still staying there, not having found an apartment, as she had told Ron on their date about a week ago. They had sent a few e-mails to one another, but both of them stayed true to their word and did not meet again until the battle.

Allen went to the desk clerk, flashed his badge and asked, "Do you have a Lani Jorgenson registered here?"

The clerk, a squirrelly looking kid in his early twenties, with bad teeth and short hair, colored green, stuttered as he said, "Is sh—sh—she in trou—trouble, officer?"

"Why, son? Do you know her?"

He shook his head, but said, "I saw her one time in her room, and it looked like she was dr—drinking bl—blood from a plastic ba—bag. You know like th—the kind you see at bl—blood banks."

Allen said, "Son, within the next day or two, you will read and hear things about this woman that you would never believe. Is she still registered here?"

He searched the computer and said, "Ye—yes, officer, r—room 107."

"Good, now would you be kind enough to give me the key to her room, please?"

The young man, not knowing that Allen would have needed a search warrant, handed him the passkey and watched him leave the office.

The pair of soon to be lovers, in Allen's mind, as he looked at Kate, went to Lani's room and Allen unlocked the door, not knowing what they might find inside.

The room was spotless, but they did find some interesting things. Allen found several bags of blood inside a cooler of dry ice. He also discovered several empty bottles of mouthwash and tins of Altoids inside a suitcase, along with some clothing, and Kathleen made the discovery of the day, Lani's laptop and a case full of disks. Each disk was labeled journal, along with the dates each one covered.

"Jesus, Allen! Look at what I found." She showed him the disks. It appeared as though there were at least twenty in the case. "These are records of Lani's life, going all the way back to 1840. What a fucking story these will make. I'm going to see if I can get one to come up on the screen. Hopefully they won't require a password, but I wouldn't bet on it."

She placed the laptop on a table and plugged it in to a receptacle. When it warmed up, she inserted the disk labeled 1840-1850 and waited for it to come up. The blank screen was suddenly filled with the words, The Journal of Lani Jorgenson. Please enter the password. Kate slapped the table and uttered, "Shit!" She scratched her head, finding a piece of glass from the car window and after pulling it from her hair, seeing it wasn't bloody, she tossed it into the trashcan.

As Allen kept rooting through Lani's things, the reporter began to fool around with the computer, entering different words, numbers, and phrases, hoping to come up with the key to open Lani's world, but everything she tried came up empty. She wrote each attempt on a notepad, and one sheet of paper was full when the Allen finished up his search.

Allen walked up behind Kate, placed a hand upon her shoulder, and said, "Any luck, yet, babe?"

She shook her head and looked up into his eyes. As soon as she had some free time, when this was all over, she wanted to get together with him. *I would also love to get together with David.* She took his hand in hers and said, "I'm going to take this all home with me and maybe I'll crack this yet."

❧❧

After several beers and two sheets of paper full of attempted passwords, Kate was ready to give up, when she decided to look at the two different sketches of Lani, to see if they would trigger a possible password, unfortunately neither did; then she remembered the necklace.

She got up and walked into the bedroom. Her purse was lying upon the bed with the necklace inside. Kate reached in and pulled it out, staring at it, hoping it would reveal a clue to the password. The necklace was merely a silver chain with a heart shaped locket dangling from it. A raised silver cross adorned the front of the heart and when she opened the catch, inside were two aged pictures. One was obviously Lani, but the other was difficult to make out, although it was probably her father. Inscribed on the back of the locket were the words. To Pumpkin From Dad. Her eyes lit up and she hopped from the bed and raced to the computer, typed in the word Pumpkin and watched the screen fill with Lani's words.

It is the day after my 21st birthday and I am no longer human. Marcus has turned me into a vampire, but he is dead, a large piece of glass having taken his head from his body. He told me he was nearly two thousand years old and I wonder if that is how long I will live.

Kate digested this piece of information, expelling a huge breath of air. Her creator lived for two thousand years. No wonder the legends and myths had gone back so far into the past. He had been obviously seen on numerous occasions, fueling the pens of long dead writers, giving them a new type of character to grace their pages. She continued reading, only stopping for a bathroom break when necessary.

After several hours of reading, she was deeply engrossed in her work, having gone through two complete disks and several pages into the third, now telling of her life in the eighteen eighties, when the doorbell rang. She looked at her watch and saw it was eight o'clock in the morning.

On the other side of town, a van bearing the logo of the local TV station was parked in the Gerancher driveway, the cameraman and reporter pacing, hoping to get an interview with one of the heroes, but Ron wanted to stay inside and not talk to them. He didn't want to talk to them, not after the stupid questions they asked last night. "What was it like watching your father put the stakes into her, and then knowing they would do no good? How did you feel when she drank his blood and let some spurt on to you? Do you think your dad was a hero? How did you feel when he turned into a vampire and the cop took his head off? Reporters sometimes asked stupid questions, and right now he and his mom were hurting, missing husband and father. Ron would never write a story about vampires, not after what he had participated in. Ron would not sleep for a long time to come.

She walked over to the intercom and pressed the button. "Who's there?" She asked.

"Kate, it's David. May I come up?"

After pressing the buzzer, David opened the door and took the steps two at a time, arriving at her door in short order. She was waiting for him, having opened her door immediately after buzzing him up.

He smiled when he saw her and gave her a kiss on the cheek and a hug.

"David, this is such a pleasant surprise. I thought they were going to keep you hospitalized longer than this. You lost so much blood."

"No way, Kate. You can't keep a good man down for too long, especially a man of my age. We senior citizens tend to stiffen up a bit when we lay around too long, you know."

"Come in. Can I get you anything to eat or drink?"

"I just had a great meal at the hospital, but I sure could go for a beer, if you have any handy?"

"What kind would you like? I can offer you Old Milwaukee, Sam Adams or Vitamin Y."

He shot her a quizzical look and said, "What the hell is Vitamin Y, Kathleen?"

She laughed and replied; "I said the same thing myself the first time I heard that from a friend of mine. He's a corrections officer at a prison near Philadelphia and one night when I was there to have dinner with him and his wife, he offered me a choice of pilsner or Y. I thought, what the hell, be bold and try something new, so I told him Vitamin Y sounds good. Turns out that's what he calls Yuengling Lager."

"That sounds great. I haven't had a lager in years. I actually gave up beer for a while, but lately I've been enjoying it again. Can I use your bathroom, please? Pardon my French, but I have to piss like a stallion."

"Sure, it's right around the corner. Just put the seat back down, okay?"

While David was in the bathroom, Kate pulled two cold ones from the fridge and took them into the living room. She sat down on the sofa and took a sip, waiting for David to join her, rubbing her neck to get the stiffness out. It had been a long night and day so far and she realized she hadn't been to bed in almost twenty hours, and the lack of sleep was beginning to catch up with her.

David joined her on the sofa and took a few healthy pulls from his beer, wiping the foam from his mouth with the back of his hand. "This really hits the spot, Kate. Thanks. So what have you found out about Lani since going to the motel?"

"How did you know I went to the motel? You were really out of it."

"Allen stopped by to visit me before I was released and told me you guys had been there and that you found her journal on disks. Did you crack the code to open them, yet?"

"Yeah, come on over and check it out. It's astonishing. She was created by a two thousand year old vampire."

"Two thousand years", David muttered softly as Kate sat down. He stood behind her, looking over her shoulder at the screen, reading.

"David, would you do me a favor, please and massage my neck and shoulders. I think I've been at this too long. *Am I going to wind up in bed with this handsome old man?*

"Sure, no problem." He began kneading sore muscles, listening to her moans of delight.

He turned her head just a bit to massage her neck on the right side, his fingers deftly loosening her. When he stopped, she felt his breath just below her ear. He was going to kiss her and she had been hoping he would, even though he was old, he was in fantastic shape. *I am going to wind up in bed with David!*

Closing her eyes in anticipation, she suddenly felt white hot pain as his teeth found their way into her carotid artery and he drank her dry. Afterward he took her into the bedroom and laid her down on top of the quilt, waiting for her to awaken to her new life.

About the Author

Larry Deibert is a letter carrier for the United States Postal Service. He hopes to retire in December of 2007.

He is also the manager/independent distributor for Fuller Brush. Larry's Fuller website is www.Fullersales4u.com.

He is a Vietnam veteran, having served with the 557th MP Company in 1970.

Larry is a life member of Veterans of the Vietnam War, Post 75, in Macungie, Pa., and VFW Post 9264, also in Macungie. He is also a member of Vietnam Veterans of America, Lehigh Valley Chapter 415.

Larry served as first president of the Lehigh Northampton Vietnam Veterans Memorial.

He is a member of First Presbyterian Church in Bethlehem, PA.

Larry has two adult children, Laura and Matthew, from his first marriage. He married Peggy Deets in 2005.

Larry continues to write in his spare time. He is presently working on several novels and short stories.

Larry invites the reader to visit his website www.larrydeibert.com.

THE BEST IN FANTASY

PIERS ANTHONY

The ChroMagic Series
Key to Chroma
Key to Destiny
Key to Havoc
Key to Liberty
Key to Survival

Of Man and Manta Series
Omnivore
Orn
OX

Macroscope

Tortoise Reform

Under a Velvet Cloak
(Incarnations of Immortality Book 8)

PIERS ANTHONY & ROBERT E. MARGROFF

The Roundear Prophecy Series
Dragon's Gold
Serpent's Silver
Chimaera's Copper
Orc's Opal
Mouvar's Magic

VISIT US ONLINE

Mundania Press

WWW.MUNDANIA.COM

Elaine Corvidae

Lord of Wind and Fire Series
Wolfkin
The Crow Queen
Dragon's Son

The Shadow Fae Trilogy
Winter's Orphans
Prince of Ash
The Sundered Stone

The Tyrant Moon Trilogy
Tyrant Moon
Heretic Sun
Sorceress Star

COUPON SALE
10% Off Any Purchase

Shop online at www.Mundania.com
and save 10% off your next purchase.
Just enter the coupon code
"200710" when you check out.

Printed in the United States
89562LV00005B/1-66/A